MW01450002

An AMATEUR SLEUTH'S GUIDE to MURDER

Books by Lynn Cahoon

The Tourist Trap Mystery Series

Guidebook to Murder * Mission to Murder * If the Shoe Kills * Dressed to Kill * Killer Run * Murder on Wheels * Tea Cups and Carnage * Hospitality and Homicide * Killer Party * Memories and Murder * Murder in Waiting * Picture Perfect Frame * Wedding Bell Blues * A Vacation to Die For * Songs of Wine and Murder * Olive You to Death * Vows of Murder

Novellas

Rockets' Dead Glare * A Deadly Brew * Santa Puppy * Corned Beef and Casualties * Mother's Day Mayhem * A Very Mummy Holiday * Murder in a Tourist Town

The Kitchen Witch Mystery Series

One Poison Pie * Two Wicked Desserts * Three Tainted Teas * Four Charming Spells * Five Furry Familiars * Six Stunning Sirens * Seven Secret Spellcasters

Novellas

Chili Cauldron Curse * Murder 101 * Have a Holly, Haunted Christmas * Two Christmas Mittens

The Cat Latimer Mystery Series

A Story to Kill * Fatality by Firelight * Of Murder and Men * Slay in Character * Sconed to Death * A Field Guide to Homicide

The Farm-to-Fork Mystery Series

Who Moved My Goat Cheese? * Killer Green Tomatoes * One Potato, Two Potato, Dead * Deep Fried Revenge * Killer Comfort Food * A Fatal Family Feast

Novellas

Have a Deadly New Year * Penned In * A Pumpkin Spice Killing * A Basketful of Murder

The Survivors' Book Club Mystery Series

The Tuesday Night Survivors' Club * Secrets in the Stacks * Death in the Romance Aisle * Reading Between the Lies * Dying to Read

The Bainbridge Island Mystery Series

An Amateur Sleuth's Guide to Murder

An AMATEUR SLEUTH'S GUIDE to MURDER

LYNN CAHOON

KENSINGTON PUBLISHING CORP.
kensingtonbooks.com

This book is a work of fiction. Names, characters, businesses, organizations, places, events, and incidents either are the product of the author's imagination or are used fictitiously. Any resemblance to actual persons, living or dead, events, or locales is entirely coincidental.

To the extent that the image or images on the cover of this book depict a person or persons, such person or persons are merely models, and are not intended to portray any character or characters featured in the book.

KENSINGTON BOOKS are published by

Kensington Publishing Corp.
900 Third Avenue
New York, NY 10022

Copyright © 2025 by Lynn Cahoon

All rights reserved. No part of this book may be reproduced in any form or by any means without the prior written consent of the Publisher, excepting brief quotes used in reviews.

All Kensington titles, imprints, and distributed lines are available at special quantity discounts for bulk purchases for sales promotion, premiums, fundraising, educational or institutional use. Special book excerpts or customized printings can also be created to fit specific needs. For details, write or phone the office of the Kensington Special Sales Manager: Kensington Publishing Corp., 900 Third Avenue, New York, NY 10022. Attn. Special Sales Department. Phone: 1-800-221-2647.

KENSINGTON and the KENSINGTON COZIES teapot logo Reg. US Pat & TM Off.

Library of Congress Control Number: 2025932701

ISBN: 978-1-4967-5209-3

First Kensington Hardcover Edition: July 2025

ISBN: 978-1-4967-5211-6 (ebook)

10 9 8 7 6 5 4 3 2 1

Printed in the United States of America

The authorized representative in the EU for product safety and compliance is eucomply OU, Parnu mnt 139b-14, Apt 123
Tallinn, Berlin 11317, hello@eucompliancepartner.com

To my love and my life, Jim.

An AMATEUR SLEUTH'S GUIDE to MURDER

An Amateur Sleuth's Guide: Tips and Tricks

1. What doesn't kill you counts as work experience.
2. Thinking about committing a crime isn't the same as doing it.
3. A person's history tells a story.
4. Don't expect professionals to take you seriously. Prove them wrong.
5. The best clues come from under rocks or from people you hate.
6. Dead men tell no tales, but their social media accounts tell plenty.
7. Never wear your best outfit to go sleuthing. Or heels.
8. Strike when the iron is hot—or interview your suspects early, since people's memories fade with time.
9. If you can get access to the murder site, take pictures of the area. Don't rely on your memory or sketching skills.
10. Everyone is a suspect. . . .
11. Everyone's a suspect . . . including your friends and family.
12. Having too many suspects is a good thing.
13. The clopping of hooves is rarely from zebras.
14. Sometimes the answer is in plain sight. Cameras are everywhere.
15. You might catch more flies with honey, but who wants flies?
16. Know your victim, find your killer.
17. Nancy Drew made this job look easy.
18. A good investigator sees the details that others blow off.
19. Changing your plan midstream isn't failing. It just feels like it is.
20. People may not like you or your questions during an investigation. Including your friends.

21. Sometimes going back to the beginning helps you see what you're missing.
22. Even when you think you're right, you may be wrong.
23. Sometimes the Fates put you on the exact path where you need to be.
24. When you're done, you find out you have more questions....

Chapter 1

What doesn't kill you counts as work experience.

Meg Gates studied her empty apartment through bleary eyes. It was her and Watson. She sank into the papasan wicker chair after moving the empty wine bottle from last night next to the other one on the floor. Meg had kept a case of Queen Anne White from the shipment that was supposed to be used to toast the happy couple at her wedding reception in two days. Instead, her father had scheduled an appreciation party for his Stephen Gates Accounting clients. He'd taken the wine, the reception location, and her caterer and charged them to his company credit card. Now her wedding failure could be a tax deduction for his company rather than another hit to his bottom line, like when she'd left college to work for that start-up. As her father always reminded her, since they weren't related to *that* Gates, they had to make sure the lemons turned into lemonade. Or, more likely, imitation lemon-flavored water.

As Meg sat staring at the Space Needle and drinking water, trying to get rid of her hangover headache, she realized she was now a three-time loser. She'd failed at college, work, and now love. But who was counting? Besides her, her family, and everyone she knew?

Last night she'd sat in this same chair, listening to John Legend and Bruno and any other artist with a sad song she could find on her phone. She'd never figured out how to pair her phone to Romain's pricy Bluetooth stereo, which was tucked on a bookshelf in the living room. All his belongings were here, surrounding her. Waiting for Romain and Rachel to return from their Italian vacation, which was supposed to be her honeymoon. Romain Evans had been her fiancé. A few weeks before the wedding, he'd changed. He'd been distant. Cold. She'd thought it had been pre-wedding jitters. It hadn't been.

Rachel had been a bridesmaid and a sorority sister. What she hadn't been was a true friend.

Mutual friends had whispered to her that Romain was moving into Rachel's condo down by the sound. She hoped he tripped and fell off the dock. Maybe he could drown, too. But that seemed unlikely. Tripping on the way to happiness was more Meg's style.

Several times last night, Meg had considered throwing the sleek black stereo over the side of the balcony, but it had seemed like too much work to commit to the failed relationship. Besides, at the time, she still hadn't finished the task at hand, drinking the wine in her glass.

By the end of the night, or maybe sometime this morning, she had been playing Barry Manilow, Joni Mitchell, and the Carpenters, her mom's favorites. As the music played, Meg spent the time cutting her designer wedding dress into pieces that matched her shattered heart. The lights from the Space Needle sparkled in the window and kept her company while she destroyed the dress. Worse, she vaguely remembered possibly making a few Facebook Live posts during the night.

Her eyes felt dry from all the tears and probably also the wine. Looking at the pile of chopped white lace on the floor by her chair didn't make her feel better. She loved the dress. Destroying it was symbolic of what Romain's betrayal had done to her soul.

Meg had been called dramatic before.

Today, she reminded herself, was the start of a new chapter. Twenty-six wasn't too late to start over. Again. Or at least she hoped it wasn't. She might be single, unemployed, and sans degree, but there had to be real jobs out there for someone like her. She was alive, young, and though not vibrant this morning, she could fake it.

To tide her over, her mom had hired her to work evenings at Island Books, the family bookstore on Bainbridge Island. Meg figured it was her mom's way of keeping her out of trouble as her heart healed. Today was moving day. Moving home. One more indicator that her life was in the toilet. At least she wasn't moving back in with her mother. Instead, Aunt Melody and Uncle Troy had let her have the apartment over the garage. She groaned and leaned back into the chair, closing her eyes. Maybe she could put moving off until next week. The hangover should be gone by then. Or at least the wine would be.

Waiting meant she'd run the risk of seeing Romain. And probably Rachel. She didn't know if she could stop herself from throwing things at them or, worse, projectile vomiting like in that old movie. Today was as good as any day to run home with her tail between her legs.

Watson, her tan cocker mix rescue, jumped onto her lap and licked her face. He must have read her mind about the dog analogy. Watson liked sleeping in, so if he was awake, it was time to take him outside for a walk.

"You know I'm destroyed, right? Heartbroken and worthless." She stared into his deep brown eyes as he whined his request. "If you want to be a Seattle dog, you should break free of your leash and run as far away from me as possible. Go toward the Queen Anne neighborhood. Maybe someone rich will adopt you."

Watson patted her chest. He didn't care about her heart; he

needed to go out. She pushed him off her lap and finished the water in one gulp. Then she grabbed Watson's neon blue leash. It matched his collar and his bed. Watson's dog accessories were stylish and expensive.

"Don't wear these out, buddy. For the next year or so, we're only buying essentials."

Watson stood at the door and whined again. He wasn't impressed with her cost-cutting ideas.

"Fine. I'm hurrying." Meg checked to make sure she had her keys. No one was around to come to save her if she locked herself out except for the building's super, who usually slept until noon. She had people coming at ten to move her back home. And she hadn't paid this month's rent yet. She'd let Romain deal with that.

Home. She'd planned on this apartment being her and Romain's home until they got pregnant. Then they would move out of the city and closer to his job in Bellevue. They'd buy a cute cottage with a fenced yard for Watson and the new baby. She'd become a tradwife with a side hustle, some sort of craft that would sell like hotcakes online. They'd be a perfect little family. She'd even make homemade baby food. She'd be the yoga mom who wore crazy-colored jumpsuits and Birks, except on date nights, when she would shimmer in designer dresses and heels, having magically dropped the baby weight. Romain would never even look at another woman, he'd be so in love with her.

So that fantasy had a few holes. Romain hadn't even made it to the wedding night.

Watson did his business, and she cleaned up, using a biodegradable bag. Just like a good dog mom. She'd done everything right. So why was she being punished?

"Wishes and horses," she said as she found a trash can on the street and deposited the bag. A homeless man leaning against the building glared at her. Her pity party was over. It was time for a new life and a new song. She sang out quietly, "What doesn't kill you makes you stronger."

Thank God for Kelly Clarkson's anthems.

When she turned the corner toward the apartment building—*Not home*, she corrected herself—she saw her moving crew. Her mom, Felicia Gates; Aunt Melody; and Natasha Jones all stood by her mom's bookmobile van. Someone was yelling at her brother, Steve, whom everyone called Junior. His head stuck out the window of his Ram truck as he tried to parallel park on the street. Dalton Hamilton, Junior's best friend, motioned him back near the curb. Mom's van was parked in Romain's spot, since his BMW was at the airport.

"Felicia, she's across the street with Watson." Her aunt poked her mom and pointed at Meg. She called out, "Meg, we're here, darling. Don't you worry anymore. We'll have you back on the island and home in no time."

Meg smiled, hoping she didn't look as bad as she felt. She should have jumped in the shower, but it had felt like too much.

Bainbridge Island was a thirty-five-minute ferry ride away from Seattle in distance and more than fifty years behind the city in lifestyle. Residents and tourists hiked and had picnics in the forests that covered most of the island. Lately, large tracts of land were being sold with a single house built in the middle of the wooded land. Or on the waterside of the property. Houses that longtime residents like her parents and aunt and uncle could never imagine owning.

In Seattle Meg had lived in an apartment building where no one knew her name, including the super. She loved that freedom. Now she was moving back to the island to the apartment over her aunt Melody's garage. An apartment where her bedroom window overlooked the backyard and her every move could be watched.

Natasha Jones met her halfway as she and Watson crossed

the street, and handed her a large coffee. "You look horrible. I should have come over last night."

"Then both of us would be hungover, and we'd have one less bottle of wine to move." Meg hugged her friend.

"One? I'm disappointed that you think so poorly of my ability to comfort drink." Natasha squeezed her back. "Are you sure about moving back? It's a big step."

Meg nodded, looking around the neighborhood she'd called home for the past five years. She loved it here, but she couldn't afford the apartment on her own. Not since the start-up she'd worked at had shut down. She had applied for a job at Romain's workplace, but she'd put off her interview until after she returned from her honeymoon in Italy. Now, that career step was totally out of the question. "It's a big step backward, you mean."

"Not even close. Seattle's not good enough for you." Natasha put her arm around her as they finished crossing the street.

Natasha had been Meg's best friend since they'd found they had matching Malibu Barbie dolls at preschool. Natasha had warned Meg that Rachel was a player, but Meg hadn't imagined that her sorority sister would go after Romain when she'd asked her to be a bridesmaid. Or that he'd jump on the offer. Until the day she'd got Romain's phone call from the gate at Sea-Tac, before he and Rachel boarded their rescheduled flight. She pushed away the memory and smiled at Natasha. "Thanks for coming. I hope you haven't started the wedding cake yet. I'll pay you for it if you have started. We can feed it to the ducks in the park."

"Cake isn't good for ducks. Besides, I called the couple I'd turned down last week and sold it to them. She thought your design was beautiful." Natasha owned her bakery, A Taste of Magic, on Bainbridge Island. She catered to the tourists who liked having fancy cupcakes to eat along with her coffee while they walked through the small town's streets. For the past year, she'd also been making wedding cakes. "I have a check for your deposit refund in my purse."

"I hope the cake doesn't bring them bad luck." Meg unlocked the door to the lobby, and the group followed her into the elevator. Finally, she unlocked the door to her apartment. As they entered, they stood around behind Meg, staring at the chaos.

Last through the door was Dalton, who'd been her big brother's best friend since he'd arrived on the island. Before passing through the doorway, he hugged her. His arms felt safe, making her want to lay her head on his chest. After an hour or two in that position, she'd be fine. She reconsidered, since it was probably not the best look for a jilted, brokenhearted fiancée.

"He wasn't good enough for you, anyway." Dalton stepped back, breaking contact. Then he punched her in the arm. "Welcome back to the boonies, Magpie."

Dalton was the only one who ever called her that. Typically, she found it annoying, but today she was so grateful for the extra help, he could call her anything. "Come on in, brat, and help me move my meager belongings home."

She pointed out the furniture she was taking, including her grandmother's china cabinet, her desk, and the papasan chair she'd bought in college. The rest of the furniture was Romain's. He hadn't liked her mishmash of yard sale furniture finds, so she'd sold most of it when they moved in together. She handed Junior a pile of blankets to protect the furniture. Especially the china cabinet. Then he and Dalton started moving the larger items into the truck.

"Mom, will you and Aunt Melody pack up the kitchen?" Meg didn't even look up as she told them the few things not to box up. The kitchen had been Meg's domain. Right now, she was on autopilot, and if she stopped to think, the tears would start to flow. Again. Biting her lip, she refrained from crying. Not in front of her family. "All the dishes, silverware, glasses, pots, and pans. And all the appliances except the Keurig on the counter. It's all mine."

Natasha went into the living room and started boxing up Meg's complete series of Nancy Drew, Trixie Belden, and the Hardy Boys titles. "I'm assuming *all* the books are yours?"

"Exactly. I should have realized that before saying I'd marry the guy. You can't trust a man who doesn't read." Trying not to run, Meg headed to the bedroom to pack her clothes. At least in here she didn't have to worry about someone seeing her crying. She taped up a box for her shoes, but most of her clothes fit into her three suitcases. She needed to remember to check the coat closet. She had a North Face puffer in there that she'd paid too much for to leave. As she emptied her side of the closet, she froze.

Romain's new tuxedo hung by his suits. She ran her left hand over the smooth fabric, imagining him standing there, watching her. The engagement ring on her finger still sparkled even as pain dulled her senses. She could keep it. Wasn't the rule if she didn't break the engagement, she got the ring? She took off the ring, studying the marquise-cut diamond and platinum setting. He'd picked out the perfect ring. He just wasn't the perfect man.

Meg tucked the ring into the breast pocket of the tuxedo. Romain had bought his tuxedo. He'd shuddered when she'd suggested getting a rental for the day to save money. *Someday when he puts this suit on, he'll find the ring.* Meg imagined the moment when he pulled it out and realized he'd made a horrible mistake. He'd try to call her, but Meg wouldn't answer. Romain was dead to her. Just like her fantasy of a perfect life.

She ran her hand across the top shelf to ensure she hadn't missed anything. Her fingers brushed a bundle. She pulled it down and realized it was a money clip with five hundred dollars in it. Romain's cash stash. Their just-in-case money. She'd contributed to what used to be their fund. He'd probably forgotten to take it on vacation with him.

"You should take the money. It will help pay for your moving expenses." Dalton stood at the doorway, watching her consider the cash. He walked inside and stood next to her. "He owes you at least that."

Meg fanned out the money. "He does, but I'm not taking all of it." She peeled off a hundred-dollar bill and tucked it and the money clip into the tux pocket with the ring. Then she handed two hundred to Dalton. "Share this with Junior for your time and gas money."

Dalton stood close enough that she could smell the aftershave he'd used since he'd been a teenager. Musky and woody at the same time. Like he'd stepped out of the forest on his way to build a log cabin.

"Meg, I'm sorry about this. But he wasn't the guy for you." Dalton pushed a lock of hair back away from her eyes. "You deserve so much more."

A cough made her jump.

"Hey, Meg." Natasha stood at the doorway, watching them. "Your mom wants to know what you're doing with the wedding gifts."

"I'll come and sort them. I'll be responsible for sending back the ones from my relatives and friends, but the others, Romain's going to have to deal with." She stepped away from Dalton, clearing her head of his forest smell. She had work to do. "I'll need another box."

Meg returned to the living room and saw her mom sitting on the papasan chair, putting all the lace pieces of her wedding dress into a garment bag. "Mom, leave that."

Mom searched the floor for the last few pieces of lace. "I'm not letting you throw this out. You paid too much for it. Maybe we can save it."

Meg picked lace off Watson's fur and put it with the rest of the dress. "I don't think even a miracle could save this. I was furious last night. I'm glad the dress distracted me."

Aunt Melody snorted, "Felicia has always believed in a patron saint of lost causes."

Ignoring her sister, Mom zipped up the bag and headed to the front door to take the pieces of the dress downstairs to the van. Meg watched her go, knowing that she couldn't say anything to change her mind and reeling from her mom's guilt trip that still hung in the room over destroying the expensive dress.

It didn't take long to sort and pack the wedding gifts, so after cleaning out the pantry and boxing up what she could save from the fridge, Meg looked around the apartment. She stepped out on the balcony to retrieve her fern, which was somehow still alive, and paused to take in the view. "I'm going to miss you, Space Needle," she declared as Natasha joined her on the balcony.

"Bainbridge Island has views, too. Including of the Space Needle and the rest of the skyline. We can walk to the dock every time you want to see it." Natasha hugged her. "Come on. If we're done here, the guys want to catch the next ferry home."

When they got settled on the ferry, Meg went up to the observation deck to get a cup of coffee and to keep Watson happy. She found a rear-facing seat at the stern and watched the city disappear into the distance. She would be living less than an hour away, but it might as well be across the world. They'd gone outside to sit, and the spray from the fog stung her face as she fought the tears. She'd cried enough over Romain's betrayal, but now she realized, it wasn't the man she was grieving. It was her life.

She was desperately searching for a silver lining in all this. Then it came to her. The book she'd been talking about writing since she was in high school. A real-life guide to solving mysteries. Not how to be a private investigator. But instructions for a normal person like her—a way for all people who wanted to crack cold cases or figure out who trashed the park by using a well-proven method. Or at least it had worked when they were in high school. Her mood started to lift, but then she had a thought.

She hadn't even seen the signs of her fiancé's betrayal. She felt a wave of depression overwhelm her again.

A man's angry voice brought her out of her anguish.

"The woman doesn't know what she wants or what she has, for that matter. Don't worry about the advance. She'll be grateful for even the part we tell her about," the man continued, his tone even harsher as he stood by the rail near Meg, his back to her and Seattle.

What a jerk. Meg scooted closer on the bench as she wiped the tears from her face. Mom had always said the best way to get over something was to get involved in something else. Maybe she could help the woman this man was trying to cheat. Unless he wasn't going to Bainbridge to meet with her. He could be talking about someone somewhere else. Maybe she had her mom's love of helpless causes, as well.

"I brought you hot chocolate to warm you up," Dalton said, suddenly appearing on the deck. He held out the cup. She turned toward him and saw the man give them both a dirty look. Like she'd been trying to listen in on his conversation. Well, she had, but he was the one who'd interrupted her pity party.

"Thanks," she said as she watched the man go back inside the passenger cabin. She took the cup but didn't take a drink. Hot chocolate was always too hot when you first got it. She'd learned that lesson years ago. Still, the warm cup felt good in her cold hands. It was late May, but warm weather typically didn't arrive in Seattle until late June. Being outside on the ferry only made it colder.

"Do you know him?" Dalton followed her gaze.

Meg shook her head. "No. I overheard part of his conversation. He's not a nice guy."

"I got that feeling from him, too. It's funny how you know sometimes." Dalton leaned on the railing, watching Seattle disappear. "Look, Magpie, Bainbridge isn't that bad. And who says it's forever? You'll be back on your feet sooner than you think."

Meg sipped her still too-hot hot chocolate, not sure what to say. She could tell him that she felt broken. That she needed a whole new life. A new purpose. In other words, she could open up and let him into her head. But Dalton was only trying to be nice. He wasn't offering a free counseling session. "You're right, of course. But it feels like a step back. At least I'll be employed again."

"I heard you're going to be working at the bookstore." He moved to stand closer to her, his back to Seattle, breaking her view of what she was leaving behind.

It didn't occur to her until later that he might have moved to that spot on purpose.

"I'll be manning Island Books from three to ten Thursday through Saturday and sometimes on Wednesday and Sunday. It's too bad I'm not a writer. I bet I'd get a lot of work done." She stopped trying to watch Seattle disappear. Bainbridge was her new life. Not there. "Thanks to Aunt Melody, I also got a second gig. I'll be working as an author's assistant for Lilly Aster."

"L. C. Aster, the mystery author? I just finished her last book." Dalton looked impressed. "Her summer home is beautiful. I helped my uncle with the flooring when it was being built."

"Well, if there's anything I do know, it's how to solve a mystery. My name might not be Nancy, and this isn't River Heights, but I think I can be useful to Ms. Aster. Besides, it will get me inside that house. I'm looking forward to seeing it. I wonder what my first assignment will be. Researching what it's like to be a spy with the CIA or maybe tracking down jewelry heists that haven't been solved?" Meg had imagined several different topics her first assignment could involve, and she'd also envisioned having coffee with the author as they discussed their favorite books.

"I haven't seen that look on your face since you solved the mystery of who was spiking Coach Bailey's energy drink. Did you ever tell him it was the cheerleader adviser?" Dalton glanced around her at the upcoming dock. "Hold that thought. We need to get back in the vehicles. We're almost at Bainbridge." Dalton worked on the ferry, so he knew all the whistles and noises.

The announcement came after they were already on the stairs. She followed Dalton down to the vehicle level and climbed into her car. Watson sat in the front, with the rest of the space in the Honda Civic taken up by plants and boxes. While she waited for her turn to drive onto the island, she thought about working for Ms. Aster. Maybe this was the start of her new life. She'd joked about writing at the bookstore, but maybe she'd try her hand at a guidebook about solving mysteries as an amateur.

She might have missed all the signs between Romain and Rachel. But that had been her heart talking. She knew she could do this investigation thing. And after some time working with the famous *New York Times* author, she'd have even more tools and maybe some experience.

Now all she had to do was convince Uncle Troy, the town's police chief, to let her help investigate the next murder on Bainbridge Island. Unless the dead guy was Romain. Because if her ex-fiancé ever showed his face again on the island, she'd be at the top of the suspect list. With good reason.

Meg Gates is no loser. She stared into the rearview mirror and rephrased her badly phrased affirmation. "Meg Gates, that's me, is on the way to being Bainbridge Island's top consultant for murder investigations."

The woman in the mirror didn't look convinced. Maybe she'd start small, like trying to find a missing clock.

It worked for Nancy.

Chapter 2

Thinking about committing a crime isn't the same as doing it.

Tuesday morning Meg rode her bike to Lilly Aster's house, Summer Break. A lot of the houses on the island had names, and as she pedaled down the street, she made note of them. Isn't that one of the tenets of being a good investigator? Paying attention to the little stuff? That was good; she needed to write that down. The house was on the outskirts of Winslow, just north of Island Bookstore and the ferry terminal. Meg rode past a house called Happy Hour and wondered what the owners had been thinking. Seagull Roost and Moose Island were next, and then she turned onto the street that would take her to the edge of the island and the Gothic-style house overlooking the sound.

Meg wondered if Ms. Aster could see Seattle from her living room. Or, better, from her office. Maybe she'd let Meg call her Lilly. They'd have tea—no, coffee—in the room and watch the ferries sail back and forth as they chatted about the upcoming book Lilly was struggling to write. Which was why she had hired Meg.

Meg continued to daydream all the way to the front of the house, where a large stone entrance invited her to climb the stairs and knock on the oversized door. She grabbed her notebook out of the basket that Aunt Melody had installed on the bike, glad she'd left Watson with her mom at the bookstore. He'd made himself at home there for the past week, ever since Meg had started working there. It was nice to have a job where she could bring her dog.

Maybe Lilly would invite Watson to come with Meg to their work sessions. As she climbed the stairs, she noticed a black sedan parked on the circular driveway. She recognized the sticker in the back window. It was a rental car from the only shop here on the island.

She found a doorbell, and as she reached to push it, the door flew open. The irritable man she'd seen a few days ago on the ferry rushed out and almost knocked her down.

He squinted his eyes, recognition hitting him. "What are you doing here?"

"Well, excuse you. I was about to ring the doorbell before you tried to run me over." Meg put her hand on her heart. She wasn't kidding; the guy had scared her.

"That doesn't explain what you're doing here. This is private property. I'll call the police chief if you don't leave immediately." He pulled out his cell phone and made a show of dialing the nine and the first one. "Why aren't you running?"

"Because I have an appointment with Ms. Aster." Meg nodded to the phone. "Say hi to Uncle Troy for me."

He put the phone in his pocket. "Locals are always inbred."

A woman appeared in the doorway. "Oh, Bobby, leave the poor girl alone. Just because you're mad about our discussion doesn't mean you have the right to browbeat my newest employee. Or insult her and her family." Lilly Aster turned toward Meg. She wore jeans and a silk tank top. Her long blond hair was pulled back in a ponytail, and she wasn't wearing makeup. Meg almost didn't recognize her as the same woman from the book covers. "You must be Meg Gates. Your aunt told me to expect you. Come on in."

Meg walked into the large foyer, which had a real-life knight in shining armor on one side of a grand staircase that looked like it had been used on the movie set for *Gone with the Wind*. Okay, so she was mixing her literary metaphors, but the place was huge and cool.

"Lilly, you need to be reasonable. They aren't going to give you a bigger advance," the man said as the door swung shut on him.

Meg heard his swearing through the heavy door.

Lilly must have also heard it while she walked into the living room and sat. She motioned Meg to sit in another chair. "I was told that the door was soundproof, but I guess that isn't true. That was my agent cursing out there on the porch. Robert Meade III. I call him Bobby because he hates it. I should get another agent, but that's a lot of work. Anyway, let's chat about what I need from you."

Meg wondered if she should tell Lilly about the phone conversation she'd overheard on the ferry. On the one hand, she didn't know who Bobby had been talking about or to. And, on the other hand, she didn't want to look like a snitch on her first day. She'd bring it up later. "Your home is beautiful. I've always wanted to see the inside."

"We'll do a tour on another day. I've got a deadline coming up, and I'm not close to being ready. So you went to the University of Washington? What was your major?"

"Mostly general studies. I wound up leaving junior year to go work at a tech start-up." Meg saw the look on Lilly's face. She wasn't measuring up, yet. Nervous that Lilly Aster would think Meg was a loser, she started to sweat as she added, "I took a lot of literature and English classes. I guess I wanted more to learn than to prepare for a career."

Lilly's eyes blinked. Meg's answer appeared to have surprised her. "Lifelong learning is an admirable trait. Have you read any of my books?"

"I've read all of them. My mom owns the bookstore on the island, and your thrillers sell very well." She paused but then added, "I'm working at the bookstore in the late afternoon and at night, but it won't interfere with any assignments you give me. I go to work and go home."

Great. Now she sounded like a nerd with no life. Which was true. "I have a dog, Watson. He's a cocker mix rescue. And I don't know why I told you that."

Now Lilly smiled. "If I were to guess, you didn't want to look pathetic for not having a social life. Believe me, I understand. I work in my office most days for at least eight hours. And when I go on a book tour, it's mostly one bookstore after another. I have to make sure I know what city I'm in before I go onstage. Then I come home and start the next book. It's a hamster wheel life."

"You still love writing, though?" Meg asked.

"That's what keeps me going. When I get done and read the whole thing, front to back, I'm always amazed at what I created." She stared at Meg for a long second. Then she handed Meg a folder. "I think you'll do. My attorney sent a tax form, a contract, and a nondisclosure form for you to sign. There's an envelope for you to mail the papers off to him once you sign. You'll get paid once a week for twenty hours unless I call my accountant and add more. It depends on what I need. But you'll always get the minimum. It's all in your contract. And your first assignment is in the front."

Meg opened the folder. "You want fifty choices of synonyms for the ten words listed below? Like *restaurant*? And *murder*?"

Lilly stood and reached out her hand. "Exactly. Can you drop that off on Thursday? Then I'll have another assignment. Just let me know if the assignment is taking more than twenty hours. Being creative sometimes is time-consuming. Welcome to the team."

She ended the interview by walking toward a second doorway opposite the one that led to the foyer. "Jolene will show you out. Give her a bottle of water for the road, will you?"

Meg turned toward the entrance where she'd come in, and a short woman with dark hair in a suit stood there, watching her. Jolene walked over to a cabinet and took out a bottle of water. "Can I get you a snack for the road?"

Meg stood and hurried over to Jolene. Shaking her head, she took the water and said, "This is great. Thanks. Hey, do you know what time Lilly—I mean, Ms. Aster—wants the assignment back on Thursday? I didn't have time to ask."

"I'd say early. She'll probably have your next task ready by seven. But you'll meet with me. Ms. Aster is a very busy woman. She writes in her office for hours." Jolene opened the oversized door to the outside and waited for Meg to walk through. "Just push the buzzer and I'll come get it when you arrive."

As Meg rode back to the apartment to drop off her bike and then walked to the bookstore to pick up Watson, she thought about her new job. Meeting Lilly Aster had been amazing, but the assignment? It was less than what she'd expected. Maybe this was a test. The good news was that being an author's assistant paid well. Even with the twenty hours a week, Meg would be able to save enough money that by the end of the summer, she would be able to go back to college and earn her BA. Now she needed to figure out that plan.

She had four years before she turned thirty, and she wanted to be on her way to a real career by then. Thirty wasn't a bad age to start your life. Again. She pushed harder on the bike pedals to climb the small hill in front of her.

One step at a time. One hill at a time. And she'd completed a giant step today. Several, in fact, since she'd left Seattle. She was on her way. Now she needed to figure out where exactly she was heading.

Dalton was at the bookstore when she got there. She glanced at her watch. "Aren't you supposed to be at work?"

"This is my 'weekend' this week. Today and tomorrow. A bunch of us are going to Point White Beach for a bonfire tonight. We can take the mutt. You haven't been around in a few years. You need to meet some people your age. That don't dress like they're ninety years old." He picked up a new release and scanned the back cover. "I need this, too. Two birds, one stone."

"Is that a jab at my former fiancé?" Meg took the book from him and went behind the counter. "I don't know. I've got an assignment for my other job."

"If the wing-tip shoe fits, then yes. This is your first assignment from Lilly Aster? Even better. You can tell me all about your meeting as we boat out to the beach. We can't clam. There's a biotoxin warning. The pollution's pretty bad now. But I'm going over to the coast to get some razor clams this fall. You can ride along then if you're still here." He handed her the same one-hundred-dollar bill that she'd given him the day of the move.

She smiled as she gave him change and put the book and receipt into a bag. "I guess we can go. Watson did okay on the ferry. It was his first boat ride."

"The ferry's a lot bigger than my little scooter. But we'll keep him safe." He glanced at his watch. "I'll pick you up at six, and we can grab dinner first. Bring a jacket."

"Thanks. I appreciate you getting me out. This afternoon, I told Ms. Aster I was almost homebound." Meg saw her mom come out of the back room, where Meg knew she'd been eavesdropping.

"Well, I do what I can." He nodded to the back door. "Thanks for letting me wait, Mrs. Gates. See you at six, squirt." He turned and headed across the room.

"I'm assuming that comment was aimed at Watson," Meg called after him.

"Think what you want," Dalton said as he left through the front door.

Mom came around the counter and wrote down the name of the book Dalton had purchased and the author in a notebook. It was her ordering system. When a book went out, she would put it on the list, and then when she made an order, she would decide if she wanted to keep it in stock. Reviewing the order notebook was one of Meg's Thursday night tasks. "Are you ready to date so soon? Maybe Romain will come to his senses and you two can get past this."

Meg closed her eyes. When she opened them, she wasn't seeing red anymore. Her mom meant well. "One, Romain cheated and then spent our honeymoon with Rachel. Two, there is no going back. Which reminds me, I need to drop off wedding gifts to the neighbors. If they ask, I'll be over tomorrow, and I apologize for the delay as I get my life together."

"And go on a date," Mom sniffed.

"We're leaving now. I'll see you Thursday at three." Meg hooked Watson's leash on his collar and left the bookstore. Sometimes her mom could be exasperating. As she walked the few blocks to her aunt's house, she thought about Dalton's offer. He clearly hadn't asked her on a date, right?

Well, she'd clear that up as soon as he arrived at her apartment. The one thing Meg Gates didn't need in her life, messing up her four-, well, maybe five-year plan, was a man.

When they got back to the apartment, she put her bike, which she had leaned against the wall earlier, inside the garage, next to her Civic. She should have sold the car before leaving Seattle, but she might need it when she went back to school.

The campus was too far to bike, and she didn't want to figure out a bus schedule.

She and Watson climbed the stairs and went into her apartment. Meg read the paperwork that Lilly had given her and signed the papers. She made copies and then put them in a neat pile on her desk. She needed to order some office supplies, so she went online and did that as well as updated her address on her Amazon account. Thank goodness she hadn't started merging her accounts with Romain's. It would make this breakup even more distressing. Thinking about the things she needed to do, she took out her planner and started writing them down.

First up, kill Romain. She looked at the sentence, then crossed it out. If her mom or aunt saw that, they'd totally freak. But it felt good to let the negative feelings out. She felt a smile tugging at her lips. Besides, she hadn't written out an actual plan to do him in.

Now for the real list. *File a change of address. Update my address on all of my bank accounts.* As she thought about all the financial housekeeping things she needed to do, she remembered that she needed to deal with the 401(k) she'd started with her former employer. She had been going to take the money out and plan a six-month second honeymoon as a surprise, but now she thought maybe she should roll it into an IRA before the start-up tried to pull back some of the funds. If they could even do that.

Now that she was freaking out about that possibility, she went to the account holder and opened a new account with the financial company. Thankfully, it was a big one. Then she closed out her employee account and sent the funds to the new account.

One crisis averted. She got up and grabbed the last soda out of the fridge. "Okay, maybe I need to add *Go grocery shopping* to my list."

Watson looked up from where he'd been sleeping on the old

couch that had come with the apartment. Meg had thrown an old quilt over the leather to make sure Watson didn't destroy it. But she was missing her old furniture. The pre-Romain stuff she'd sold. She started a grocery list and added a newspaper to the list. This weekend was yard sale day. Thinking about all the possible finds made her smile.

She scanned her planner. It had been a productive day. After losing her job, some days it had been hard just getting out of bed. The wedding planning had helped, but now she was rebuilding her life. She was gainfully employed, even if she had had to cobble two jobs together for full-time hours. She wasn't living on the street. With family, yes, but not on the street. And she had a list. Lists were good.

Returning to her desk, she pulled the folder from Lilly Aster over to her and wrote down the time on the front. Someone, probably Jolene, had written in ink on the front of the folder, *Keep track of your hours here, including your travel time out here to meet Ms. Aster.* She'd even given an example. Meg glanced at her planner and tried to estimate when she'd arrived back in town to pick up Watson. She wrote the information down. Then, after checking to see if she still had an hour or so to work before Dalton arrived, she wrote down the current time.

Then she started playing with the list of words Lilly had given her. The first ten synonyms for the first word came easy, so she dropped down to the next word before digging into a thesaurus. She'd worked on half of the words before she realized she needed to get ready for the non-date.

Hanging out at the beach meant possibly getting wet, so she didn't want to wear her best jeans. Dalton had told her to dress warmly, so she went digging through her suitcases to find the right outfit. Layers, they worked every time.

Before they went to the marina, Dalton took her to a fish

and chips restaurant, and they sat at an outdoor table, looking out at the sound. She sprinkled malt vinegar and salt on her basket of fish, fries, and a bit of minty mushy peas. "I forgot how pretty it is here."

"Seattle's nice, if you like concrete and brick. The island is more pastoral, don't you think?" He met her gaze.

She laughed at his description. "Pastoral's more country. Like farmland? This is rural, yes, but forested and set more on the water. Everything is about island life. If it was on the coast, you could use #saltlife on social media."

"So the author hired the right person to edit her books." He picked up a fry. "I was trying out a word I read in a book last week. I guess I got it wrong."

"No worries. I'm not her editor. Or even a beta reader. I'm a researcher, I guess. However, right now, I think she's testing me with busy work. I feel like I'm back in Mrs. Scott's sixth-grade class, doing the dictionary search. Remember that assignment?"

"No, because I never finished my real assignment. You were always doing extra credit. She made up things to keep you busy." His gaze met hers. "You were always years ahead of the rest of your class."

"And look how far that got me." Meg held up her hand. "No, I don't want to go through a list of my failures, at least not tonight. Who's going to be at the bonfire? Anyone I know?"

He considered her statement, then nodded. "A few from school. Several new guys who think saving the island from newcomers is their personal life mission."

"But you said they were new, as well," Meg said as she finished her fish and handed Watson one fry since he'd been quiet while they ate. "That doesn't make sense."

"They aren't rich. So, therefore, they think they're one of us. Mostly they're jerks. Maybe don't talk about working for Ms.

Aster. I've heard them rag on her and her house before. Everyone hates the rich until they become wealthy."

As they left the restaurant and headed to the marina to take Dalton's fishing boat out to the beach, Meg wondered how much Bainbridge Island had changed since she'd left to live in Seattle.

Chapter 3

A person's history tells a story.

The sun was low in the western sky, and the bonfire in the middle of the sandy beach was already lit. So were several of the young men gathered around it. From what she could see, there were more men than women. Meg spied the group of women hanging out next to another boat that had been beached on the shore. Natasha waved her over. When Meg and Watson walked over, Natasha hugged her.

"I didn't realize you were going to be here." Meg glanced around at the other women. Three were from her class, but they hadn't been friends. This was the old stoner group from high school. At least that was what the band kids had called them. Meg still had her flute.

"I told him to invite you. This is the gathering spot for everyone under thirty on the island. Unless they've already married and are living the boring settled life." She introduced the other women. "So remember that singles bar in Seattle, Harbor Bay Hannah's? The one we used to go to after we turned twenty-one? This is Bainbridge Island's equivalent."

"Except the men at that bar were way cuter," the woman standing next to Natasha added. She glanced over at the group of men. "And usually less trashed than these guys. I swear, they must start drinking at noon. I'm not sure why I even come anymore. I'm not that desperate. I'm Luna, by the way." Luna hadn't been in Meg's graduating class.

A cheer went up around the fire as someone threw an empty bottle into the flames. It was going to be a long night. Watson whined at her feet.

"I think I need to walk him." Meg smiled at the group. "I'll be back in a few minutes."

Luna followed her. "I'll show you the property lines. Most of the residents are cool, but some of them can be touchy about someone crossing the invisible line onto their precious private beach. We don't want the cops out here arresting people. Most of these guys need to go to work tomorrow. So you came with Dalton. He's sweet."

"He's my brother's best friend. We've known each other since we were kids. He's being nice." Meg turned her head and caught sight of Dalton, who was talking with another guy. And watching her. He raised a soda bottle in greeting.

"He never brings anyone to the beach, and he never leaves with anyone, either. At least not since I've been here. And believe me, I've watched the guy. He's hot." Luna looked back and smiled at him and waved, but he turned away. "See? He's guarded. Except with you."

Meg thought about her mom's earlier question. *Are you ready to date so soon?* Dalton had been a part of her life as soon as he'd become friends with Junior. *History tells a story.* She paused as Watson watered a small bush on a dune. "I just got out of a serious relationship. I'm not ready to date yet."

Luna looked back again and saw that Dalton was still watching them. "Have you told him that?"

When they walked back to where they'd left the group of women, they saw that everyone had gathered around the fire. Dalton waved her and Watson over to a pair of chairs he'd set up outside the ring of people. "I've got soda or water. Or if you want something else, I'm sure someone has extra."

As he said that, Natasha came over with a six-pack of hard

lemonade drinks. "I hope you still drink these, Miss Fancy Pants. I couldn't afford one of those bottles of wine you were drinking last week."

"I'll have one. You should come over one night, and we'll open a bottle of that wine and order Chinese food. I think my delivery service app is still attached to Romain's checking account." Meg took one of the black cherry–flavored drinks. "Bring over a chair and chat with us. I haven't seen you since my walk of shame home."

"Moving home isn't a walk of shame. You should have left that jerk a long time ago." Natasha handed her the bottle. "Girls rule, boys drool."

"What are you, twelve?" Dalton leaned back in his chair. He had been watching the conversation. "Natasha, do you want my chair?"

"No, I don't. I want to sit in the sand and give Watson my full attention. He's the only guy here I can trust." Natasha sank to the sand and patted her leg to attract Watson. The dog looked up at Meg, then went and cuddled on Natasha's lap.

"Traitor." Meg reached down and rubbed Watson's head. "He's all confused, but he loves Aunt Melody's backyard. He thinks we're on vacation or something."

"So how did the interview with Ms. Aster go? Are you working with a famous author now? Do you have a fancy title?" Natasha opened a bottle of the hard lemonade and took a sip of her drink.

"Researcher. But the pay's great, so I don't care what she calls me." Meg added to herself that she hoped once Lilly trusted her, maybe she'd get better assignments. "Twenty hours a week, when I can fit them in, or more if I need it. With the bookstore hours, I'm full-time, with bare bone benefits. I need to figure out insurance before Mom can't cover me anymore. She says insurance is crazy expensive and—"

Suddenly, a man stood over her, interrupting their conversation.

"Nate, what's going on?" Dalton asked, standing up to meet the guy.

Meg could see it was a power move, but maybe Dalton was more worried about the weaving guy falling on her. He was drunk to the gills, a phrase her dad used all the time. Which told everyone how often island residents were drinking.

Nate pointed his finger toward her. "You're working for the witch on Haunted Cliffs? Aren't you a local?"

"I was born here, not like some." Meg sipped her drink. She knew Nate must be one of those newcomers that Dalton had warned her about.

"Meg," Dalton warned as he put his hand on her shoulder. His voice was low and commanding. She was poking the bear, and he didn't like it.

"Well, you should know better, then. Rich people come here, build big houses, then tell us where we can go. It's not fair. I can't even use my favorite deer-hunting tree stand anymore. It's on private property. What about us? Where's our private property?" Nate swayed as he took another drink, finishing off the whiskey bottle he held. He threw it toward the fire but missed and almost hit another guy.

"Nate, you need to slow down." Dalton stepped in between him and Meg's chair.

From the other side, Meg could hear Watson growling. She looked over and saw Natasha had him on a short leash, keeping him out of the fight.

Nate leaned around Dalton. "Mark my words, you're going to be sorry you're fraternizing with the enemy. All they want is to take over our homes."

A male voice called from the fire, "Nate, leave Meg alone before Dalton flattens you and I have to drag your sorry butt into the boat and back home."

Nate waved his hand at the advice giver, then leered at Meg. "You're kind of cute. You should come over and sit with me. I'd teach you the ways of the island."

"Violet's waiting for you. Besides, Meg's already taken." Dalton took Nate by the shoulders and aimed him toward the fire and his waiting friends. Then he watched as Nate stumbled toward the fire. When Nate fell next to a woman, Dalton sat down again. "Sorry about claiming you. I know this isn't a date. I needed to put it in words that Neanderthal would understand. Your mom called this afternoon, after I left the bookstore, and read me the riot act about my intentions and your fragile state. Is it true she thinks Romain will come crawling back?"

Meg felt her shoulders relax as she leaned back in the chair. She hadn't minded Dalton's words and was glad Nate had left. "My mom called you?"

"She did. She's worried about you jumping into something before you have time to think." He held his hand up, warding her off as she sat straighter. "Her words, not mine. Don't kill the messenger."

"I'm going to kill my mother. Isn't matricide legal if there are extenuating circumstances? Like driving a daughter crazy." Meg took a long drink as she leaned back in her chair. "There's no chance Romain's coming back, and if he did show up, I won't be going back. He had his chance with all this."

Watching Meg run her hands up and down her body to show off what a catch she was sent Natasha into giggles. "Yeah, you go, girl. Who needs a man, anyway?"

If she'd asked Meg that question a month ago, she would have raised her hand. Maybe both hands. Today she was a stronger, more independent Meg. And she was going to stay that way.

Dalton was quiet as he guided the boat back to the marina two hours later. After he docked and tied the boat to the moorings, he held out a hand to help her up on the dock. Instead, she handed him Watson. The dog had slept all the ride back.

"He's tired. I think the upheaval has been a little too much for him. He never bonded with Romain, but I thought with time he would grow on him. Except it's clear Watson likes people here a lot more than he ever liked Romain."

"That's saying something, right?" Dalton took the dog and set him on the dock, holding Watson's leash in his hand. Then he reached out to help Meg up onto the dock. "Except Nate. Watson didn't like him at all."

"He seems like a blowhard." Meg took the leash, and they strolled toward the marina exit. The water gently slapped against the rocks. "Nate hates Lilly Aster."

"He hates a lot of people. Don't let him get in your head. He likes stirring up trouble, but he's harmless."

"If you say so. His girlfriend wasn't happy with what he said to me. What's her name? Violet?"

"Violet's a real islander like us, younger, though. She graduated from Bainbridge High a few years ago. She seems to like hanging out with the bad boys. Her dad's the mayor, so it makes life interesting for your uncle. I bet he has lots of stories." He opened the door to his truck and reached down to pick up Watson, then lifted him inside. "Okay if you wait here while I grab some things off the boat? I don't like to leave things out, especially since I'll be at work tomorrow."

"I thought you were off for the weekend," Meg asked, but either Dalton didn't hear her, since he'd already walked away, or he didn't want to answer the question.

As he drove her home, they talked about the bonfire and the people who'd been there. Natasha had been right; it was like an outdoor singles club. She thought about what Luna had said about Dalton.

"So are you dating someone?"

"That's a strange question coming from a woman I'm not supposed to be dating." He grinned at her. "According to your mom."

"Luna likes you. She thought you were interested in me. She

said you don't bring girls to the bonfires or leave with them." She pointed out what she'd learned about Dalton tonight.

"Until today." He pulled the truck in front of her aunt's garage and left the engine running. "I'm not interested in Luna. Have a good night, Meg."

Her dog in her arms, she got out of the truck, and she and Watson watched as Dalton drove away. He hadn't answered her question, except to tell her that he wasn't interested in Luna. Meg found herself smiling as she and Watson headed upstairs to go to bed.

Meg had been awake since five, thinking about Dalton. Then she compared him to Romain. Frustrated with her focus on men, she went to the pile of wedding gifts she needed to return. Nothing better than dealing with returns to push romance out of her head. There were several she needed to mail back, but she wanted to call each giver and make sure they didn't want her to take the gift back to a store to get a refund on their card. It would make it easier on both her and the giver. The only problem with that plan was she'd have to listen to how sorry everyone was that she and Romain had called off the wedding.

She decided that she wasn't ready for that much sympathy. She'd pay the postal charge.

Meg pulled out ten of the gifts. Five were from island residents, and she could stop by their houses and drop them off this morning on her way to get coffee and see Natasha. The other five she wrapped in boxes to send back to the givers. She needed to go grocery shopping, but that would wait. She needed to get all the final canceled wedding to-dos off her list. Every time she looked at the gifts, she felt stupid.

She wrote down a plan for the day, which included finishing the assignment for Lilly and stopping at the post office.

With a fresh cup of coffee, she sat down at her desk and pulled out the folder from Lilly. She would call her Ms. Aster at the house, but in her head, she liked calling her Lilly. It made it sound like they were already friends. "I know. I'm projecting again. Romain would have a field day with this."

Watson jumped off the couch and went to get a drink of water, ignoring her comment.

Meg got to work. Without Romain to tell her what she was doing wrong, she needed to become her own conscience. Watson clearly wasn't going to help.

When she reached Natasha's bakery a few hours later, she was pleased with her progress. Lilly's assignment was done, so she'd be ready to head up to Summer Break tomorrow. Since she was at the post office, she'd mailed the signed paperwork to Lilly Aster's attorney. She'd dropped off the five wedding gifts from local residents. The packages she'd left at the post office made her a lot less emotional. If there was no way her mom would find out and have a cow, Meg would have mailed all the gifts back, including the few she had left from island residents. She needed to suck it up and do it. Her new motto. *Suck up the sucky and go on.* Or maybe, *Every BODY has history.*

Not bumper sticker material, but this was her life now.

"Good morning, sunshine," Natasha called out from behind the counter. "Coffee? Black?"

"Please, and a large. Okay if Watson's in here?" She leaned in the doorway until she got an answer.

"Of course. Come on in. Just stay out of the back kitchen. I don't want to get in trouble. Does he need some water?" Natasha filled a travel cup and grabbed a dog bowl for water.

"He'd probably appreciate it. I've been doing the apology tour this morning and dropping off the wedding gifts." Meg sank into a chair at a table near the front window.

"You should let someone else handle that. It feels punitive. You didn't call off the wedding. Romain ruined your day." Natasha set the coffee on the table and the water bowl under the table.

"I've got a system. And maybe feeling all the feelings until it's done will speed up my mourning for losing what could have been. Can you sit?"

"For a few minutes. We'll have a rush as soon as the next ferry docks." Natasha glanced at the clock. "But we've got fifteen minutes before that happens. Did you enjoy last night? Did Dalton sneak a kiss when he dropped you off?"

"No." Meg felt her face warm as she remembered their discussion last night. "Anyway, I'm ready for tomorrow's meeting with Lilly Aster. I'm working tomorrow night at the bookstore, but I'm done at nine. Do you want to grab dinner with me? Mom said she'd take me shopping on Monday morning. So I'm enjoying eating out until then."

"Sure." She stood up and went back to the counter. She came back with a bag. "I've got some day-old pastries and bread that you can have. It's a lot of sugar, but you won't be hungry."

"You don't have to do this," Meg protested.

"We're friends." Natasha hugged her as a noise sounded outside.

They looked up and saw Uncle Troy's truck, followed by the only police car on the island, take off from city hall. Meg stood and watched them go by. Before she could ask Natasha anything, she saw the ambulance following the police car. "What on earth is going on?"

"I don't know," Natasha said.

Then a man stepped into the bakery. "Quite the show, right?"

"Todd, what's going on? Do you know?" Natasha stared at the ambulance, which was followed by another truck. "Isn't that Kevin Call following the ambulance?"

"I was chatting with him at city hall when the call came in. A body was found at the Aster place out by Haunted Cliffs. Jolene called it in. She sounded shocked."

Meg froze. She couldn't believe this was happening. "It wasn't Lilly Aster, was it?"

Todd shook his head. "No, Jolene said it was a man. That he must have fallen off the dock. I'm betting it's a tourist."

Natasha helped Todd with his coffee order, then rejoined Meg at the table. "You move back, and everything becomes interesting again."

"Natasha, someone's dead. That's horrible." Meg glanced at her watch and made a note of the time. That was important in an investigation. What time law enforcement was called in versus the time of death or, worse, the time of discovery. If Jolene hadn't called right away, there might be a reason. "I guess I'll find out more tonight, when I have dinner with Aunt Melody and Uncle Troy. I'll let you know what I learn."

"It's like back in high school, when we used to solve mysteries. Just like in the Nancy Drew books. What did we call ourselves?" Natasha grinned at her friend. "The Mystery Crew?"

"I don't think we settled on an actual name. We never investigated a death. We just figured out what we didn't know. Like who was stealing the band treats, which we found out was Mr. Higgins, the band teacher."

Meg wondered what she'd find out tonight. She hoped Jolene was right and the victim wasn't Lilly Aster. Selfishly, she didn't want her job to disappear before she could even prove herself to the mystery author. And, worse, she couldn't see a future without the author's books.

CHAPTER 4

*Don't expect professionals to take you seriously.
Prove them wrong.*

The next morning, as she rode her bike to switch out her assignment folders, the roads up to Lilly Aster's house were packed with cars. When Meg got closer, she saw why. News vans lined Summer Break's circular driveway, and a bunch of men in black uniforms blocked the entrance to the house. Meg left her bike by the side of the driveway and pushed her way through the crowd of journalists. When she got to the security line, she tapped on the crossed arms of the very muscular guard who was staring over her head.

"Hi. I'm Meg Gates, and I work for Ms. Aster. I was supposed to check in this morning."

He looked down at her, and she held up a folder.

"You can search me. I have my phone in my backpack, but that's it. Well, my wallet and a few pens, but I left Watson at home. I didn't know what to expect when I got here." She rattled off more than the guard needed to know.

"Who's Watson?" At least now he was looking at her.

"He's my dog. He's a cocker spaniel. Of course, he could be a mix, since I got him at the shelter, but he looks like a purebred. I think someone dumped him as a pup." Meg rambled when she was nervous.

A smile teased the man's lips. "Hold on a second."

He leaned into a small microphone on his black blazer. "I have someone here who says she works for Ms. Aster. A Meg Gates?"

Meg couldn't hear the response, but all of a sudden, he lifted the caution tape the police had stretched across the steps.

"Go on in. Jolene is expecting you." He smiled now since his face was turned away from the news crowd. "I wish you'd brought Watson. I have a Golden Doodle at home named Roger. He's a card."

Meg heard the reporters yelling after her.

"Who's that?"

"Did she have something to do with the murder?"

"Is that his daughter?"

Had the man they'd found been murdered? She'd thought it was an accident. Meg hurried up the stairs and knocked on the door.

Jolene opened it a crack, then saw it was her and pulled her inside. "I didn't know if you would come today. It's been a zoo here. But Lilly said you'd come. She had a feeling, and I guess she was right. Is that the completed assignment?"

Meg looked down at the folder in her hand. "Yes. I followed your instructions and kept track of my hours on the front of the folder."

"Great. I'm sure you won't misrepresent your time, but it makes me feel better." She took the folder and opened it. She was still reviewing the work when she asked, "Have you mailed off the paperwork to the attorney?"

"I dropped it at the post office yesterday, when I was in town. What happened here?" She looked around the foyer. "Someone fell off the dock?"

"Well, I found someone on the beach. The problem is the cops and vultures want to make it into something it's not. Lilly's quite upset, and strong emotions affect her writing." Jolene took the other folder off the table and handed it to Meg. "Here's the next assignment. She wants you to find thirty to a hundred places in the Santa Barbara area in which to hide a body. Real places, not in a generic flower bed or on a beach."

Meg nodded, not bothering to open the folder or check the assignment inside. Not the fun or even challenging assignment she'd hoped for. Maybe this was all a test. Lilly must need to know what she was capable of doing. Without complaining. "And when is it due?"

"Tuesday. You'll mostly be returning assignments on Tuesdays and Thursdays. Those are Lilly's research days. Thank you for coming." Jolene paused and stared at Meg. Clearly, she'd forgotten her name.

"Meg. Meg Gates."

"Jolene, someone's at the back door. Can you make sure it's locked? Please?" Lilly Aster stood at the top of the grand staircase, looking down. She wore what looked like silk pajamas, and her hair was mussed.

"Of course, Ms. Aster." She opened the door and gently pushed Meg outside.

Meg stuffed the folder into her backpack before turning around and facing the crowd. As she headed toward the spot where the guard had let her cross under the caution tape, reporters pelted her with questions.

"What were you doing at the Aster house?"

"Do you know Ms. Aster?"

"Did you know the man she killed?"

At this question, she glanced up. She felt the shock on her face. But then the guard who had let her in took her arm and led her through the crowd. "Don't react to them. It will feed the frenzy. Where's your car?"

"Bike," she responded, keeping her head down. She pointed to where she'd left it. "It's over on the side of the driveway."

He walked her over and stood close as she got on the bike.

The news crews had already forgotten her as someone was looking out a window in the house. She pedaled out of the driveway and headed down the hill toward Winslow. No one seemed to notice her leaving. That happened in Seattle, too. If you were on your bike, you were invisible. So much so that an inattentive driver had hit several of her friends who biked to get around. Today there were no cars on the road, which wasn't unusual for this area of Bainbridge Island. But instead of it being a slow day, Meg thought all the cars were probably parked at Summer Break.

At the bookstore, the gossip was all about the man who had been found on the beach. "I bet it was Aster's ex-husband," Meg's mom guessed. "He's been showing up on the island the past few months. Sally said she saw them eating dinner together at the pub the last time he was here, and Lilly wasn't happy to see him. Rumor is he came back for more money."

"Now, Felicia, you know you can't get your news from Sally. That woman makes up half of what she talks about. Troy says that the department is hosting a press conference to release the information tomorrow morning, after the next of kin has been informed. He's pulling out his dress uniform tonight for the cameras. I hope it still fits." Aunt Melody sipped her tea. "So, Meg, how are you liking working for Lilly? Did you hear anything when you were up at the house this morning?"

"How did you know I was at the house?" Meg took Watson's leash off, and he went straight to the dog bed under the counter.

"You were on television, dear. Walking up the stairs. The announcer called you an unknown visitor. At first, all I saw was your back. And your curly hair. On your way out of the house I could see your face. You looked stressed. You look much better now."

"I wasn't stressed, except for all the people yelling at me.

Like I'd know anything." Meg poured herself a cup of coffee as she settled in for her shift. Usually, her mom left as soon as Meg walked in, but tonight the sisters were going out to dinner. It was a weekly event, designed to help them keep in touch, even though they lived less than three blocks from each other. Meg thought it was cute. She sat down at the table where they had gathered. "I don't know anything more than you two do. I don't think Lilly Aster had anything to do with the man's death, though. There's no way."

Aunt Melody sniffed. "I agree with you, but I'm worried. Troy won't tell me anything, but I heard they are bringing her in for questioning tomorrow afternoon. They don't do that unless they think you're a suspect. Sorry about your job and getting you involved in all of this. Oh, and your uncle said to stay away from his crime scene."

"There's no way Lilly Aster killed anyone . . . outside her books, that is." Meg thought about the woman she'd met this week. She was smart, self-assured, and was definitely not a murderer. Besides, Meg had started her own book last night. A "how to be a detective without the badge" guide. Working for Lilly Aster, or L. C. Aster, the queen of mysteries, would add substance to her proposal. If she worked for her for only a week, that would ruin any street cred she might obtain. It wasn't like she wanted to have the same agent as Lilly Aster; that man was horrible. But maybe Lilly knew some other, nicer agent who would take her and the book on. This was one project she wasn't going to fail at.

Unless she did. Or Lilly Aster went to prison.

She watched as her mom and aunt gathered their things to walk the two blocks to the restaurant where they had a standing six-thirty reservation.

Her mom kissed her as she pulled on her jacket. "There's a list of things on the counter that need to be done. Don't worry about the job with Ms. Aster, dear. If she goes to jail, we'll find you another job."

"That makes me feel so much better." Meg hugged them both, then went to the counter once they were out the door. Watson snored in the corner. She read over the list, then pulled out her laptop and scanned the local news for any stories about the body. There was a video of her walking out of Summer Break, her backpack clutched tightly to her chest.

"There's my fifteen minutes of fame, Watson. And my life is over. Again."

Watson snored louder. Apparently, he didn't care.

The bell rang over the door, and Natasha came in with a box from her bakery. "I figured you needed some sugar after your day. Did she kill the guy?"

"No, she didn't—" Meg's denial was interrupted when Dalton followed Natasha inside the bookstore. "Dalton, I didn't expect you."

"I'm checking in. I heard Aster's going to jail. What's going to happen with your job?" Dalton greeted Natasha and opened the box. "Apple turnovers?"

"Of course." Natasha sat the box on the table that Meg's mom and aunt had just deserted and went to the back. "Is it too late for coffee?"

"Mom made a fresh batch before she left. And Lilly's not going to jail." Meg felt like she was trying to corral cats. She grabbed the notebook she always carried and took it and her cup back to the table. The list could wait. "So what has everyone heard?"

After they all had drinks and were eating the turnovers, they talked about all the rumors they'd heard around the island. By the time they'd finished, Meg had a whole sheet of notes. "So did anyone see Lilly Aster's ex-husband on the ferry yesterday?"

Meg and Natasha both looked at Dalton.

"I was off yesterday, remember?" He pulled out his notebook from a coat pocket. "I can ask, though. And maybe look at the logs. Cissy, the girl at the ticket counter, writes down any celebrities that she sees buying tickets or getting on or off."

"And, of course, you two are good friends," Natasha teased.

Dalton turned a little red as he answered, "We talk sometimes. I'm not dating her."

Meg saw the look he gave her, then glanced back at her notes. "Would she recognize Lilly's agent, Robert Meade? He was there Tuesday and didn't look happy. On the ferry I heard him talking about stealing money from someone. Maybe Lilly found out he was skimming."

"Which makes her a suspect again," Natasha pointed out. "I thought you were trying to keep your job?"

"Best-case scenario, it was a random tourist who got lost and fell off the dock. I guess we won't know that until Uncle Troy gives his press conference tomorrow morning." Meg leaned back, thinking about the list of tasks her mom had left.

"Or you could ask him if you see him at home. What time do you get off?" Natasha asked.

"Nine. I could stop by the house. Aunt Melody might still be out with Mom, though. And Uncle Troy isn't going to leave confidential police information lying around for me to find. I thought we were grabbing dinner." She stood and refilled her cup. "Anyway, I need to get busy. Mom won't be happy if I don't finish her list."

"Fine, kick us out. No dinner for me. I have a big order that came in that I need to work on tonight. Sorry." Natasha went to the back, put her cup in the sink, and threw away the now-empty box. Dalton had snagged the last turnover and was polishing it off as they said their goodbyes.

Natasha strode quickly toward the door.

"Hold up, Natasha. I'll walk you home." He paused at the door and met Meg's gaze. "I'll be back at nine to walk you home, too."

"Not necessary. I know my way back." She sipped her coffee.

He snorted. "I know you do, but a man was killed on the island. I'm a little freaked out. Let me play good guy to a damsel in distress."

"Except I'm not one," Meg reminded him.

His mouth quirked into a smile. "Too bad. I'm still coming back to walk you home. At least until we know who was killed and why. Let me be a Boy Scout, okay?"

"If you want to waste your time, Watson and I will close the shop at nine. If you're here, you can walk with us as we go home." Meg headed to the counter to look at her mom's list again. Dalton waved and left the shop. Meg watched the door for way too long after it closed.

After she got all the books sorted and shelved, she finished the last task on the list, and she still hadn't had a customer come into the store. Not even a tourist. The ferries back and forth from Seattle ran until midnight, but the tourists started leaving around five. Time to go back to Seattle and do other things than wander the island.

Since she didn't have anything left to do from the list, she pulled out the folder that Jolene had given her. Inside was the new assignment. She checked the time and wrote it and the date down on the front of the folder. She also wrote the time she had left home to pick up the folder. She hoped Mom and Lilly wouldn't compare her work hours. But Mom didn't care if she read while on the job at the bookstore, so she guessed that she wouldn't care if she did work for someone else there.

Satisfied with that logic, she pulled up a map of Santa Barbara on her laptop and started thinking about murder.

Chapter 5

The best clues come from under rocks or from people you hate.

True to his word, Dalton showed up at the bookstore right at nine to walk her and Watson home. He passed her a cup of hot chocolate as they walked uphill to the road that would take her to Aunt Melody's. Meg needed to start thinking of it as her apartment, if not home.

"Your girl isn't looking good in this thing. The dude who died was her agent, that Robert Meade guy." He carried her backpack for her. When she stared at him, he added, "I heard it from Fred at the sandwich shop, who was told by someone who works for your uncle."

"So almost from the horse's mouth? Anyway, I don't believe it. There's no way she killed anyone." Meg pulled gently on Watson's leash as he had got stuck on a scent near a tree.

"Says the woman who just met her and has spent less than an hour with the suspect." He met her gaze. "You're that convinced she's innocent?"

"I am. I met this agent guy twice, in fact. You saw him on the ferry on the day I moved here. He was a jerk then, and the day I saw him at the house. He'd be more of a killer type than Lilly."

"Except she's not dead," Dalton reminded her. "He is."

"But he was a jerk, and maybe someone else wanted to kill him." Meg tried to logic it out as well as walk faster, but the incline was getting her. She had thought she'd lived in a hilly area of Seattle. The hike up the hill from the bookstore was even steeper. "I don't know what to tell you. I know what I know."

"Those are your Nancy Drew powers? Knowing who killed who?"

She knew Dalton was teasing, but she took Nancy Drew and all the other amateur sleuths in books seriously. "That's not funny. Besides, I'm not saying I know who killed that horrible man. I know Lilly Aster didn't kill him. Maybe this is my first real sleuthing case. I can write my book while I'm working on the case. It will give me the ability to add real-life examples."

"Where you change the names to protect the innocent?" They had arrived at her apartment. Meg noticed that Dalton had left his bike leaning against the steps up to the front door. He must have left it here before walking down to get her. The man was thoughtful.

"Something like that. So if you think Lilly's going to be arrested tomorrow, when Uncle Troy does his press conference, why did you walk me home? The world's safe now." She saw the confusion on his face. He had a bit of a five o'clock shadow accenting his cheekbones. No wonder Luna was in lust with him. With his blond hair, he looked like a modern-day pirate. In all the good ways.

"I was the clicker today on the ferry."

The sudden change of subject caused her to lift her head to meet his gaze. "What?"

"I was the clicker. I got to watch people leave Bainbridge Island on the ferry, clicking the counter as they walked past. Parents, kids, older people, young adults. I count them all. Except for the dogs. They don't get counted. I always thought that was sad. If the ferry goes down, they'll know how many people to rescue, but not how many dogs."

"You're messing with me." Meg walked Watson over to the patch of grass by the garage.

"Not really. I wanted to change the subject. And tell you how truly mind-numbing a job can be. You've been lucky and had great jobs." He leaned against the stair railing, watching her. "You should feel fortunate. Your résumé is diverse."

"My résumé makes me look like a flake." She walked back to the stairs, Watson dragging himself behind her. "But thanks for the positive outlook. Besides, I'm good for right now. I'll start looking for a real job in a month or so. Mom probably won't need the help much in the fall. I'm pretty sure she doesn't need me now. I'm renting the apartment for only a year. Aunt Melody doesn't care, but Uncle Troy made a point to ask me how long I'd be here. It's a money thing. They're charging me the friends and family rate. The market rate almost pays their mortgage. I don't want to be a drain."

"They love you. It's nice to have people who care about you." He grabbed his bike and wheeled it over to where Meg was standing.

Dalton didn't talk much about his family. Junior, Meg's brother, said he never did. It was like Dalton had arrived at Bainbridge Island Middle School for seventh grade after being dropped on the island by aliens. Meg assumed the real story was a little more sordid than that. Rumor was that he and his mom had been living on the streets, and when she'd disappeared, he had started riding the ferry. He had ridden it for hours. That was back before the ferrymen made you get off at each stop. Finally, Uncle Troy's boss at the time had been called, and the next day, Dalton had become part of his family. And a new Bainbridge Island resident.

For Junior, Dalton became the best friend he'd been missing his entire life. Dalton was always over at their house. Meg's parents treated him like he was one of their own.

And in a way, he was, because he belonged to all the residents at the time.

She reached for his hand. "You have people who care about you, too."

He looked up and met her gaze. He moved his hand away. "I'm the lucky one. Anyway, I've got to go. Early call at work tomorrow. What are your plans?"

"I've got the night shift at the bookstore again. Hopefully, I'll get more walk-ins than I did tonight. I'll work here at home until I'm finished with the Aster assignment, and then I'll call her." She leaned against the garage wall. "That's my life, except for the nights I don't work at the bookstore. No wonder I'm looking for a mystery to solve. My life is boring."

"Your life isn't boring." He held his arms out wide as he stepped away from her. "Think of it this way. You could be a clicker."

She chuckled, then, on that light note, wished him a good night. As he rode away, Meg made her way upstairs. When she got there, she turned to see if she could see Dalton or his bike. All she saw was the flash of his headlight as he turned the corner toward the little house on the other side of the island. He'd been at the same place since he bought the house a few years out of high school. At some point while Meg was living in Seattle, Dalton started working for the Washington State Ferries system and became an adult. Unlike Meg, who'd bounced around from college to the start-up, to a fiancée, and finally to home, where she was starting all over again. There was something to be said about consistency.

Her cell rang as soon as she got inside the apartment. She picked up the call with an answer to the unasked question. "Yes, I locked the door."

"Were you outside, honey?" Her dad sounded concerned. She had thought it was Dalton calling.

"I just got home from the bookstore," she explained. "Dalton walked me here."

"That was nice of him." Her dad got right to the point. "Sweetie, I heard there was a killing on the island. Is everything okay? Maybe you should move back to Seattle and live with me and Elaine."

Elaine was her dad's new wife. She'd been his secretary for years, but they both swore that nothing had happened between them before the divorce. Her dad didn't like change. "Sorry. I thought it was Dalton calling. He walked me home from the bookstore."

"What a nice young man. But isn't it a little early to be dating? Romain may—"

Meg interrupted him. "Dad, if you think I'm taking Romain back after his little jaunt to Europe with one of my bridesmaids, you don't know me at all. You should be hating on the guy, not making excuses for him."

"Sometimes there's two sides to a story." He must have realized how that sounded, because he hurried to add, "Of course, I believe your side."

"There's no sides here. He didn't want me, and thank goodness he figured that out before we were married and had kids. I don't want my kids to go through a divorce." Now Meg was throwing stones. She closed her eyes and pinched the bridge of her nose. "Anyway, I'm fine, even with a killer who may or may not be on the island. How was your party?"

"Very nice. Your caterer did a great job of taking out all the wedding touches. I'm sorry you couldn't make it. It would have been nice to see you before you moved back to the island. But we're only a ferry ride away."

And a taxi or an Uber across Seattle and into Bellevue. Which would run her another hundred dollars round trip. But she didn't want to gripe. She'd chosen to live on Bainbridge due to the extremely low rent her aunt had offered her. She felt safe on the island. Even with a murder happening right after she'd moved home. "I'll come over soon." Meg crossed her fingers on both hands behind her back, hoping he wouldn't hear the lie in her voice.

"We'd like that. Elaine enjoys talking with you." He was piling on the guilt now.

"Oh, my cell is almost out of juice. I better go." Meg closed her eyes. Two lies in one conversation. Her dad never brought the best out in her. "Have a good night, and thanks for checking in on me. It was nice to know someone cares."

"Of course I care. Just because your mom and I aren't married doesn't mean I'm not your father anymore. I love you, Meg."

Meg felt drained. She didn't want to fight with him, so the easiest thing to do was to back down. "I love you, too, Dad."

After she ended the call with her dad, she plugged in the phone and then went to her desk to look at the list of Santa Barbara body-stashing sites she'd compiled. She'd done good. At least in her mind. She realized she probably didn't need to add more sites, since she was already over the thirty required. And some of them were unusual. She texted Jolene to see if she wanted the list dropped off before Tuesday. Which would give her a chance to ask casually about the murder. Especially if the victim was Robert Meade, as Dalton had said.

Satisfied with her Santa Barbara assignment, she opened a new notebook and wrote *Murder on Bainbridge Island* on the front and on the first page. Then, under the heading on the first page, she wrote all the things she knew, including a possible victim and the fact that Lilly was being questioned by Meg's uncle. She found the notebook in which she'd written down what Dalton and Natasha had told her. *Keep all your notes in one spot.* That should be another piece of advice for the book. She grabbed a second notebook and wrote that down. On the front of the second notebook, she wrote *Guidebook Ideas* with a Sharpie.

If she didn't watch it, she'd be out of notebooks soon.

She thought about the interview with Lilly Aster. If Lilly had killed Meade, she had seemed okay about him and his faults on Tuesday. Why the sudden change? Had she found out he was planning on screwing her? Again? She needed to tell Lilly what she'd heard on the ferry.

A text came over her phone. She was being summoned to the house tomorrow morning. That was fast. She tried to remember everything she'd overheard during the trip on the ferry. Maybe if Lilly knew what he'd said, she'd be able to acquit herself well when up against Uncle Troy's interview skills. She sent a quick answer back, letting her know when she'd be there. She was probably texting Jolene, but it could be Lilly. And that would be ultracool.

She looked over and saw that Watson had climbed up his stairs onto the bed and was already asleep. He was gently snoring.

Meg walked over and locked the door. It was better to be prepared than to worry about her safety and security later if she heard a noise. There were a lot of animals, besides the humans, on the island. No need to make it easy for anyone or anything to get inside her apartment.

She wrote down the idea about not making it easy on scratch paper. It seemed to be the start of one of her mystery-solving rules, but it needed tweaking. She'd figure it out tomorrow. Then she went to bed. She dreamed of walking on rocky shores, looking for something.

Uncle Troy's press conference was breaking news for the Seattle news stations. The reporters loved covering sordid activities that weren't set in the city. For one, it meant a ferry ride to and from Bainbridge Island, and pancakes with huckleberry syrup or lunch at Proper Fish, all on the company clock. The island was known for its great food.

Meg decided to stay home and watch the press conference from the couch while eating a bowl of cereal. She reread *The Mystery at Lilac Inn* as she waited. When the news cameras went to the favorite local reporter, Vi Chin, Meg turned up the volume on the TV.

"We're here today to get a report from the Bainbridge Island police chief, Troy Miller, on the body found near local author L. C. Aster's mansion. This is the first murder or unexplained death on the island in over fifty years." Vi turned and saw Uncle Troy at the podium. "And now for the announcement."

Uncle Troy had a few index cards in his hands, and he put them on the lectern in front of him. He barely fit into his dress uniform, but the camera panned in on his face and not on the bulging buttons on his coat. "Ladies and gentlemen," he started, then introduced himself. "On June fourth, at ten o'clock, we got a nine-one-one call from a home in the Haunted Cliffs subdivision. A man was found floating in the shallow waters of the sound and appeared to be unconscious. The caller saw the man from the beach when she'd gone for a walk."

He paused and turned the card. "When our emergency crews arrived, the paramedics, after trying to revive the man on-site, transported him to the hospital, where he was pronounced dead. Further investigation determined that his name is Robert James Meade III, from San Francisco. He had been visiting a resident before his death."

Gasps came from the crowd. A hand went up, and without waiting, Vi Chin asked, "Did he kill himself?"

Uncle Troy waved their hands down. "Please let me get through my prepared notes first. Then we'll answer questions. Mr. Meade appears to have gotten turned around and to have fallen into the water from a dock, hitting his head on a rock sometime when he was submerged. At this time, that's all we know. A coroner's report will be presented when available."

"Who was Mr. Meade visiting on the island? Can you verify his connection with L. C. Aster?" Vi Chin asked. Before Uncle Troy could answer, she followed up her questions with a more pointed one. "Wasn't he L. C. Aster's agent?"

"I know what you know about that. We can Google names, too." He looked around. "Any other questions?"

Meg listened to the rest of the press conference, but it didn't last too much longer. Uncle Troy said what he could and then shut the reporters down. She'd made notes during his talk, and she glanced through them after turning the television off.

There was a chance that Meade had fallen into the water. That it was an accidental death. But bad things usually didn't happen to bad people. They seemed to have a way of avoiding the karma from their misdeeds. Lilly needed to know what her agent had said on the ferry.

He'd been visiting someone, probably Lilly. Meg wondered what had brought the agent out so many times in a couple of weeks. She'd seen him twice, and Uncle Troy had mentioned a third time. Why had he come back the day he was killed?

How come none of the reporters had asked that question?

At least she had a reason to be visiting Lilly Aster's house today. Maybe that should be one of her sleuthing rules. Always have a cover story for when you're investigating. Depending on how much spare time she had between her two jobs, this book should start writing itself. Especially with a murder right here on Bainbridge Island to help her hone her craft.

That sounded horrible. Meg was a horrible person. Or she would be if it was anyone but Robert Meade who had been found on the beach.

Her earbuds beeped, alerting her to a text. It was from Natasha. The computer voice read it aloud. **Come have lunch with me. The bakery is dead today.**

When the computer asked her if she wanted to respond, she said yes and told Natasha she'd be there by noon. Riding out to the Aster house from downtown took a little time. But it gave Meg lots of time to think about the current state of her life. Including Dalton's role in her life during the past few weeks. He'd been there for her even more than her mom or brother had been. Of course, Junior was always busy. He'd asked her to come to dinner with him at Dad's a few days ago. So she couldn't fault her brother for trying. It was going to Dad's that she had trouble with. Not hanging out with Junior. Her brother seemed to have no issue with Dad's new life. Was it because he had already left home when the divorce was announced? Or maybe he didn't remember when their family was happy? Or was it a male thing? He didn't feel the betrayal like Meg did.

Before she knew it, she had arrived at Summer Break. There was still a guard outside the house, and he nodded to her when she got off the bike.

"You didn't bring Watson again, I see." It was the same guard.

Meg smiled as she took off her helmet and put it in her basket, then fluffed her hair as she walked. "No, sorry. The ride's a little long with him on the bike. The dog weighs almost thirty pounds. I think my riding freaks him out a little."

"He doesn't like the hills, I bet." The guard walked her toward the house.

Meg nodded, surprised. "He doesn't. What is it about hills?"

"You go fast, then slow." He explained his theory about dogs. "Or slow, then fast. Maybe he doesn't know what's going on."

"Or he thinks I'm going to crash." She pointed to the front door. "Is it okay for me to knock?"

"They're expecting you." He held up his phone. "You are the only visitor on today's list. I'm not sure how much longer they'll keep me on, but for right now, it's a great gig. The scenery is amazing here. I'm usually stuck in the middle of a skyscraper in Seattle. I like being outside."

"Until it rains. Then you'll wish for the tan walls of a boring corporate office," Meg pointed out as she headed up the stairs to the front door. Jolene must have been waiting for her, because the door opened before Meg even knocked.

She waved Meg inside, then glanced at the folder and the times written on the front. "You're doing fast work. Ms. Aster is happy with the quality. So, good job."

Meg watched as she set the folder on the table and picked another one up. Jolene held it out, but before Meg took it, she said, "I need to talk to Ms. Aster. I saw Meade, her agent, on the ferry. She needs to know what he was saying."

Jolene frowned but shook the folder. "Take this and stand right here. I'll go see if she has time for you. She's very busy."

After taking the folder, Meg stood right where Jolene had left her. She was worried that the woman would notice if she moved an inch to the left or the right. She opened the folder. This time the note was handwritten.

> *Meg, I need fifty ways to poison a victim. Please also include a list of side effects of the poison as well as the length of time between ingestion and death. I'm looking for something fairly undetectable, if possible, as well as some time to pass between ingestion and death, so my killer can get away before the person feels the effects. You're doing great work. So glad to have you as part of the team. Lilly.*

Meg couldn't help it; she felt her lips stretch over her teeth. Lilly had called her by her first name *and* said she was doing a great job. Of course, Jolene had said the same thing, but it hadn't made Meg positively giddy when she said it. Maybe something in her life was working out. She was an effective author's assistant. Or she'd been one for almost two weeks now.

Instead of Jolene coming out of the office, Lilly hurried over to where Meg was standing. She'd hoped to be invited into Lilly's actual office. The place where the magic happened. It was probably huge, with big windows looking out on the water. And floor-to-ceiling bookshelves lining the walls.

"Meg, I'm sorry. I don't have much time. I'm expected in town in less than an hour. What do you need to tell me? Jolene said it was about Robert. Please tell me he didn't give you a hard time that day." Lilly looked at her with sympathy.

"Oh, no. I wanted to tell you I saw him the week before we met. I was on the ferry, and he was on the phone. I don't know who he was talking to or about, but he said he was going to shortchange someone with the advance. That she wouldn't know the real offer." Meg saw Lilly's face go white.

"He was skimming. I always thought so, but he must have doctored the contracts before he sent them to me to read. And, of course, I always scanned only the last page when I sent them back." She closed her eyes for a second and took a deep breath. "I hate to say I hope he was talking about someone else, but I don't think that's true. Thank you for telling me. I'll look into this."

Meg saw she was being dismissed. "I appreciate the job and working with you. If there's anything I can do, let me know."

Lilly nodded. "Thank you, Meg."

Immediately, Jolene was standing with them, and she opened the door. "We'll see you on Tuesday unless you text before that. Thank you for the great work."

Meg walked out and felt the door slam behind her. Hopefully, she hadn't ruined her job. Some people didn't like to be told they'd been wronged. Even when they'd kind of known it all along.

She glanced at her watch. Time to grab lunch with Natasha. And after today's bike ride, she needed the fuel.

CHAPTER 6

Dead men tell no tales, but their social media accounts tell plenty.

Natasha let her assistant, Candi, know she was leaving for lunch, then met Meg in the small dining room of her bakery. "I'm dying for some fish and chips. What about you?"

"Dalton and I ate there before the bonfire, but you know me. I could probably eat fish and chips every day. Especially those from James's shop. Is he still around?" Meg followed her friend out the bakery door.

"He went back to England a few years ago. His son, Tommy, runs the place now. I guess James wanted to retire." She linked her arm with Meg's. "Remember how we used to eat there every Friday night, before we'd go into Seattle? It was so much cheaper than the places in the city. And so good."

"James used to kid us that we were going fishing for husbands when we'd go into town." Meg remembered the older British man's teasing fondly. "He said we'd be old married women in less than a year. And look at us now. Do you think he'd be disappointed? In me, I mean?"

"I think he'd be disappointed if he'd ever met Romain. He was a jerk to you. Not only this last over-the-top, jerky thing. He never listened, and it was all about him. You're better off alone and stranded on a desert island than married to that tool."

"Seriously, you need to start opening up and telling me how you feel. This holding back is horrible for your health." Meg grinned at her friend.

Laughing, they turned right and started up the hill.

"Sorry. I guess I am speaking a little too frankly lately. Since I have you in a good mood, what's going on with you and Dalton?"

"Who?" Meg raised her shoulders, faking incomprehension. "I'm kidding. He's being nice. Nothing is going on between us. I broke off my engagement to a man I'd been with for two years. I'm not ready to jump into something this quickly again."

"Keep telling yourself that," Natasha said as she turned into the walkway leading to the small restaurant. The smell of fried fish must be pumped out into the street to bring in more customers. "So did you see your uncle on television today?"

"Yes, and I also talked to Lilly about what Meade had said on the ferry." Meg and Natasha stepped up to the restaurant's window and ordered, and then they found a table in the outdoor area surrounding the small porch. Once they were seated, Meg leaned over and updated Natasha on what she'd learned.

"Interesting. I heard Vi Chin talking to her cameraman today at the bakery. According to her, your boss, Lilly, hired a new agent last week and was supposed to cut ties with Robert the day he died. Maybe he committed suicide over losing his cash cow. Wasn't she his biggest author? What's fifteen percent of a boatload of money?"

"A rowboat or a cruise ship?" Meg's phone beeped, alerting her that she'd received a text. She glanced at the message. "It's Mom reminding me that I need to be at the bookstore at three today. It's like she thinks I don't have a calendar or I'm sleeping my day away."

"Maybe she thinks you're depressed. You've had a lot going on."

Before responding, Meg waited for the woman headed their way with a loaded tray to drop off the food. "She and Dad both think Romain is going to come crawling back to me. That I need to wait for him."

"Seriously? If he did, you should push him into the sound. Maybe off the ferry, so he could swim with the fish. Isn't that *The Godfather* line?" Natasha opened her tartar sauce container.

"It's sleeping with the fishes." Meg sprinkled malt vinegar over the top of the long strip of fish. "At least that's what I remember. We should ask Dalton. He and Junior watched those movies over and over."

"Yeah, but he'll do it in that bad imitation voice he does . . ." Natasha tried to imitate a character from the movie. Which made them both break out laughing.

As they were finishing up lunch, Meg remembered something else that she'd heard. "What about Lilly's ex-husband? Was he around the day Meade died? He could have found out that Lilly's agent was stealing from her."

"But why would he protect an ex? I don't think they were looking to get back together. In fact, the last time I remember him being on the island, he left his girlfriend at the bakery to wait for him while he went up to Lilly's house. She looked like a Miss Georgia or something. Right down to the big hair, Southern twang, and tiny waist. She ordered a muffin, cut it into fourths, and then threw away all but a sliver of the muffin. Before she even ate a bite." Natasha waved a fry for emphasis as she talked. "My triple chocolate muffin. Most of it wound up in the trash."

"They are addicting. I don't think I could have the discipline to eat only a fourth of it." Meg finished her water.

"That's what I'm saying. He's dating a psycho." Natasha put her napkin over the rest of the fries in the basket. "Maybe I'm jealous of her willpower. Anyway, I need to get back. I've got to set up tomorrow morning's bake schedule for Serena. I'm so glad I found her. Otherwise, I'd be up at three getting the cupcakes ready for the day and in bed by eight."

"I need to get back to the apartment and make a shopping list. Aunt Melody's heading over to Poulsbo, to visit a friend and go grocery shopping. Mom bailed on taking me to the store. I'm out of almost everything besides capers, canned crab, and dried pasta. Which gives me something to make tonight for dinner and leftovers. Especially if I raid Aunt Melody's herb garden." Meg stood and waited for Natasha to go first. The walkway to the restaurant was wide enough for only one person coming or going.

"I can send you home with more day-old muffins," her friend offered. "I think we have several apple cinnamon ones. I'll be closing the shop at three. I'll drop them off at the bookstore. I'd hate to see you starve."

"More likely I'm going to eat my troubles away around here. Between your day-old pastries and eating out, I'm not going to fit into any of my clothes. Especially the ones I bought for the trip to Europe." Meg tapped her hand. "And there I go again, talking about the Romain disaster."

"What's with you slapping your hand?" Natasha asked.

Meg felt her face warm. "It's a habit-breaking technique. Every time I think of the person who must not be named, I slap my hand."

"Oh, like snapping a rubber band when you want a cigarette. Does that even work?" Natasha paused, and Meg realized they were already back at the bakery.

"I'll let you know in a few weeks." Meg hugged her friend. "I guess I'll see you later at the bookstore?"

"Sounds fun. I'd love to work on the case of the angry agent.

Maybe that's the title of this caper. Or *An Island Killing*?" Natasha's eyes sparkled as she teased Meg.

"Maybe. I'm not writing a novel. I'm writing a 'how to investigate when you're not a professional' book." She considered what Natasha was saying. "Maybe Lilly's new agent, whoever that is, will want to help me sell it. After I prove myself to be indispensable as an author's assistant."

"You have some lofty goals. Or maybe we should call them dreams." Natasha held up a finger. "Sorry. Candi's waving at me. Something must need my skilled hand. The bathroom toilet is probably acting up again."

"Oh, the joy of owning your own business," Meg called after her as she headed up the street toward her apartment.

Upon arriving home, she quickly took care of the things she needed to do, including compiling a grocery list and starting a load of laundry. And then she looked at Watson. "You know, at least when we were in Seattle, I had someone to report back to when I got something done. Now, unless it's about work, you're the only one who gets my daily reports."

He lifted his head, then dropped it between his front paws.

Meg laughed. "You're probably as interested in my daily life as He-Who-Must-Not-Be-Named was. The only difference is you won't run off."

She didn't slap her hand, because this time, the mention of her ex-fiancé didn't have the sadness hanging around the words. It was more about her new life. She glanced at the clock. "Time to head to the bookstore. Are you ready?"

Watson jumped off the couch and stretched. At least they were both getting a lot of exercise with the walks and her bike riding to Summer Break. She packed her tote with a few treats and grabbed her shopping list. She'd stop by Aunt Melody's and drop it off before she went to the bookstore.

As she knocked on her aunt and uncle's kitchen door, she heard arguing through the open window. She prayed the fight wasn't about her. She couldn't afford to find a new place in downtown Bainbridge, and she didn't want to live with her mom. Not at twenty-six.

"I can't believe you are treating Lilly this way. We're friends. There's no way she killed that rat of an agent." Aunt Melody talked even louder when she wasn't happy, and this was one of those times.

"Mel, I didn't say she killed him. I needed to interview her and find out if she had a motive and what he was doing there that day. It doesn't look good. She'd fired him." Uncle Troy's voice was smooth and calming.

"Yes, she fired him. Which is what you do when you find out someone is stealing from you. There was no reason to kill him, because she'd already fired him and fixed the situation." Aunt Melody did have a point.

"As I said, Mel, I'm not charging her with anything." Uncle Troy let the *yet* hang unspoken, but Meg knew it was there, and so did Aunt Melody. "Look, I've got to go back to the station. Thank you for making lunch. It was thoughtful."

As Meg stood there, the door opened, and Uncle Troy almost ran into her. "Meg."

"Oh, hi. I was dropping off my grocery list. Aunt Melody said she'd pick some things up for me when she ran to the store. I'm paying for them myself."

He blinked at the barrage of information he hadn't asked for but then nodded. "Your aunt is in the kitchen. Have a nice day, Meg."

Meg made her way into the house with Watson by her side. Her aunt and uncle were dog people, but they were in between dogs right now. As her mother told the story, Uncle Troy wanted a German shepherd, but Aunt Melody wanted a toy poodle. Their last dog had been a terrier. So they were waiting to see who would cave first. Or, if Meg knew her aunt, when Aunt Melody would find the perfect dog and bring it home.

She found Aunt Melody cleaning out the refrigerator. "I brought you my shopping list."

Jumping at the sound of Meg's voice, Aunt Melody hit her head on the fridge door. "Ouch! Don't sneak up on me. I suppose Troy let you in."

"He was leaving as I came up the walk," Meg lied. She didn't want her aunt to know she'd been eavesdropping.

She rubbed the back of her head and reached out to take the list. "Are you sure you don't want to go shopping with me? It will be more fun with two."

"I don't want to leave Watson that long. And I've got a new assignment from Ms. Aster. She's keeping me busy. It's not quite what I'd expected, but the money's nice, and she seems to like what I'm doing."

"Is the work too hard? I know Lilly's books are filled with twists. Maybe it will take a while for you to learn her style." Aunt Melody put my list up with hers on the fridge. "I know you weren't planning on being a writer."

But Meg had back in high school, when she thought she could do anything. Only when people had started talking about being practical and getting a degree that was worth something had she changed direction.

Aunt Melody didn't know about Meg's book. Neither did her mom. And she wanted it to stay that way. "I could do more. She has me doing things I hadn't expected. Like looking up ways to kill people or places to hide the body. I thought maybe I'd be an early reader or work on marketing."

"I think she has people for that. Honestly, I think she needs someone to bounce ideas off who won't be using them to write their own book. She had an assistant who was stealing plotlines for her book last year. Lilly was heartbroken. She liked this girl but had to fire her. Since you're not in the book business, she agreed to take a chance on you."

Meg blinked. So much for her dream about chatting about

writing and Lilly helping her find an agent for the how-to book. Now she needed to keep it secret from one more person. Maybe she should tell Natasha and Dalton not to tell anyone. She'd see them at the bookstore after Mom left tonight. They could talk then.

"Well, Mom's expecting me. I forgot to ask, how was your dinner last night?" Meg tried to carefully steer the conversation away from Lilly Aster before she said something that would get her fired.

"You know your mom and me. When we get together, we have a lot of fun. I'm sorry that your mom didn't have another girl, so you could have a partner in crime. Junior's an all right kid, but he's more like his dad. And you two don't seem to spend a lot of time together."

Aunt Melody was right about that. Junior wasn't that much older than her, but he'd always felt like he was in a world of his own. And he'd had Dalton to hang with. They hadn't wanted a baby sister hanging around.

"I have Natasha," Meg said, and it was true. Unlike Rachel, who'd probably pretended to be friends to have someone to gossip with about the other sorority girls, Natasha had always been there for her. "Anyway, let me know what I owe for the groceries. I've got cash in the apartment."

She had the money she'd taken from Romain's money clip as well as her own cash stash, which she'd started to pay for the next vacation. At least she wouldn't starve if her family kicked her out of the garage apartment.

Mom had already left the shop when the bell rang and Natasha and Dalton came in together. Dalton was carrying a box from Natasha's bakery.

"If you keep bringing treats, we'll all be too fat to go sleuthing, anyway." Meg watched as her friends made their way into the shop.

Natasha flashed a smile. "You're going to become my new taste testers. Serena and I adjusted our coconut lemon cupcakes today, and I brought three for us. I need to know if they work."

And as Meg gathered with her friends, she wondered if Lilly had people like this besides Aunt Melody. People who believed in her no matter what. And Meg added one more criterion. People she wasn't paying to be there.

Chapter 7

*Never wear your best outfit to go sleuthing.
Or heels.*

While Meg, Natasha, and Dalton were gathered at the bookstore, it bustled with customers. Between the three of them, they could suggest the right book and find it on the shelves, which got people in and out of the bookstore quickly. At about seven, Dalton left to grab their Chinese food order from the Terra-Cotta Soldiers restaurant down the street. They did takeout but didn't deliver.

They had only a couple of hours left to talk, and there had been people in and out all night. No wonder Mom hadn't given her a list of tasks for today. Tomorrow the bookstore closed at eight. Sunday nights the world started to slow down. At least on Bainbridge.

A group of teenagers who had been hanging out most of the night left as Dalton came back into the store. Meg took a quick walk around the shelves. Then they all gathered around the couch and coffee table.

"I think we're alone. Finally." She opened her honey shrimp and took a big whiff. "This place serves the best Chinese in the Puget Sound area."

"I'd up it to the Pacific Northwest." Dalton waved a bite of broccoli and beef at her as he settled back into his chair. "So what did anyone find out, if anything? We know who was killed, but your uncle hasn't confirmed yet if it was murder or an accident."

"It was murder. I heard Uncle Troy and my aunt talking. She's upset that he's focusing on Lilly Aster. I am, too, if that's what he's doing. There's no way she would have killed Meade. Besides, she didn't know at the time he was stealing money from her."

Natasha looked up from her chicken chow mein. "How do you know that?"

"I told her what he said, and she said she'd suspected as much. I think she was going to ask her publishers for copies of the contracts she signed and match them up to the ones in her files. She seemed upset." Meg put some white rice into the larger honey shrimp container and sprinkled soy sauce over the top. Oh, so good.

"Maybe she already knew that, and you gave her the excuse that she learned it after the guy's murder," Dalton pointed out.

"What is it with men wanting a woman to be a killer?" Natasha asked as she focused on eating.

"It's crazy sexy," Dalton said, looking around the room. When neither woman answered, he looked over and found both of them staring at him. "For some guys, but not me, obviously. I'm not into crazy stalker girls. Which is why I never even talked to Luna. That girl has a rep."

"Speaking of women you know . . ." Meg was almost full, and she still had half a container of honey shrimp left. She put the rest of her rice in the larger container and closed it up. She'd take it home and have it for dinner tomorrow. "What did Cissy say about Lilly's ex-husband? Has she seen him lately? And what days?"

"Cissy didn't work today. And tomorrow I'm going across

the sound to work security for the Seattle side. Maybe one of you can head over to talk to her?" He finished off his food.

"Natasha has the shop. I'll run over in the morning. What time does she work? Do you know?" Meg pulled out her notebook with tomorrow's list in it. She'd told her mom she'd go to church with her. Then she had to make sure she was home when Aunt Melody was so she could pay her for the groceries. And she had to be back at the bookstore at three. "I'll take Watson on a walk down to the ferry terminal after church."

"Don't rush off after church. Those women know a lot about what's going on. Especially if it's juicy gossip, like a death. And Lilly's divorce." Natasha put her food away in a bag, as well. She must have felt their gazes, because she continued. "Don't blame me. I used to go to church with my grandmother, and those women knew everything about everyone. It's probably a little harder for them to be busybodies now since there are so many new residents."

"Leave it to the gossip tree to know about a killer on the island," Dalton said dryly.

Mom was waiting for her outside the Bainbridge Island Community Church when Meg arrived. She'd walked down the hill from her apartment, so she'd worn flats, but with the look her mom gave her, she slipped them off and replaced them with the black heels she had in her tote. She'd been hoping to keep wearing the flats, but apparently, that wasn't going to happen.

"Good morning, Mom."

Her mother leaned in and kissed her on the cheek. "Stay away from Agnes Murphey. Unless you want to give her a blow-by-blow about Romain and his misdeeds, I'd keep my distance."

"Noted. Which one is she again?" Meg followed her mom's

finger as she pointed out Mrs. Murphey. Now Meg remembered her. Every time she'd come home from college, Agnes Murphey had cornered her and asked pointed questions about her progress in her classes, whom she was dating, and if Meg had seen any of the other island kids during the semester. The woman had wanted all the dirt Meg knew. Natasha had been right. "I can't believe I forgot about her."

"Telling Agnes is better than putting an ad in the newspaper." Mom saw the woman looking their way and waved. "Let's go inside and you can say good morning to Pastor Sage."

Pastor Sage stood near the chapel doors as Meg and her mother greeted her. "Meg, I'm so sorry about what happened, but it's better to find out early, before you have to tear up an entire life built around the wrong person."

Her words were like a knife cutting into Meg's heart. If people didn't stop talking about Romain, she'd never get over him. "I am lucky that he showed his true colors as a cheating"—she switched her words from a less than polite descriptor and kept going—"swine before we had three babies together and I'd have to figure out how to raise them on my own."

Pastor Sage's eyes widened. She hadn't expected Meg to agree with her so vividly. "Exactly. I need to get ready for my sermon. You might find it comforting and useful."

"That's what I'm here for, to find comfort and learn practical skills to get by in life." Meg paused when she felt her mom squeeze her hand tightly. She must have sounded snarky. "It's nice to see you. Thank you for offering to officiate at the wedding."

As they walked into the chapel, her mom leaned closer. "Did you have to be so direct?"

"Mom, I was telling her what she wanted to hear. I am over Romain, and I would never go back." She scooted into their regular pew and then turned toward her mom. "A statement maybe you need to hear, as well."

A hand squeezed her shoulder, and she looked up into the face of Agnes Murphey. Great. "Good morning, Mrs. Murphey."

"Now, Meg, you're an adult. Please call me Agnes." The woman smiled, and Meg noticed her hat was off-center on her head. "I wanted to thank you for returning my wedding gift. Although I would have been fine if you'd kept it. You should get something out of this disaster your horrible fiancé created. Women always have to clean up men's messes. Anyway, if you ever want to chat, you know where I live."

Meg turned back to face front and saw her mom staring at Agnes's back as she left to go sit by her husband. She whispered to her mom, "That was unexpected."

"I can't believe she was supportive. She's always snarky at the book club about everyone." Her mom turned back to face forward and took Meg's hand. "If you're sure about Romain, then I'll stop bringing him up."

As the service progressed, Meg was able to breathe around her mom for the first time in a long time. She'd finally accepted Meg's situation. She'd call it her decision, but Romain had made the choice. As Mrs. Murphey had said, now she had to clean up the mess.

After service, Meg and her mother made their way out into the warming day. "Your aunt is having brunch over at her house. Troy probably won't be there, what with the investigation."

After they got into the car and turned on the air-conditioning, they had to wait for traffic to clear for their turn to get out of the parking lot. Mom turned the radio down. "Do you want the name of a good therapist? There's one in Poulsbo."

Meg rolled her shoulders. Sunday with the family might not be the most relaxing way to spend a day. "Mom, I'm doing fine. I'm getting a handle on working the two jobs. I'm making plans to go back and finish my degree. I don't need a therapist. Natasha is here if I want to talk."

"Natasha's a sweet girl, but she's not trained in seeing depression or anxiety." She pulled a card out of the cup holder. "Here's the woman's information. She has an opening next week. I can drive you if you want."

Meg took the card and put it in her purse. "No, thanks, but I'll keep this in case, and thank you for caring about me."

"You're my baby girl." She waited for a couple to cross the road before turning toward Aunt Melody's house. "I was listening to this podcast about divorce on Monday at the shop . . ."

Meg tuned out and thought about the rest of the day. She'd change and take Watson for a walk, then put him in the backyard so she could see him from Aunt Melody's window. She had to work at three, so she could use that as an excuse to leave brunch early, unless Uncle Troy was there. Maybe he'd answer some questions about Meade's death. There was something else she said she was going to do. What was it?

"Are you going to sit there all day?"

Meg looked up and realized they were parked at Aunt Melody's. "Sorry. I was thinking about my day."

"I knew you weren't listening to me. Why listen to your mother?" Mom shook her head and got out of the car. "Anyway, if you need me, you know where I am. Come inside. Melody texted that the food's on the table. Troy is actually here but needs to get back to the station."

Meg hurried and changed, but as she was waiting for Watson to do his business, she saw papers in the front seat of Uncle Troy's official vehicle. She moved a little closer and tried to read what was lying there. It was a coroner's report, and she read the name Robert Meade III. She stepped closer, then leaned inside the window so she could read the medical jargon.

Fifty-five-year-old male, five feet seven and two hundred thirty pounds. The body was found . . .

"Anything interesting?" Uncle Troy had come out of the house without Meg noticing and now stood next to her and his Jeep.

"I'm waiting for Watson," she replied as she jumped away from the door, hitting her head on the top of the window opening. "Ouch!"

Watson was sitting next to her, watching the two of them talk. Okay, so that white lie didn't work. She changed the subject, asking, "Leaving so soon? I thought we were having Sunday brunch together."

"Almost a nice save." He stepped around her and opened the door. "I've got to report to the district attorney tomorrow, and I'm still going through the evidence. On a non-case-related subject, I don't want you to worry about the apartment. You needed to come home. I never liked the guy. He wasn't good enough for you. Anyone could see that."

"I needed to hear that." She hugged him. Turning the subject back to the investigation, she asked, "You know I'm working for Lilly Aster, right? Any chance I'm going to keep my job?"

"I knew you were snooping." He chuckled as he blocked her view of the papers on the passenger seat. "You always did have a nose for investigation. I remember when you and your friends used to try to find missing dogs in the area. Didn't you earn enough for a summer camp one year?"

"We did. We're good at finding clues." She fiddled with the handle on Watson's leash. "I know it's not the same, but I don't think Ms. Aster killed that man. He wasn't a nice man. There had to be others that he cheated, too."

"You think he cheated Ms. Aster? Why?" Now her uncle was all cop, and he was using his investigation voice. "Meg?"

Great. Now, instead of turning her uncle on to other suspects, she'd turned the spotlight on Lilly. Not what she'd wanted. She told him about what she'd heard on the ferry and informed him that she'd relayed the conversation to Lilly.

He stared at her, waiting for anything else she needed to tell him.

"That's it. Except Natasha said Lilly's ex-husband has been on the island a lot with his new girlfriend. He has her camp out at the bakery while he goes to talk to Lilly." Meg knew that this information also didn't clear Lilly of killing Meade. But if she hadn't killed her ex for being a jerk, why would she kill her agent?

Uncle Troy started to get into his car. "I'm thinking that telling you to stay out of this investigation is useless, but this isn't finding lost dogs. Someone could get hurt. Be careful, and don't do anything stupid."

She watched him leave and waved when he turned back to look at her. She'd been given a message. Stay out of his investigation.

Meg had never taken orders well.

She went inside the gate and let Watson off his leash. Then she went inside to have lunch with her mom and aunt. Maybe they'd know more about the murder.

Meg had been busy with customers since she'd arrived. Her mom had a woman, Glory, who worked only Sunday mornings. She didn't want a lot of hours, just enough to keep her employee discount on books. Meg assumed with the number of books she bought each week that she was buying more than her check even covered.

Glory had finished with the customer at the counter. Then, after hugging Watson, she took off. "Got to grab the next ferry to Seattle. I bought a subscription to the shows at the Paramount Theatre. See you next week."

Meg watched the older woman hurry out of the door as Dalton held it open for her. They exchanged a few words, and then he came into the shop. "Hey, I'm on my lunch break. How did the chat with Cissy go?"

Meg groaned. "I knew I was forgetting something. My mom dragged me to lunch after church, where Uncle Troy Jedi Mind–tricked me into telling him about what I'd heard Meade say. Then I came here. Is she working tomorrow?"

"Hold on. Let me text her." He pulled out his phone and typed in a message while Meg helped a customer. When he came back, he shook his head. "You're not going to like this, but she's gone after five for a week. She's going to Florida to visit family."

"Who goes to Florida in June?" Meg glanced around the shop. "Maybe you could watch the bookstore and—"

"Sorry. I've got to get back to work. I'm catching this ferry back to Seattle." He tapped his hand on the counter. "I've got Tuesday and Wednesday off this week. Do you want to do something on Tuesday night?"

"Sure. I guess I'll see you then." She waved as he headed out the door.

A customer came up and put two books on the counter. "I'll take these. Your boyfriend looks like one of the heroes in my favorite fantasy romance. Tell me he likes to LARP."

"LARP? What's that?" Meg rang up the books.

The young woman handed over her credit card. "Live-action role-play. There's a guild in Snohomish that meets at the Renaissance Faire site."

"Not that I know of." Meg handed her the bag and her receipt and her card. "But he's not my boyfriend."

"Oh, I thought I sensed a vibe there. Maybe you two haven't found the spark yet. Friends to lovers is my favorite trope—"

Another customer came up and interrupted them. "Do you have the new Jack Reacher book? I know his brother took over the writing, but I can't remember his name."

"I'll be right there." Meg turned back to the woman, but

she'd already left the store. She walked around the counter and met the man near the new-in-fiction shelves. "The new author is Andrew Child, so the books are still shelved in the same place."

By the time she closed at eight, she'd had plenty of time to kick herself for not going to talk to the ferry ticket girl. And to think about Dalton. They'd become friends when Meg was in middle school and they'd formed the sleuthing club. But was there something more?

She locked the store and, with Watson leading the way, headed home. She had a couple of advanced reader copies of new novels in her tote and plenty of time to read. Unless Lilly started giving her more complex assignments.

A job is a job, she thought, then she added, *Be grateful for what you have.* If her uncle had his way, there'd be no assignments at all, because Lilly would be in jail.

Chapter 8

Strike when the iron is hot—or interview your suspects early, since people's memories fade with time.

Monday morning, Meg was still kicking herself for missing out on talking to Cissy. So after she'd finished up Lilly's assignment, she texted Jolene. The text back told her to bring it by tomorrow morning and she'd get another assignment. Then a second text said, **Thank you.**

Jolene wasn't the most personable in face-to-face conversations. Her texts were even more blunt. And Mom thought Meg was direct.

Meg wrote a note on her new weekly calendar that she'd ordered online last week. She could see her entire week at a glance and had room for a running to-do list. She added her bookstore work schedule, and on Tuesday, she added, *Drop off Aster's work*. Then she wrote, *Meet up with Dalton*, at the bottom of the Tuesday square. It wasn't a date. She wrote *Mom* with a question mark on Sunday's morning square.

Feeling guilty, she added, *Call Dad,* to her to-do list. Making time to see her parents was important, even if Dad wasn't home anymore. And as a bonus, if she called, she didn't have to see Elaine.

She looked at the date. If Romain had kept to their honeymoon schedule, he and Rachel would be back next Friday. He'd probably call as soon as he visited the apartment to get his things. "Why are these presents still here? Why didn't *you* take care of them?" She mimicked his mad voice.

Watson woke up from his second nap of the day and looked around, his eyes wild.

"Sorry, dude. That was me being funny." She slapped her hand. Watson had never warmed up to Romain. A sign she should have taken seriously. Dogs knew who was a good person and who wasn't. Watson loved Junior, Dalton, Uncle Troy, and Dad. Which was a point in her father's favor. And proved that Romain's explanation of the dog not liking men was wrong.

Oh, so many signals she'd ignored.

Never again.

She finished her to-do list, adding a column for things she needed at the store so she wouldn't have to make a quick list and forget something, like she had on Saturday. She added, *A facial scrub*, on the first line, with the brand name. Then she went to her fridge to see what she had to eat.

She had the pasta she'd made sometime last week and leftover Chinese from Saturday. Maybe? She needed to write what she planned to eat and when, especially when she brought home food. She put the pasta in the freezer and then wrote that down in the Thursday square for a quick late lunch. Then she warmed up the Chinese. Romain didn't like leftovers, so if she hadn't eaten them for lunch the next day, they had got thrown away.

She slapped her hand again as she got a soda out of the fridge. She needed to stop comparing her new life to her old one. It wasn't that she missed Romain. She didn't. She missed the life she'd imagined. The one that would never have happened, but she would have convinced herself that everything was okay even when it wasn't.

This was her life now. And she liked it.

Watson whined.

"It's true." She stood and clicked a leash on him to take him outside. "I like this new life. I need to make sure I get to keep it."

Her phone rang as soon as they got back upstairs.

"Get down here now," Natasha whispered.

"The bakery? Why? I heated some lunch." Meg took the hot bowl out of the microwave. The honey shrimp smelled as good as it had Saturday night.

"She's here. The ex's girlfriend. Which means he's coming back soon. They always have a coffee and share a treat when he gets back. Probably so they don't wait at the terminal." She said something to a customer. "Get down here."

Looking longingly at the food, Meg covered it with aluminum foil and put it away in the fridge. Maybe this was why you never read about Nancy Drew eating dinner. Unless she was grilling with her father. Or celebrating that they'd figured out the mystery. Investigating was too involved for her to eat. Maybe that was why she stayed so skinny in the drawings. Meg wondered why she didn't pass out at a crime scene from low blood sugar.

"Come on, Watson. We might as well get your walk in for the day, as well." She clicked the leash back on her dog, who looked longingly at the couch. "We all want something we can't have."

He looked a little confused and tried to head toward the couch. It must be time for nap number three.

"Sorry, buddy. Natasha wants us to visit." She grabbed his walking bag, with necessities like poop bags, treats, food, and several collapsible bowls, and then took a full water bottle from the bottom shelf of the fridge. She reused bottles and rotated them until they looked like they were going to break. Romain, or he who must not be named, had griped about her putting them in the fridge. He'd been using them for a while when Meg had asked him where Watson's bottles were so she could refill them. He'd been appalled that he'd been drinking tap water meant for the dog during his runs.

She'd thought it was funny. After that, she'd kept the bottles for Watson on the bottom rack of the fridge. And the other guy—Meg kind of liked that euphemism better—had switched to a more expensive water with minerals for runners. And had kept count of the bottles. Meg had watched him write the date on the bottles when he put them in the fridge. He'd wanted her to take over the task, but she'd never got around to it. Another one of her many faults, according to him.

When she got to the bakery, Natasha handed her a cup of coffee and a scone. "Does your dog want water?"

Meg blinked, then realized Natasha was trying to act like Meg was a random customer. "That would be great. No ice and I have a bowl."

She waited for Natasha to pour water into a glass; then she went over and sat in the woman's line of sight. She poured the water into the bowl. The woman was leaning in, watching. Meg's plan had worked. Everyone wanted to chat about dogs.

"What kind of dog is that?"

"Watson's a cocker spaniel. I think he's a purebred, but I got him as a rescue. I'm not sure." Meg reached out her hand. "Oh, and I'm Meg. I'm always giving people the whole story on my dog but never even my name."

The woman laughed as she shook Meg's hand. "I know the feeling. I know every dog on my block, but I have no idea what their humans' names are. I'm Tabitha."

"What are you doing on Bainbridge today? Touristing?" Meg focused on watching Watson drink, hoping the question would sound conversational.

"My fiancé has some business with his ex-wife. I swear, some relationships never end. Do you know what I mean?" Tabitha reached out and rubbed Watson's ears as he sniffed her hand.

"Gah, I hope that's not true. I only recently got out of a bad relationship. I'm wishing that I'll never see that loser again." Meg leaned back, sipping her coffee. "I guess visiting Bainbridge Island isn't a bad way to spend a Monday morning. I work at my mom's bookstore part-time. I need a real job, but I've been trying to find myself after the breakup. I can't believe there's so much to do. Moving out was step one. My list keeps growing."

"You'll be fine. I've had my share of heartbreaks, so I know when someone is on the other side of the hill. Josh is sensitive, but it's obvious he doesn't love the woman anymore. He still cares about her, though, and she's going through a bad time." Tabitha leaned closer. "Since you live here, I suppose you've heard about the man who died? It was Josh's ex-wife's manager or something. He handled her money. Josh said that the guy was a real jerk, but Lilly couldn't see that. She thought everyone was fighting their own battles. Such a stupid motto, right?"

Meg nodded, trying not to stand up for Lilly. She was in sleuthing mode, not author's assistant mode. "I heard about that. He went swimming or fell off a dock or something."

"He drowned, but he also had been hit on the head. Josh thinks someone killed him and set up Lilly to take the fall. Now, I don't like the woman, mostly because Josh is always more worried about her than our future, but that's horrible. I hope the police find out who did this soon. We're supposed to go to Cancún in July for a week. If this is still going on... Well, I guess I shouldn't complain, right? At least we're alive."

"What does Josh do?" Meg broke open the scone. "You

guys have a lot of free time, being here on a Monday. Maybe his company has a job for me?"

Tabitha laughed and sipped her coffee. "I am a bit of a lady of leisure these days. I'm an actress, and I'm waiting on the next assignment. My agent is negotiating a part in a series for me. It's going to be on Netflix. Josh, he's a writer. He's working on his next book. Lilly broke out before he did, but he gets a nice alimony check. I saw his last contract. Writers don't get paid as much as you would imagine, working at a bookstore."

Her phone beeped. "Oh, I got a text. I'm meeting him at the terminal. I guess I better get going. Thank you for sharing Watson with me. He's a lovely dog."

"Oh, no problem. Maybe we'll run into each other again soon." I took out my phone and pretended to scroll through my social media accounts, but as soon as she walked out, I snapped several pictures of Tabitha.

Natasha came over with a cup of coffee and another scone. "What do you think? Could this Josh be the one who set up Lilly?"

"How much did you hear?" Meg was still watching Tabitha as she made her way down the street to the ferry walk-on bridge.

"All of it. You are a great actress. I'm surprised she didn't recognize the craft." Natasha grinned and then took a bite of the huckleberry scone. "This is so good."

"Yes, you make great treats."

She shook her head. "This was all Serena. She's a wizard in the kitchen. She should have her own place."

Meg blinked. Natasha never complimented her staff, at least not to her. "Anyway, Tabitha said that they were living off Josh's alimony more than money from his books. Unless she's the major breadwinner in the family. They're going to Cancún in July."

"It's the offseason. They get a lot of rain then. So it's cheaper," Natasha said as she finished her scone. When she looked up, she saw that Meg was watching her. "What? I like to plan travel vacations."

"Have you gone to Mexico?" Meg finished her coffee and checked on Watson, who was sleeping under the table.

"No, but I went to Vancouver, BC, last fall. I closed the bakery for a week. It was heaven." She leaned against the back of the chair. "Running your own business is harder than I expected. You're hands-on all the time."

"Maybe you should hire a manager." Meg threw out the suggestion, but she was still thinking about Lilly's ex-husband. "It sounds like Josh is still very involved in Lilly's life. Maybe too involved. What would happen if she was arrested for this murder? Would his cash cow dry up, or would someone else step in to keep the mystery series going? Like the Jack Reacher series, which was transferred from one person to another."

"Or the Nancy Drew series. Didn't several people write that?" Natasha pointed out.

"I got to go," Meg said as she stood. "I've got lunch at home. I'm going to write all this down, and maybe you and Dalton can come over Thursday, and we can talk about what we've learned since last week."

"I hear you missed talking to Cissy on Sunday," Natasha said as she followed Meg to the door. "Dalton stopped by this morning for coffee, before getting on the ferry."

"Thanks for reminding me." Chilled, Meg rubbed her arms. "The good news is I have a new calendar, where I can write down all my to-dos. Including those for our not-so-secret investigation. Uncle Troy caught me trying to read one of his reports through the window of his Jeep. He came up behind me and scared me. I hit my head on his truck door."

Natasha laughed at the image. "Did you find out anything?"

Meg shook her head. "Just that they have the coroner's report now and Meade was overweight and fifty-five. I didn't have time to read the rest before he caught me."

"Maybe you could check his vehicle at night, after he gets home," Natasha suggested.

Meg laughed as she opened the door to leave the shop. "I don't think he'll be leaving anything out like that again. He even brought up how I made enough money investigating to pay for summer camp. At least he recognizes I have skills, even if he's trying to keep me out of the investigation. Or, I should say, keep us out."

"We're a powerhouse when we put our heads together." Natasha waved goodbye as Meg headed up the street and back to her apartment. If anything, her thighs and calves would stay in shape here. She walked everywhere, it seemed. Today she'd check off *Move* on her daily to-do list since she and Watson had gone down to the bakery. The scene probably erased any positive effect of the walk, but at least she'd done something besides read today.

Because that was all she was doing when she got home.

When she went up the stairs, she found an envelope leaning against the door. She picked it up, then opened the door and let Watson inside. As he ran to get water like he was thirsting to death, she shut the door behind them and sat at the small table.

She opened the envelope. A ring box, a hundred-dollar bill, and a note fell out.

She didn't have to read the note to know that Romain was on or had been on the island. She opened the box first. Her engagement ring sparkled at her, and she took it out of the box and slipped it on her finger. It still felt right, and it glittered like it had the day he'd proposed, but she didn't feel the joy she'd felt then. Instead, she felt sad. She took it off and put it away in the box. Then she opened the note.

Meggie, I'm sorry. You didn't deserve what I did, and I feel horrible that we ended that way. I was cleaning out our apartment and found these in my tuxedo. You should keep the ring. I gave it to you, and I broke my promise. Keep it, sell it, or throw it in the sound. I don't care. It's yours. But you could make a nice deposit in your IRA if you sold it. The money was for our honeymoon. I'm not sure why you left part of it for me, but you should have all of it.

I'm sending back the gifts that were left in our apartment. I hope you find a good man, and I'm sorry that wasn't me.

I'll always be yours,
Romain

"Except you aren't mine, Romain," Meg said to the note. What was he thinking coming here? Had he expected to make up and go on with their lives together? What about Rachel? Had she tired of him so soon, or had he kicked her to the curb? Or had he come to return the ring and say he was sorry? That he and Rachel were over-the-moon happy? But he'd come home early from Italy. Maybe they weren't happy.

She went to slap her hand, then stopped. This wasn't her pining over some man who'd broken her heart. It was a normal reaction to a guy sticking his nose into her life. Again. She took the ring and the money and tucked them both away in her desk. His suggestion about selling the ring was a good one, and she'd have it appraised soon. Then she'd put the money away—her severance pay for the relationship. Every girl should get one.

She checked the lock on the door, then flopped on the couch, moving Watson to the end. Then she picked up her book and started reading. Nancy never had these kinds of problems with Ned. He was always there by her side. Willing to take a drive to the scary house at night or take her to the beach to unwind and play volleyball.

Like Dalton.

Meg groaned and pushed away the image of Dalton on the beach with a volleyball. She found her place and started reading again. She'd be finished with the book before dinner. And since she hadn't eaten all the Chinese for lunch, she still had leftovers.

Tabitha had man troubles, too—a man who was still in love with his ex-wife. Maybe Tabitha needed to read some Nancy Drew and figure out her own life. If Meg knew her address, she could send her a book.

Meg focused on reading and got lost in solving the mystery.

CHAPTER 9

If you can get access to the murder site, take pictures of the area. Don't rely on your memory or sketching skills.

Tuesday morning, on the way to Summer Break, Meg stopped her bike on the road near the place where they'd found Robert Meade's body. She glanced up at the house, then imagined herself walking from the front door to the dock. She couldn't see either the dock or the front of the house from here.

The scenario didn't make sense if Meade had been walking back into town, to a rented house or room or even to the ferry. He'd brought his car the first day she'd seen him. She had watched him take the stairs down to the ferry's lower level to get into his car before they docked at the island. And the day she'd first come here, there had been a silver BMW convertible on the driveway. She'd assumed it was his.

So why had he been walking from town to Summer Break? And had he stayed over and rented a room? Or did he own property here or know someone besides Lilly who owned property? The more she thought about his death, the more questions she had. And, not to be mean, but the guy was in no shape to hike up the hills from the ferry terminal to this house. Or even walk down.

Last night Meg had been working on the chapter on how to investigate a crime scene in her guidebook. She'd drawn a crude picture of Lilly Aster's dock, her house, and the road, but she'd assumed that the dock was a lot closer to the road than it actually was. She needed to update her chapter after this because she'd made a lot of faulty assumptions regarding where Meade's body was found.

She left her bike at the curb, then went to find the trail that led down to the beach and the dock. When she got to the dock entrance, she found a locked gate and a fence blocking the way. There was a numbered keypad, but she didn't know the code. She could see the dock from where she stood, as well as a small boat tied to the end. She turned to the left and saw a boardwalk that went from a deck off the back of the house to the dock.

If Meade had been on the dock and had slipped and fallen, unless he knew the code to the gate, he'd reached the dock from the back of the house. He hadn't missed a turn on his way back to town. And where had his car been? She took pictures of every angle she could see from the gated dock entrance.

She walked back to her bike, but before getting on it, she pulled a notebook out of her backpack. She wrote down what she'd found and drew a horrible sketch of the house and the two access points to the dock. Maybe Dalton or Natasha could see what she wasn't seeing. And she had the pictures.

If, for some reason that she couldn't fathom, Meade *had* walked from the ferry terminal, his car should be parked either in Seattle or in the island's ferry parking lot.

She decided to walk down there after she got back home to search for the silver BMW.

It wasn't much, but at least she had something to investigate. You always started with the victim, and she'd forgotten that tip. She'd been so worried about Lilly's possible involvement in her agent's demise that she'd forgotten to look at Meade and try to determine what had happened with him. This could have nothing to do with Lilly at all, except for the fact that he had been at her house before his untimely death. It was possible. She tucked everything away in her backpack and finished the last of the ride to Summer Break.

This time there was no security guard. Meg parked her bike in front of the house, then walked up the stairs and rang the bell. When no one answered, she rang again. To her surprise, Lilly answered the door herself.

"Oh, Meg, sorry. I'd forgotten you were coming today. Jolene took off for a personal emergency, so I guess it's me today. I swear, that woman is my brain—outside of the writing, of course. Come in. I have your next assignment right here."

Meg followed her into the house and stood while Lilly looked at the empty table by the door.

"I think I must have left it in my office yesterday. Like I said, Jolene is my brain. Come on in." She motioned toward the doors near the back of the foyer. "I'm sure it's right where I left it. I've been writing this morning. I tend to get lost in the words."

"I'm sorry I'm bothering you," Meg said, following her into the office. Her entire body vibrated with excitement. She took a breath and exclaimed, "Your office is beautiful. I mean, I'd imagined it being like this somewhat, but this is amazing."

The white room was bigger than Meg's apartment, and as she'd expected, it had a wall of bookcases behind Lilly's desk. A couch and love seat set was clustered around a stone fireplace on the other side of the room. But the draw was the wall that faced the sound and the Seattle skyline. Glass sliders gave Lilly an unobstructed view and made the view look like a photograph. A balcony was perched outside the windows. Meg stepped over to the sliders and looked out. She scanned the rocky beach below and the dock she'd seen from the outside gate.

"How do you work here? I'd be staring out the window all the time."

"I still spend time staring out, but I seem to be lost in the book when I watch the water and the boats. It's very calming, and with the books I write, I need a bit of calming at times. Especially during the murder scenes." Lilly sat at her oversized white desk, which held a laptop and several piles of paper. It also had a bottle of vitamins, along with two other bottles. The label on one said it was for the immune system, and the other one contained collagen. Lilly followed her gaze and laughed. "If they aren't right here, I don't remember to take them. I have a pill container in the bathroom that has all my other supplements. As I age, it seems my doctor suggests I take more and more."

She dug through the papers on her desk and pulled a folder out from under papers bound together with a clip and rubber bands. "And, because I'm not busy enough, my ex wants me to write a blurb for his upcoming book. I read enough of his works when we were married, so it's not fair that I have to read anything he writes now. But I'll be the better person. Karma . . . It all comes back. Am I right?"

Meg thought about the contents of yesterday's envelope and Tabitha's comment about some relationships never dying before she answered. "I try to do the right thing, even when I feel put upon. Sometimes, though, the right thing is hard to determine."

Lilly sank farther into her chair. "You're very wise for someone so young."

"I'm good with tidbits," Meg corrected. She handed her the folder. "Here's what I did. I hope you like it."

"I appreciate your work. The nice thing about sending you on these wild-goose chases is that sometimes you catch a goose, which gets my creative juices going. This assignment's a little different. I want some funny situations people get themselves into. The stranger the better, although the book is set in California, so you might want to use that as a parameter. But if you find a good 'stuck in a snowdrift because you jumped out of a window when the husband came home' story, I might be able to work something in. Or, like I said, it will get me thinking. And, hopefully, laughing." Lilly handed Meg the folder.

Lilly began to talk about her characters for the book. Meg sank down on a chair and grabbed a pen from the cup on Lilly's desk.

She took notes on the blank piece of paper that Lilly had included in the folder. But one thought kept ringing in her head like the Liberty Bell before it cracked. This was what she'd imagined the work to be like. Sitting here in this freaking amazing office and chatting about books and words and characters. Okay, there was coffee in the daydream, but Jolene was gone for the day. So no coffee.

"Do you have any questions?" Lilly leaned back, watching her.

Meg had been daydreaming about the office, and Lilly had caught her. "No. I mean, this is great. It will be fun. I don't know that I'm funny, though."

"That's the benefit of research. You don't have to be. I'm looking for funny situations for my characters. And you're my second brain." She stood and motioned to the door. "I'd ask if you wanted coffee, but Jolene's not here, and I'm afraid I drank what she left me."

"Do you need me to make another pot?" Meg turned as they were walking. "I'd be glad to help out."

Lilly shook her head. "I'm pretty sure I don't need any more coffee today. But thanks for offering. My chef will be here for lunch, and Jolene's expected back from the ferry terminal anytime."

"She took the ferry into Seattle?" Meg hated small talk, but she loved every second of chatting with Lilly.

"Yes. She had an appointment in town early this morning."

Lilly opened the front door and followed Meg outside. She smiled when she saw Meg's bike. "It's a beautiful day for a bike ride. We're so lucky to live on the island."

And with that, Lilly waved, turned, and disappeared back inside her mansion. Meg was dismissed.

She biked home to get Watson. After entering her apartment, she tucked her phone in her jeans pocket and grabbed Watson's leash. "We need to take a quick walk into town. Then you can take a nap before Dalton comes over."

She'd had Watson at the word *walk*.

When they got to the ferry terminal, they walked through the parking lot instead of taking the direct route to the ferry landing. A security guard glanced at her and Watson but nodded. He must have either recognized her as a local or thought she was more about walking the dog than breaking into cars.

When she found the BMW, it had a notice on the windshield. She took a picture of the vehicle and sent it to her uncle. Why had Robert Meade left his car here? Had someone picked him up and driven him to Summer Break? She could bike there, but Meade had thirty years on her and had not been in the best shape. She didn't think he'd get up the first hill. Besides, during Uncle Troy's press conference there hadn't been any mention of the police finding a bike. Visiting a client on the island was an odd time to start an exercise routine. Someone had to have driven him to the house.

It felt like a clue.

She needed to get home and get ready for Dalton to "stop by," whatever that meant. She was glad to have someone to spend time with. She'd been lonely when she'd moved home. Natasha was great, but she had a bakery to run. And Meg had a lot of spare time.

When she got back to the house, Mom's car was in the driveway. Meg put Watson in the backyard, then knocked on Aunt Melody's kitchen door.

"Come on in," Aunt Melody called out.

When Meg walked in, her aunt and Mom were sitting at the table, playing cards. Wine had been poured, and there was a charcuterie board on the table. "I thought Wednesdays were for wine?"

"Don't be a smarty-pants." Mom rolled her eyes. "We're adult women who like a little wine and cheese in the afternoon. And before you ask, Glory needed some hours. She's hooked on fantasy romance right now, and she wants a few series in full before she starts reading them."

"I'm not the boss of you." Meg got a glass and poured a little bit of the wine for herself. "I think you're my boss."

"I know, but sometimes it feels indulgent to leave the shop in the middle of the day." Her mom set down her cards. "Your dad always thought I was reading at the shop, anyway. He wanted me to work harder, like he was in his business."

"Stephen never understood the joys of living. He's still in the rat race, trying to buy a newer house or rack up more money, which he won't spend while he's alive. I'm sure you kids are going to be rich when he passes." Aunt Melody refilled their wineglasses and then went to set the bottle on the counter.

"I don't want to think about anyone dying." Meg sipped her wine. "Especially not my parents."

"Sorry, dear. Sometimes I speak before I think." Aunt Melody nodded to the charcuterie board. "Eat. Have you even had lunch yet?"

Meg's stomach growled in response. She made herself a cracker sandwich with pepperoni and cheese. "No, but Dalton's coming over later, and I think we're going to dinner."

"You need to eat more than once a day." Her mom not so subtly pushed the board closer.

"I went up to drop my work off at Lilly Aster's, and I actually got to talk to her today." She made a second sandwich, this time using prosciutto. She felt gleeful about the time she'd spent with Lilly, and wanted to tell someone. "Jolene was at an appointment in Seattle."

"Lilly works too hard. She's always writing," Aunt Melody added. "And now she has to deal with her agent's death? I told Troy there was no way she pushed Meade into the drink. But with all the trouble she's had working with him, I couldn't blame her."

"What trouble?" Meg asked as she sipped her wine. Then she made another sandwich. Maybe she'd learn something new about the slimy agent.

"She caught him lying about a publisher not wanting her next manuscript. He'd tried to get her to switch publishers, until her editor flew out to Seattle to have lunch with her. Then the real story came out. It's always good to get both sides of an argument." Aunt Melody looked away as she added, "The things women put up with in a business situation."

"You think he was stealing from her?" Meg hoped the answer was no, because that would mean that Lilly had less motive.

"I know he was. The man bragged about it to another agent." Aunt Melody had been in the literary agent business before she'd married Uncle Troy a few years ago. They'd been high school sweethearts, but when she'd left the island to make her name in New York, he'd stayed behind and made a life here in downtown Bainbridge. When Meg's parents divorced, Aunt Melody had come home to lend moral support and had fallen back in love with her soulmate. It was a great story. And mostly true.

"Anyway, she's better off without him. I know her new agent, and she's a powerhouse. I'm sure Lilly's going to be so much better off now. Maybe she won't have to write so much." Aunt Melody finished her glass.

Nothing was giving Meg any hope that Meade had been

killed by someone else. No wonder Uncle Troy saw Lilly Aster as his primary suspect. She would, too. "Who else was a client of Robert Meade?"

"Oh, he had a few big names and lots of little ones. I never knew why he'd take on so many debut authors, but I guess he thought with the numbers, at least one or two would become successful. But then if they didn't, he'd drop them like a hot potato and sign up more. They were like cogs in a wheel. If they didn't perform, he didn't want them on his list." Aunt Melody closed her eyes. "I would hate to be his webmaster. He had people going up and down monthly, or at least it seemed that way to me."

"So if I had a book, he'd sign me, then try to sell me. And if I didn't work out, he'd dump me?" Meg was trying to understand the process.

"Exactly. Now, a lot of agents weed out their client list frequently, but most of us . . ." Aunt Melody smiled at including herself in the group still. "Well, we give new authors a little more time to find their groove. I never took anyone on I didn't fully believe in at the start. I don't think Robert even read their books before signing them. Especially if they wrote in a hot genre."

"I hear cozy fantasy is hot right now. Dwarves and elves drinking tea and solving mysteries," her mom interjected.

Meg excused herself and took Watson up to the apartment. She needed to shower and think about what her aunt had told her. If another author had been mad at Meade, at least there was a different suspect to bring up to her uncle. But from what her aunt had told her, the suspect pool may be too deep to even see the bottom.

Chapter 10

Everyone is a suspect....

Dalton showed up at six and took her to dinner at a new-to-her restaurant, the Local Crab. She called it Americana as the offerings felt upscale but home-cooked. As they ate, he told her about his day working at the ferry. "The thing I like the best is I'm always doing something different. If someone calls in, they pull me over to cover. My supervisor says I'll be up for promotion soon. I'd love to get to captain someday, but that might be me dreaming."

"So you'll stay there for your entire career? What about your dreams of joining the service?" Meg asked. When they'd been kids, Dalton had talked about joining the Navy or the Coast Guard, so when she'd heard that he'd taken a job with the ferry system, she'd been surprised.

"I already did four years with the Coast Guard when you were in college." He smiled as she reacted in surprise. "I guess Junior didn't mention that."

"He might have. That period was a little crazy. The folks got divorced right after my senior year of high school, so it kind of messed with my head about home and family," Meg admitted. "I was too locked up in my pity party surrounding my family not being perfect. No wonder the ferry service jumped on hiring you, with your experience."

"Not everyone likes jumping from one place to the next," Dalton pointed out. "I'm more of a 'stay and grow where I'm planted' type. I hope I'm going to be able to afford to stay on Bainbridge Island for the rest of my life." He sipped his overpriced beer. "But it's getting harder. I bought my little house when I left the service. I thought I'd remodel or buy something bigger later. Now, I could pay off my mortgage and fill my retirement fund if I sold the house. But where would I live?"

"I know my dad's regretting letting Mom keep both the bookstore building and the family home in the divorce. At the time, it was a fair distribution. Now she's probably got enough right there to keep her on a cruise ship for life if she wanted that life. But she likes what she does. I walked in on her having a wine and cheese card party with Aunt Melody this afternoon. I think she hired me so she could have more free time." Meg held up a forkful of the crab-stuffed fish she'd ordered. "I have to say, this is good."

"The chef is out of Los Angeles . . . Emmett Harding. He wanted a slower lifestyle, so he moved here. Now he's bringing in foodies from all over the Pacific Northwest. We get a locals discount, and he let me call in a favor for tonight's reservations."

"You know the chef?" She smiled as she leaned back and looked around the cozy restaurant. "Only on Bainbridge."

"Emmett is taking sailing lessons from me. He bought a sweet boat last summer. We'll have to go out on it one night." Dalton smiled as he cut another piece of his steak. "He lets me borrow it because he knows I won't mess it up."

"My favorite sailor is in the house," said a man at the side of the table. Meg hadn't seen him walk up. "And this is the woman you called in a favor for? I have to say, I approve."

"Emmett, this is my friend Meg Gates. She's a local, but she moved back from Seattle after seeing the error of her ways. Meg, this is Chef Emmett. Two Michelin stars, if I'm correct?"

"My restaurant's glory, not my own," Emmett replied, demurring to the compliment. "Now, the three James Beard Outstanding Chef Awards, those are all mine. Meg, it's nice to meet you. I hope you won't be a stranger here at the restaurant. A lot of you locals feel like I'm intruding and bringing in outsiders, who fall in love with the island as much as I did."

"We are an insulating bunch, but when you're serving food this good, I'm sure you would be welcome anywhere. They'll get over it in a decade or so," Meg teased. It took some time for the locals to accept a new resident. Especially if their business brought in more new residents. Tourists were fine; it was the ones who decided to stay that upset the balance. "I loved my dinner."

"I'm so glad." He was looking at the entrance rather than at her. "Sorry. I've got a take-out order walking in, and my hostess is confused. We don't do takeout as a normal process, but I adore Lilly Aster's books, so what she wants, she gets. We'll see you tomorrow morning, Dalton?"

"I'll be at the boat at six. Will you?" Dalton reached out and shook the man's hand.

"Such a slave driver. But for you? I'll be there." He squeezed Meg's shoulder. "I hope to see you again."

When he walked away, Meg followed him with her gaze up to the hostess stand. Jolene was back on the island and picking up dinner. "That's odd. Lilly said her private chef was here today."

"Emmett's cooking's so good, she might give her chef the night off from time to time. It seems like he's doing it as a favor to Lilly." Dalton frowned as he watched her. "Something bothering you, Nancy Drew?"

"Stop calling me that. But it feels strange." She took a sip of her wine. It was much better than what her aunt had at the house. Which was expensive. What was this friendly dinner costing Dalton? "Anyway, did you know that Meade's car is still parked at the ferry? How did he get from the ferry to

Lilly's house? He couldn't have walked. He wasn't in that great of shape."

"You think someone picked him up?" Dalton turned and watched Jolene leave the restaurant, bags in hand.

"Yes. And I wonder why." She finished off her mashed potatoes. "Lilly had already hired a new agent. Wouldn't she have fired Meade before doing that?"

"Your aunt would know the timeline, right?" Dalton finished his dinner. "I was thinking we could go out to the boat and sit for a while and talk. I've got a bottle of wine from the Eagle Bay Winery that I won in a raffle at work last month. We won't take her out unless you want to."

"That sounds great, but can we pick Watson up first? I hate for him be alone and tear up the apartment." She set her fork down, staring at the empty dish. "I cleaned my plate. I never do that. Romain thought it made me look unladylike."

"Your ex is a loser." Dalton's lips twitched. "Come on. Let's go before I have to wheel you out."

"You're so mean." Meg swatted at him.

Their waiter came over to take their plates. "Chef has a dessert ready for you."

"Oh . . . Well, can we take it to go? And I need our check." Dalton met Meg's gaze. "You may not want more wine after you eat one of Emmett's desserts. He's legendary for them."

"I'll get that dessert packed up, and no check. The chef said to tell you thanks for the lessons." The waiter disappeared.

Dalton stared after him. "I can't believe Emmett comped our bill."

"I know," Meg teased. "If I'd known, I would have ordered the surf and turf rather than the stuffed fish. I was trying to be nice to your wallet."

After they'd picked up Watson, they made their way to the marina and Dalton's boat. He held her hand as she stepped onto the boat deck, pulling her close. A tingle started in her hand, and she looked up into his eyes. "Thank you."

He nodded, then dropped her hand and grabbed Watson from the dock. "Come here, buddy. You can curl up on my winter jacket."

As Meg made herself comfortable near Watson, the gentle rocking of the boat felt calming. She took the glass of wine Dalton poured her and waited for him to sit down with her. There were lights strung up on the dock, but most of the light came from the almost full moon. "It's beautiful out here."

"And quiet. I bet you didn't get that in Seattle," Dalton said as he sat across from her. "So what's going on with you besides work? You seem distracted."

"I'm writing this book about how to do an investigation, and the more I write, the more I realize that I don't know anything. So for this first book, I'm focusing on what a brand-new investigator would need to know."

"Like what?" He sipped his wine as he watched her.

"Like everyone's a suspect. I believe Uncle Troy is limiting himself, because he came in with a preconceived notion. He thinks Lilly killed Meade so he's trying to prove that theory." Meg rubbed Watson's head. He'd gotten up and come over to comfort her. The dog could read her emotions. "I guess I'm as bad, since I can't imagine her killing him. I need to be more in the middle to let the issue build and solve itself. Right now, I'm pushing, so the answer is what I want it to be."

"You might not like what you find out," Dalton warned. He must have seen her shiver, as he stood to put a blanket around her shoulders. "Let's get that cake eaten and get you home. You look like you're freezing."

"It's not bad. I'm not used to being outside this late." Meg rubbed Watson's fur. "Especially lately. If I'm not working, I'm typically tucked in bed by now. I know, I'm the life of the party, right? Hey, speaking of the party, isn't it bonfire night? I'm surprised we didn't go there."

"Why? Did you want to go?" He sat next to her and handed her a fork and spoon wrapped in a white paper napkin.

"No, but I thought that was where you hung out on Tuesday nights." She took a bite of the cake. "Oh, my goodness. This is heaven."

"Emmett loves making desserts. If Natasha hadn't found a loan to keep her afloat a few years ago, he would have bought her out and taken over the bakery. I'm glad he didn't, because now we have two amazing places to eat." He looked at Meg's face and saw her reaction. "I take it she didn't mention she almost lost the bakery."

"No. Not one word. And we FaceTimed that whole year, almost nightly. It was before I started dating Romain, and with the lockdown, we were both stuck inside. I even asked her how the business was doing, and she said she had enough saved for a rainy day." Meg took another bite, but this time, the dessert didn't taste quite as sweet.

"I guess it rained too long," he said. "Even for the Seattle area."

"I don't understand why she wouldn't tell me. I had my retirement money. I could have taken it out and helped." Meg blew out a breath. "Okay, so it might have helped her for a few months at least."

"You're a good friend, and she knew that. Anyway, she got through it." He pointed to the cake box. "Eat the last bite. First and last bites are always the best."

She thought about Natasha and the bakery all the way home, and when Dalton pulled his truck up to the garage, she realized he'd never answered her question. So she asked it again. "Why aren't you at the bonfire tonight?"

He grabbed Watson's leash and put him down on the ground. Then he shut the door.

Meg got out and met him on the side of the garage where Watson was wetting down a rock. "Are you going to answer my question?"

He handed her Watson's leash. "I'm not there, because I want to be here with you. I'm not that kid who used to love to party and hang out, talking about the time I threw the winning pass senior year in high school. At least not anymore. And those guys... Well, that's all they talk about. What big shots they used to be. Anyway, I'm sailing with Emmett tomorrow morning, and then I've got a double shift. Are we hanging out Thursday night at the bookstore?"

"Of course," Meg replied as he headed back to the truck. She saw that he waited for her to go upstairs with Watson and open her apartment door before backing out. She locked the door and watched his truck disappear down the road. Just when you thought you knew everything about your friends, people changed.

She wasn't quite sure what was going on between her and Dalton. He hadn't tried to kiss her or anything. She still had wedding gifts to return sitting on her table from her last failed relationship. But it was nice having someone to talk to and do things with. Even when she and Romain were doing fine, she was alone most of the time since he worked long hours.

Or said he was working.

The good thing about Dalton was he told her exactly what was going on. Something that she hadn't had with anyone except Natasha since her parents sprung the divorce on her and Junior. Except now she had found out that even Natasha was holding back.

She'd talk to her tomorrow. Tonight she was too tired for that kind of discussion.

The envelope with the money and the ring and the note still sat on the desk. What was going on with her life?

Instead of crawling in bed, she popped popcorn and turned on the television to find some home remodeling show. Here, in La-La Land, even the worst dump of a house could be turned into an upscale home in less than an hour. Meg wished her life worked that way.

The next morning she heard a knock on her door. After grabbing her robe, just in case, she opened the door and found a basket filled with orange juice, muffins, and fruits. Her aunt was walking back to her kitchen door.

"Thanks, Aunt Melody. You didn't have to do this."

Her aunt turned and waved. "It's a 'welcome to the neighborhood' kind of Wednesday basket. I didn't want to wake you. I saw your television on late last night, after Dalton dropped you off. Everything okay?"

"Yeah. I couldn't sleep." Meg knew better than to tell her aunt anything, especially about what she was thinking. Her mom would find out, and before she knew it, they would both be over here trying to fix her life. "Thanks for breakfast."

She took the basket in and unloaded the contents. At the bottom of the basket was a book. *Healing From Toxic Relationships: Learning to Love Your Life Again.* Probably from her mom. She set the book aside and opened one of the muffins. They were still warm. She'd had Aunt Melody pick up butter during her shopping trip, so now she got some out and slathered the cinnamon apple muffin with butter before starting her coffee. She poured some orange juice and then opened her laptop and brought up the local newspaper website. Meg had kept a subscription to it when she'd moved to Seattle, mostly to keep track of any festivals or weddings. Now she was watching for any articles on Robert Meade's death.

Nothing. Not even a mention of her uncle's press conference. Did the newspaper not cover the actual news anymore? Or was it more of a tourist sheet now to give businesses room to advertise?

She did see an article that piqued her interest, especially since she worked at the bookstore and didn't know about this.

Lilly Aster was doing a signing on Friday night. She picked up the phone and called her mom, hoping to reach her at home. When she answered, Meg asked, "Why didn't you tell me there was going to be an author event on Friday?"

"Good morning to you, as well, dear daughter," her mom responded. "Hold on. I need coffee."

Meg's coffee was ready, so while she waited for an answer, she made a cup for herself.

"Okay, now, why do you think it is Friday? It's not until the end of the month. Your wedding was the first weekend. Or was supposed to be the first weekend? Then we moved you home, and, oh, well, yes, the Aster event *is* Friday. It's fine. I ordered the books last month, since this month was so busy. Maybe you can call Natasha and check in on the cakes I ordered last month. I'll deal with the coffee and punch."

"L. C. Aster's new book is a big deal. We should have put something in the newsletter and up on the website." Meg thought about what other forms of marketing they needed.

"Dear, that's already done. Glory updated the website on Sunday and sent out a newsletter. I had forgotten exactly when the event was happening. We did survive for years without you in the bookstore, telling us what to do. You know that, right?"

"Mom, I didn't mean to question your effectiveness. I didn't know," Meg lied. She had thought her mom had forgotten, and she had, but Meg guessed things were okay. "Anyway, I assume we'll be busy on Friday."

"You'll need to unbox about five hundred of the books tonight, because Lilly will be in the store Thursday to sign and personalize the ones we've already sold. We'll start shipping those on Monday. Thank goodness she lives here. I might not have had the bookstore after the lockdown if she hadn't done her first event here for releases for the past five years. That awful man wanted her to open her book tour at least in Seattle, but Lilly always let us have release day. She's a saint."

"Robert Meade, her agent, wanted her to move the signing?"

"Yes. He stormed in here one day and told me that there was no way I was living off Lilly's release day push anymore. He told me that I'd been taking advantage of her due to her friendship with Melody." Mom paused a minute, probably to drink some of her coffee. "Anyway, I told your aunt about his visit, and she fixed it. I'd say it is too bad he passed on, but I'd be lying. The man was pond scum."

She asked if Meg had gotten the basket, and then ended the call, but not before telling her that she needed to be at the bookstore at noon on Thursday so she could help with Lilly's preorder signing.

Meg set the phone down and updated her weekly calendar. The only thing she could focus on was the possibility that both her aunt and her mom now had a motive to kill Meade: to save the bookstore.

That couldn't be possible, right? She focused on her coffee and wished she'd never started looking into Robert Meade's death or writing the guidebook. Nancy Drew never had to clear her dad of murder, right?

CHAPTER 11

Everyone's a suspect ... including your friends and family.

Meg kept herself busy on Wednesday working on Lilly's latest assignment. She wanted to get this done since she had to work full days on Thursday and Friday. Then she could hand the folder to Lilly when she arrived at the bookstore. Besides, if she kept herself locked up in her apartment while working, she didn't have to ask Natasha, Aunt Melody, or Mom hard questions. Like, did they kill a man?

By the time the work was done, she was starving, and she decided to walk Watson down to Island Diner to pick up a take-out order. Eventually, she'd have to unpack her kitchen boxes and cook, but today was not that day. Maybe she'd finish unpacking on Sunday and invite Dalton and Natasha over for dinner, if she'd cleared her friend of any murderous intent by then.

She could have stayed in Seattle and investigated a murder there. Then she wouldn't know the suspects, like she did on Bainbridge. With her luck, if she had, her dad, brother, and probably Romain and Rachel would all be implicated in the murder.

Ugh. Even their names were cute together. They'd probably insist on giving their future kids names starting with *R* so they could all match and have matching sweaters with a big *R* on the front in front of the tree for the Christmas card shoot.

Now she wanted to kill someone. Instead, she slapped her hand.

She and Watson walked downtown. The evening was cloudy, and it looked like it might rain tonight. Meg hoped it would hold off until after they got back home with the food. She took a shortcut on a trail that ran next to the historical museum and through the parking lot of city hall as well as the fire department. On weekends, there was a farmers market here, too. One summer in high school she'd worked for the city, handing out flyers and directing people to the art museum, the historical museum, and the farmers market. She'd directed hundreds of people a day to turn left at the second light.

The good thing about the job was they had paid her for a full eight hours a day, so she had got to read in between ferry arrivals. She'd even won an award for handing out the most maps for three weeks in a row. Jerry Glower had won the extra hundred bucks for a month before they had found his boxes stuffed in a recycling bin and Jerry smoking weed behind the parking lot.

She'd worked the job all through high school, giving her the money she'd needed to start college. During school terms, she'd worked at the Seattle Space Needle, handing out informational pamphlets on Seattle sights to tourists. She'd lived on campus and taken classes in the summer, as well, planning on graduating in three years rather than four.

Except she'd met Frank, and he'd talked her into quitting and going to work for the start-up his dad was developing. Frank's dad had already worked for Microsoft and had retired and started his own business. One he'd sold for a huge payday. So then he was starting again with a new idea. As an employee on the ground floor, Meg would be part of the next payday. Except this start-up, like most, failed.

At least Meg had put as much as she could away in her retirement fund.

Now she had no career. No college degree. And no fiancé. Maybe if the job with Lilly tanked, she could hand out maps again. She had experience.

When she got to Island Diner, several people were sitting outside, waiting for tables. She tied Watson to the bike rack, where she could watch him, stepped inside, and went over to the pickup area, which was a corner of the bar. The bartender, who also handled the take-out orders, held up a finger, indicating he'd seen her. She had to wait.

She stood there for five minutes, then went to the door to check on Watson. He was sitting by the bike rack, watching something in the tree next to the building. Meg saw the bartender wave her over and hurried back to the bar.

"Hey, I'm picking up a take-out order for Meg Gates," she said.

"I figured your type would have a private chef." He leaned closer and smiled. "Get it? You're a Gates, like Bill."

"Definitely not like Bill," Meg responded. "Sorry. My dog's outside. Is my food ready?"

"I'll go back to the kitchen and check. It's a madhouse today. One of the cooks didn't show up for his shift." He tapped the bar. "Just wait here. I'll be right back. Unless you want a beer while you wait."

"No. Like I said, my dog is outside waiting for me," Meg explained again.

The bartender glared at her. "Your loss. I'm a fun date."

"When did I say . . . ?" Meg shook her head and went back to the door to wait so she could keep an eye on Watson. Except he wasn't there. She opened the door and saw his leash was no longer tied to the rack. "What the heck? Watson, where are you?"

A bark sounded from around the side of building, and as

Meg ran in the direction from which it had come, she saw Glory walking him back. "Oh, thank goodness. How did he get untied?"

"I watched as some jerk untied him and then scared him away. I went after him, and thankfully, he recognized me from the bookstore. Are you eating here?" Glory handed Meg his leash.

"Picking up food. Can you watch him for a second while I go in to see if my order's ready yet?" Meg didn't want to leave him alone again. She guessed she'd have to leave Watson at home if she was alone and was going inside somewhere.

"He'll be fine with me. I'm waiting for a table with my friend." She nodded toward a handsome older man sitting on a bench, watching them. "Go get your food."

Meg was still steaming when she got home. Why would anyone try to hurt a dog like that? If Watson had gone out into the street or gotten lost, Meg would never have forgiven herself. Watson, on the other hand, seemed tired and went to lie down after he determined that Meg wasn't going to share her dinner with him.

As she ate, she pulled out the work she'd done for Lilly. It was good, but maybe it could be better. She worked on tweaking the words as she ate, and then she put the folder in her tote. She'd look at it again tomorrow at the bookstore if she had time before Lilly showed up to sign books. She'd gotten her first payment for work today deposited into her checking account. At first, she'd thought it was an error, a deposit put into the wrong account, but then she'd checked her email and found her "pay stub" from Lilly's financial manager. She needed to keep this job going. The money might cover her return to college.

When dinner was over and she'd calmed down, she grabbed the remote and called Watson to join her on the couch to watch some television. It was their "Sunday" since she had to work tomorrow at the bookstore. She needed to chill for a bit, or she'd never get to sleep.

Thursday morning, her mom was already at the bookstore when Meg and Watson walked down the hill. She'd made Watson a tote bag, which would get him through until she took him home at ten that night. It would be a long day for him, but she'd rather have him with her where she could watch for him than alone in the apartment. She still couldn't believe that someone had untied him last night.

"You're early." Her mom put a cup of coffee in her hand after she unleashed Watson. "I appreciate you adjusting your schedule for this. I lost track of time this month."

"No problem." Meg tucked her tote under the counter, then took a sip of the coffee. She hadn't made any at the apartment this morning, hoping the walk would wake her up before she arrived. It hadn't completely done its job. "When's Lilly arriving?"

"Jolene said she'll be here at one. I'm printing off the pre-order and signing instructions now for those who asked for the books to be personalized." She pushed a stack of paper closer to Meg. "Tuck one of these in each book and stack them on the side table. Lilly likes to sign on the title page. The ones that want only a signature, we'll handle separately."

Meg's eyes widened at the stack of papers. "And you're still printing?"

"I told you, Lilly having her release day events here saved the bookstore." Mom hit a key, and the printer started spitting out paper. "Over two hundred people signed up and prepaid for tomorrow's release party. I'll have another list tomorrow. We'll be having that event over at city hall. The bookstore won't hold that many people."

"Do you need me to help move books?"

"No, Junior and Dalton will be helping out, so they'll move the boxes. I wish we could have it here." Mom glanced around the bookstore. "I used to get a lot of impulse buying before and after the events. Now, unless I can talk Glory into working, I'll have to close the store. We'll bring over her other books, in case a reader needs one of the backlist books."

Meg saw that Watson had curled up on his bed behind the counter. She woke him and took the bed and his water to the back room, where she could keep an eye on him. Then she grabbed the papers. "I better get started if I want to be even close to ready by the time Lilly gets here."

She started opening boxes and then transferred a box to the table her mom had set up. Then she carefully put the signing instructions in each book, between the right pages to make it easier for Lilly. Man, her hand was going to be cramped up by the weekend. After this, she was probably heading out to more signings. Meg wondered if she'd leave her with assignments. Meg glanced at the sleeping Watson. "I'm worried about your expensive food, you understand."

Watson didn't respond.

When she took a break from the boxes and went out front, she grabbed her folder from her backpack and took it to the signing table. Mom had already set up three fine-point black Sharpies for Lilly's use.

Then she turned on the radio to a local station, grabbed the next stack of papers from the counter, and opened another box. She could count this as either cardio or core work, since she had been bending over, grabbing books all morning long. She'd finished the stack of books when her mom came into the room. She had more papers as well as a takeout bag.

"Lunch is ready," Mom called out. "I ordered Chinese."

"I'm starving," Meg admitted, taking the papers from her mom. "Okay to eat back here?"

"I'll be up at the counter. The ferry landed, so I may be getting some customers." Mom looked through the bag and pulled out a container. "Let me know when you're done, and I'll give you the number of books we need a straight signature on. We also need some signed stock for the store. I don't like to bother Lilly after the event. I know these things wear her out."

"It would me, too," Meg admitted. Her dad had suggested she go into sales as a career, but the idea of talking to people day in and day out, trying to sell something, was overwhelming. She knew she was an introvert, but she hadn't considered that in her career planning. Maybe in her next career, she should. She dove into her order of shrimp fried rice.

She'd finished setting up the back when she heard Lilly and Jolene greeting Mom as they entered the shop. She hurried to clean off Lilly's signing table. She'd already taken the empty food containers out to the trash bin, but you could still smell the ginger in the room.

Jolene came in first. "Oh, I'm glad you're here. When you didn't show up this morning, I thought maybe something had happened."

Guilt filled Meg. She grabbed the folder and handed it to her. "I'm so sorry. I knew you were going to be here, and Mom asked me to help her set this up for Lilly. I assumed you knew I'd be here. The next time, I'll reach out and let you know."

A smile curved Jolene's lips. She checked the times on the front of the folder. After putting the folder in her tote, she pulled out a new one and handed it to Meg. "Lilly told me you'd be here. She had no doubts. She had me bring the next assignment. So far, you've been living up to her trust. Don't abuse it."

Meg didn't have time to answer, because Lilly and Mom had come into the room. Mom pointed to the table. "We've got you set up over there. Meg's here to help with anything you need. Water, coffee, maybe food?"

"We ate before we left. My chef likes me to eat most of my meals at home so he can adjust my calories as needed. It feels like I'm always on a diet, but he's super creative with making vegetables taste good." Lilly walked over and put her arm around Meg. "And this one. Your daughter is also very creative. Did you know that, Felicia?"

Mom laughed as she nodded. "She's always been a bit of a storyteller. And not just for written projects. I'm glad she's working out for you. I love having her back home."

"Yeah, cheap labor," Meg teased as she opened another box of books. And started stacking them on the back table.

"Not only for that reason," Mom replied. "Anyway, I'll let you get busy. Coffee?"

"Please." Lilly sat down and glanced at Watson, who was staring at her, waiting to be acknowledged. "Nice to meet you, Watson. Your mom has told me so much about you. Who's a pretty boy?"

Watson beamed at the attention, then returned to his bed.

Jolene rolled her eyes at Lilly's stalling. "You've got a dinner in Seattle at seven, remember?"

Lilly threw up her hands. "Fine. I remember. I wish he'd accepted my invitation to the house. I hate going into Seattle at night."

"I'm coming with you, and we have a car meeting us at the ferry terminal. You'll be in and out in no time." Jolene nodded to the books. "Your fans are waiting."

Lilly took the first book and slipped on some reading glasses. "I love being an author. I love being an author."

"Keep telling yourself that." Jolene grinned. "You're giving Meg the wrong impression."

Lilly laughed as Meg put another pile of books on the signing table. "I am grateful for the fact that people seem to love my books and for having the chance to meet readers. I like spending time with my characters more."

"And the money. You love the money," Jolene added as she stacked the signed books after Lilly finished with them.

"I love what the money buys. Like my house. And time

with the two of you," Lilly clarified. When Watson barked, reminding her of his existence, she added, "Sorry. With the three of you."

That night, after everyone but Meg and Watson had gone home or to their dinner engagement, Natasha and Dalton showed up with pizza.

The store was quiet, so they ate in the front, on the couch, as Meg recounted her day. "I didn't realize how much work authors have to put in after the book is done. Especially those who are doing well. It's all about the social aspect."

"And you haven't even done an author event with her. Your mom usually has Junior and me at these things, running errands, moving boxes, and doing crowd control. It gets crazy. And that's before she moved it to the larger venue in city hall. Tomorrow's going to be a madhouse. The people on the ferry line are already talking about it. They add extra staff for launch days." Dalton took another slice of pizza and folded it before taking a bite.

"I worked a few smaller events when Mom bought the bookstore during high school. I remember stacking books." Meg gave Watson a bite of the pizza crust. "It was nothing like this. I think it's crushed my dream of being a huge author. Now I'm hoping that my book sells and I become a solid midlist author, where no one expects much of this event stuff."

"From what I've heard, you have to do more stuff as a medium-level author." Natasha held up her hand to block the dirty look Meg threw her way. "Don't kill the messenger. Tabitha, Josh's new girlfriend, is always talking about all the social media he has to do compared to what she does as an actress. And guess what? Josh has a type. Tabitha's writing a romance novel in her spare time."

"I guess the acting thing isn't working out?" Meg crossed her legs and stared at the pizza. She shouldn't want a third slice, but she did. Food tasted better on the island. Or she was depressed. She'd heard that people ate when they were depressed. Or stressed. She'd been through a lot, so maybe that was what was going on. She decided to stop thinking and eat the pizza.

"She told me yesterday that her agent was playing hardball with them, so she had some free time and decided to do this book thing. Since it looked so easy." Natasha laughed.

The front door opened as Meg took a huge bite of her pizza. She chewed furiously but then relaxed when she saw it was Uncle Troy. He glanced at the three of them.

"Looks like you're busy around here," he joked.

"Everyone has to eat," Meg responded after swallowing. "We have plenty. Do you want a slice?"

"Nope. But I need to talk with Ms. Jones for a few minutes. Do you mind coming to the station with me? If you're done with dinner?" He scratched Watson on the head while he waited for an answer.

Natasha's eyes widened, and she wiped her mouth with a napkin. "Now?"

"If you don't mind." Uncle Troy nodded. "We need to clear up why you were the last person seen with Robert Meade on the night he died. We have a video of him getting into your car at the ferry terminal."

CHAPTER 12

Having too many suspects is a good thing.

"What on earth is going on?" Meg stood, but Dalton grabbed her hand and pulled her back down on the couch.

"Let your uncle do his job." Dalton put an arm around her. "Natasha, call me if you need a ride home. I don't want you walking alone in the dark."

Uncle Troy shook his head. "You kids take care of each other. Maybe a little too much sometimes. Don't worry about Natasha. I'll drop her off at her house when we finish talking."

"I'm worried about her," Meg declared.

"Meg, leave it alone. I'll fill you in tomorrow morning." Natasha wiped her hands with a napkin and then stood. "Mr. Miller, I'm ready."

"Chief Miller or just Chief will work." He held the door open for her.

When they left, Dalton let go of Meg. "You can't block these things. If a police officer says to do something, you do it."

"What does he want from Natasha? And what was that about her driving Robert around the night he died?" She closed her eyes, then turned on Dalton. "And you're not surprised about all this."

"No, sorry." He took the last slice of pizza.

Meg waited for him to finish the slice, then asked, "Do you want to tell me what you know?"

"Natasha was in a bad spot when the lockdown happened. I told you part of this. Anyway, she'd remodeled the bakery and had a loan payment. She couldn't shutter it. She needed to make the payment and utilities and supplies. But the island was dead. No one was coming to visit our cute little town. Especially when they started talking about Seattle as a hot spot for the virus. That Seattle was the first place it was detected in the United States." He took a breath and closed the empty pizza box.

"I remember. I was here. And stuck in Seattle when the ferries were limited to essential travel only." Meg pushed away the memories of that time. "So Natasha was hurting. What's that got to do with Robert Meade?"

"He loaned her the money to stay afloat. The interest rate is high, but it kept her open and solvent. It was either take the loan offer or sell the bakery to Emmett. Meade kept bringing up the money she owed him every time he visited. He was mean to her. One day a few months before you moved here, she broke and told him off in the middle of Island Diner during the dinner rush. Of course, everyone was watching when she did." He rolled his shoulders and stood. "I'm surprised it took your uncle this long to bring her in for a talk. We both know she didn't kill him. Hopefully, she has a strong alibi."

"And if she doesn't? I don't get how you can be so calm." She rose from the couch, then went over and looked out the window. A few tourists were heading to dinner or the local night spot, but no one seemed to be heading to her store to grab a book. Meg wasn't sure why her mom had hired her, except to give her a job here. Like she'd told Lilly, she liked having her daughter home.

"Natasha will be fine. She didn't kill the guy, and none of Nancy Drew's friends were ever convicted of murder. We're not going to let her be the one to break that tradition." He grabbed the pizza box. "Do you have anything else that needs to go to the trash? We probably should be working on closing up."

When Meg got home, she texted Natasha and paced until she got a reply.

Just got home. I'm fine. Thanks for worrying about me. We'll talk later.

Meg stared at the message. *We'll talk later.* Natasha had to assume that Dalton would fill Meg in on what had happened. She flopped on her bed and stared at the ceiling. She needed to find out who had killed Robert Meade so the dead guy could stop messing with her life and her friends.

She went over to the desk and opened her laptop, then pulled up the file named "Meade Death." Then she started updating her notes and making a list of what she didn't know and how she'd find it out. As she typed, she highlighted parts that could go in her guidebook. Like not dismissing a suspect because they were your best friend. Still, she was sure Natasha was innocent. If Meade had been mean to Natasha, he had probably been mean to many, many others. She had to find the clues.

The next morning her alarm woke her, and blurry-eyed, she got ready for the day. She sat down at the table once the coffee was done, and started writing a to-do list for the day. She needed to be at the bookstore at three. She needed Lilly's book tour schedule so she'd know when to pick up and deliver assignments. Unless Jolene was going to be at the house to work with her. And since Lilly hadn't said anything about changing her schedule, maybe that was the plan.

She didn't want to be out of work for a month or more while Lilly was off promoting the new release.

Now she sounded selfish.

Meg opened the file on Meade that she'd updated yesterday

and highlighted one of the questions in a different color. Who was this man who would step in to help a local business but then use that help as leverage? If he'd done it to Natasha, you could bet it wasn't the first time he'd used power and influence to get his way.

She stood and looked out the window. Uncle Troy's truck was still in the driveway. When he left, she'd go to the house and talk to Aunt Melody. As a former literary agent, she had to know more about Robert Meade. Maybe enough to get Natasha out of Uncle Troy's spotlight. At least for the murder. She added the visit to her to-do list and took out one of the muffins her aunt had given her. As she ate it, she realized she still had her aunt's basket. She didn't need an excuse to visit family, but she was glad she had one today.

With that settled, she ate her breakfast and opened the new folder from Lilly she'd gotten yesterday. The page had one question. She read it aloud to Watson. "If you were going to kill someone, who would it be, and how would you stage it so someone else would take the blame?"

Lilly's questions were getting odder with each assignment, but she had said she liked Meg's creative mind. Maybe this was a way for her to determine a jumping-off place for her novels. Or perhaps she wanted to see how a normal person would plan a murder and why.

There was only one problem with that theory. It assumed that Meg was normal.

Romain's note was still sitting on Meg's desk. Why had he come all this way to return a ring that she'd practically thrown in his face? Well, without him being there. And hidden in the breast pocket of his tux, so he might not ever find it.

She should have waited for him to get home, then actually thrown the ring in his face. But that would have meant a face-to-face confrontation. Something that she was uncomfortable with. Something that she hadn't had with Romain yet. It needed to be done; she knew it. He thought he could come to her apartment and drop off the engagement ring plus some cash and she'd be happy.

What had he expected?

Now she had two mysteries on her hands. Who killed Meade? And why was Romain being so nice? She wasn't sure she wanted the answer to either question.

The problem was she needed the answer to both.

She heard Uncle Troy's truck leave after she'd gotten out of the shower. She peeked out the window after she'd dressed to confirm this. It was time to get to work.

Meg grabbed the basket and clicked a lead on Watson. She'd pop him into her aunt's backyard before they talked. Meg had some time to visit before she had to go to the bookstore. Lilly's assignment was going to take a bit of thought. Unless she planned to kill Romain. She had plenty of ideas there. But if she went there, she needed to change the name to protect the guilty.

"You look happy," Aunt Melody said as Meg walked through the kitchen door. "I'm so glad you're settling in. Your mom thought it might be a while."

Meg didn't want to mention why she was smiling, so instead she agreed. "I wanted to bring back your basket. Those muffins were amazing."

"Thanks." Aunt Melody put the basket on top of the fridge. "It's nice to have someone to bake for. Usually, Troy winds up taking a batch to the station. Those guys will eat anything. Of course, most of them aren't married. So if you're looking for a date, let me know."

"I'm okay being single for a while." Meg thought that planning Romain's imaginary death might not be the healthiest activity for her. "So has Uncle Troy figured out what happened to that agent of Ms. Aster's? Will her new agent be at the signing?"

"Oh, probably. That's tonight, isn't it?" She glanced at her calendar. "I guess I better get something in the slow cooker for Troy. He hates book events."

Her aunt had ignored one of her questions and barely answered the second. Was it because she'd been a cop's wife for too long?

"Who is her agent?"

"The new one? Sarah Townsend. She's amazing. I told Lilly years ago she should dump Meade. He had a horrible reputation in the business." She poured Meg a cup of coffee. "She finally caught him doctoring the books, which he probably had been doing for years. He begged her to forgive him. Said that he would make it up to her, but she held her ground. Thank goodness."

"Aunt Melody, don't you think that makes her look guilty of killing him?" Meg sipped her coffee. "If he was stealing from her?"

"Lilly wouldn't kill a fly. That's why she hired Jolene. Jolene was probably the one who fired Robert. Lilly tries to stay out of the business side of the writing. That's one reason she didn't see his treachery soon enough. But when Jolene started cleaning up her office and found the contracts, she realized they didn't match the ones that the publishing house had sent her when she digitized all the records. Jolene was even madder than Lilly. She came over for coffee to grill me about new agents I thought would be a better fit for Lilly."

Meg wasn't sure her aunt knew what she was doing. By expressing her faith that Lilly didn't kill Meade, she moved the spotlight onto Jolene. Meg needed to find out more about the assistant that Lilly thought she couldn't live without. And someone needed to check out the new agent. Was she around the day Meade died? Would she kill off the competition?

As Meg gathered Watson from his favorite napping spot on the back deck, by the planter with blooming pansies and tall lemongrass in the middle, she decided she might have some time with both women during the launch event this evening.

Sometimes the Fates put you on the exact path where you need to be. Even if you have to go through a cheating fiancé to get there.

The store had been crazy since they'd opened. Glory had been assigned to sell water to the waiting crowd starting at two. She also handed out a list of local restaurants that would deliver. Felicia had set up the system a few books signings ago, when she'd had two people pass out from heat exhaustion while they waited in line. She'd wanted to give away the water, but when she'd added up the numbers, she'd realized it would take a chunk out of her profits for the event. Profits she needed to keep the store open between book releases.

Dalton had made a second supply run to the grocery store for more water. He dropped off a PayDay on the table in front of Meg as she checked book boxes to make sure they were ready to move over to the auditorium. Meg held it up. "What's this?"

"Don't tell me it's not your favorite anymore," he said as he poured ice into the empty cooler he'd brought back from Glory's station in front of city hall. "Glory always goes for Hershey's with Almonds. And your mom—she's partial to anything with coconut. So I get Almond Joy bars for her."

"You buy candy bars when you're sent for water?" Meg laughed. "No wonder Mom needs this event. You all are all about the extras."

"It's not extra. It's necessary. Your mom gets hangry if she doesn't have a treat midday. And you take after her." He grabbed the cooler and opened the back door.

"I do not," Meg called after him as he left to take the now full cooler to Glory. She went over and refilled her water bottle at the water filter machine her mom had bought a few years ago.

Meg's mom came in the back room, a half-eaten candy bar in her hand, and looked around. "Who are you talking to?"

"Dalton, or I was." Meg glanced at the back door, through which he'd left, probably without having heard her witty comeback. "He left with water. The boxes are ready. What's next?"

"I'm heading over to work with Dalton and Junior on the setup. I need you to watch the front. We've been busy today with people having someone else hold their place in line as they come in to get something to read." She took the last bite of her candy bar. "I love book people."

Meg chuckled as she started moving her stuff to the front. "Do you want me to leave the back door open?"

"Please. I'll be sending Dalton and Junior back with a cart to get the books." She nodded to Watson, who was sleeping on his bed. "Do you need to take him out before I leave you here by yourself?"

"Not a bad idea. I'll get everything moved to the front, and then I'll take him out. He shouldn't be long."

"No worries. We only have the biggest event of this year happening in less than six hours." Mom laughed and shooed Meg away when she stopped in her tracks. "I was kidding. Go get set up and then take your dog for a walk. You probably need some fresh air, too."

Her mom was right about that. She needed to stretch. She hadn't sat this long since she left her job. However, working at the bookstore gave her the opportunity to engage in a lot of different activities during the day. Today was busier than normal. She hadn't had time to work on Lilly's assignment, at least not on paper. She'd been thinking about how to kill Romain, now named George, all day.

Probably not something she should admit to her uncle or anyone in law enforcement.

Walking Watson, she ran into Jolene standing by her car, waiting in the ferry parking lot. She was looking at something on her phone. Meg walked over to her and called out a greeting. "Hi, Jolene. Waiting for someone for the event tonight?"

She looked up, frowning. But when she recognized Meg, she smiled. "Lilly's new agent. Sarah's on the ferry, so I'm running her up to the house. The chef has an early dinner ready for them. Lilly doesn't like waiting until after events to eat. When we're on the road, we're always the first to arrive at some restaurant, hoping they'll feed us before the nightly rush."

"Well, Mom's busy getting the auditorium set up. She had Natasha bake a cake with the book cover on it. Actually three cakes. Mom's hoping that will be enough if we cut small slices." Meg realized she was babbling. Jolene probably already knew about her mother's plans for the event. "Anyway, I'm taking Watson out for a few minutes."

"Remind me to get a picture of Lilly with the cakes. She'll love that. We're always looking for fun photo ops from the events." She looked down at the phone when it buzzed. "That's Sarah. She's looking for me."

Meg watched as Jolene turned and scanned the ferry parking lot. A slender blond woman in a skirted suit had her phone out and was at the entrance to the walk-on passengers parking lot. She saw Jolene and headed her way. She had brought a small suitcase.

"There she is. I guess she's staying overnight. They need to review all of Lilly's old contracts and figure out what to do next with this mess Robert left," Jolene muttered as the woman walked toward them. "Hey, stay and meet her. Lilly's probably been talking about you, so you might as well meet face-to-face."

"Okay." Meg glanced at her watch. She'd been gone less than ten minutes. A few more wouldn't hurt. And it was book business. *That* Mom would understand.

When Sarah reached the car, she hugged Jolene. "I'm so excited to be here for this release. And to help Lilly clean up this disaster. Of course Robert would make a mess of things. Hopefully, her contract with him ends at his death. He didn't have any other agents in the company, so that's helpful."

When she leaned away from Jolene, her eyes lit up. "Oh, this must be the new member of the Aster team. You're Maggie, right?"

"Meg," she corrected as she was swept into a hug. When Sarah released her, Meg glanced down at Watson, who was looking at her with amusement. "And this is Watson, my dog."

"Well, isn't this a pleasure? You're related to Melody, right? It's old home week here. I can't wait to see Melody and that handsome hunk that wooed her away from the publishing world." Sarah glanced at her luggage. "Can I put this in the car?"

Jolene opened the trunk with her remote and reached for the bag. "Let me."

Then Sarah got into the back seat of the car as her phone rang. "Oh, James, I'm so glad you called. However, I'm away from my desk right now, but maybe we could chat tomorrow, when I'm on my way back to civilization? Yes, I'm out in the wilds today."

Meg met Jolene's gaze as she closed the back door. "I'll see you tonight?"

"If I'm not off running errands for the princess here. Robert might have been a pain and a thief, but at least he pretended to be a human. This one? I'm not sure." Jolene went to the driver's door and shook her head. "Off to chauffeur the new agent to the house. I'll see you later tonight, hopefully."

CHAPTER 13

The clopping of hooves is rarely from zebras.

Lilly's talk that night was more of a conversation with the other famous author on the island, a man who wrote thrillers about art. They both shared their love of the little art museum on the island. Meg made a mental note to stop in there one day soon. She'd visited as a kid, part of a school field trip, of course, but it had been a while. She sat at the signing table in the back, watching the interview. The other author, Skyler Johnson, was good at keeping Lilly talking about her book. Mom had had them bring a few copies of his latest novel over from the store, as well. The story sounded fascinating, from the hints he dropped as he asked the questions.

The conversation went wonky after the audience question and answer period started.

"Miss Aster, can you tell us what you know about the dead man found floating near your home a few days ago?" A man with a small tape recorder had stood and asked the question before Skyler could call on anyone.

Sarah must have been standing close by, because she stepped in front of the stage and shook her head. She grabbed the microphone from Skyler and announced, "I'm sorry, but this is a book conversation, not a press conference. If there are any other members of the press with us tonight, please refrain from interrupting the conversation again. Ms. Aster's official comment on the death of Robert Meade III will be released to the press tomorrow morning at eight at the police station."

As the first journalist headed out of the audience, several others stood and left with them. They'd been in the back, so they weren't any of the people who'd lined up for hours to see L. C. Aster. They would probably wait at the doorway to see if they could corner Lilly as she left the building later. Meg watched as readers filled the empty chairs. The auditorium wasn't big enough for the book signing, either. Mom would probably have to do the next one at the local park at midday to allow everyone a chair. Or hold two events.

After that interruption, the rest of the night went well. Natasha had arrived a little late, but she was in charge of getting readers' names as they stood in line to have Lilly sign their book. Then she wrote each name on a sticky note and put it in a book that she handed the customer as she explained the rules. One picture and only signatures on books bought tonight. Skyler Johnson's autograph line was much smaller. Dalton handled the line for his book signing, with Aunt Melody helping Mr. Johnson.

Meg's shoulders were starting to scream, along with her feet. She didn't understand why. She was standing and moving one book at a time. Well, sometimes four, but mostly one. Who knew being a bookseller would be so physical?

Lilly looked up at her and smiled. "It's a marathon, but it looks like the lines are starting to ease up a little. I'll be back from Los Angeles on Monday night, so I'll have another assignment for you then, unless you need a break."

Meg handed her the next book with the sticky note on the title page. "No. I'll have this one done. I've had to do more thinking this time rather than looking up stuff."

She took the selfie for the reader and then turned to the

next person in line. Romain handed her the book with his sticky note and receipt.

She was tired. She was seeing things. She blinked, then looked again.

Nope. Her cheating fiancé was here and had bought a book for Lilly to sign. Sometimes God laughs.

"What are you doing here?" Meg focused on the receipt, then shoved it back into his hand.

"I came to talk to you, but I guess I picked the wrong night. I took a chance that you'd be working at the bookstore tonight. Where's Watson?" He glanced around the auditorium. "Do you need me to take him for a walk? I can hang around until you're done."

"Watson's fine, and he's not your responsibility. You never liked him, anyway." Meg handed Lilly the book and the sticky note. "You can get a picture of you and Ms. Aster if you want."

"Not true. I liked the canine." Romain's voice went soft. "Maybe I could get a picture of you and me."

Meg glared and put the table between them.

Lilly looked at the sticky note, then up at Romain. "That's an unusual name."

"My folks love visiting Europe," he responded, then looked at Meg. "I find it's kind of boring without the right person to visit with."

Lilly looked thoughtfully from him to Meg. She signed the book and held it out to him. "And that answers the next question. Have a nice night, Mr. Evans. You can exit to your left. Meg, can you help the next reader?"

Meg nodded and stepped around the table to help the excited woman behind Romain.

"I bought all four books you had available. I have them at home, but I didn't get signed copies before. These will never be read, I promise." The woman pushed a stunned Romain out of the way as she went up to the table to talk with Lilly. "I love your books."

Meg ignored Romain's stare, which she felt in the middle of her back, and when she turned around after setting the first opened book and sticky note in front of Lilly, he'd faded into the crowd. Meg opened the next book and waited to switch the books out. When Lilly looked up at her, she explained, "I'm sorry about that. I never expected him to come here."

"Well, I guess I'll know who you're considering killing in the assignment. Don't worry about him. We all have baggage." She took the next book and smiled at the reader before signing. "Make sure you follow me on Facebook. I'll be doing posts from all my stops."

"I'm coming to the signing in Scottsdale. My mom has a condo there, and my friends and I are doing a girls' trip to see you. They're working, or they would have come tonight." The superfan came around the table, then handed Meg her phone. "Can you take two, in case the first one is blurry?"

As Meg worked with the last few people in line, her aunt came over to help her since no fans were waiting for Skyler Johnson to sign their books. He was busy signing stock for the bookstore. "Was that Romain I saw earlier?"

"It was." Meg opened another box of books behind them. She didn't want to talk about it.

Aunt Melody helped her set the rest of the books on the table. She smiled at Lilly. "Go ahead and sign all of these. Felicia will sell out by the end of next week."

By the time Lilly had finished with the last attendee, everyone who'd worked the event was gathered around the signing table. Meg's mom sank into a chair. "That was crazy. I'm sure your numbers are going to be list-worthy this week, especially with your trip to Los Angeles."

"I'm getting the buzz that she might have hit last week with the run on preorders. So technically this will be week two. Let's cross our fingers that we'll have a long run on the lists. It's a great book," Sarah added, not looking up as she typed on her phone.

As everyone cleared out, Meg noticed that Dalton and Junior were taking back boxes of books to the bookstore as well as taking cardboard to the recycling. She headed over to her mom and sat next to her. "What can I help with?"

"We're good. Go check on Watson at the bookstore. I'm sure Glory's ready to close down the shop." She leaned back and closed her eyes. "I know we need big events like this, but sometimes, I want my slow, quiet bookstore back. The next week or so is going to be busy as we send out the rest of the preorders. We'll get a rush of call-ins to see if we still have signed copies."

She pointed to Meg's bag. "Don't forget that. And take the kids out to dinner. I'll reimburse you. Unless you need my card."

Meg shook her head. "I've got credit. Don't worry. I'm sorry about Romain showing up."

"He's missing you." Her mom held up her hand. "But he shouldn't have assumed you'd be here pining for him. He made a big mistake. I don't know what he can do to fix it, but at least you know he realized it."

"Maybe." Meg hadn't heard him say that. She grabbed her tote filled with just-in-case stuff, like extra pens, mints, and a bottle of water. Her mom had given her a list of what to pack before the event. The bag felt extra heavy. She looked inside and pulled out a copy of Lilly's book.

Opening it, she saw the inscription. *To the newest member of my team. I'm enjoying getting to know you. Lilly.*

"She had it in her tote when she arrived. It's from her private stock." Mom pushed herself up out of the chair. "You've impressed her. She only hired you because Melody asked for a favor. Jolene about had a fit. But you've done good work. Keep it up and you might find your niche in the world."

Dalton was waiting for Meg outside the auditorium. He stood as she came out. "Everything okay? Junior went inside to check with your mom to see if she needed anything else."

"According to her, we're done. I need to get Watson home, but then I'm supposed to take you, Junior, and Natasha to dinner. She would do it, but she's beat." They walked slowly toward the bookstore.

"I was asking if his being here upset you." Dalton reached over and took Meg's tote. "You look beat."

"I'm physically tired, but no, Romain showing up didn't mess with my head. But it's the second time he's been on the island since I moved here. I'm beginning to think I should have moved somewhere that's not a ferry ride away. Although, in my defense, he left me. I didn't think he'd come back."

"Your mom did," Dalton replied. "I got the whole lecture on the ferry as we left the island to move you home. How you were tender from what happened, and I shouldn't mess with your feelings."

Meg opened the back door to the bookstore. "Have you been messing with my feelings?"

"What? No. I mean, I like hanging with you. Maybe someday, there could be something, but with you just out of . . ."

Meg grinned. "Stop. I was messing with you. My mother doesn't decide if I'm too fragile to have a relationship. Romain coming by to say, 'Oops, my bad,' doesn't fix things. He left me basically at the altar, then spent what was supposed to be our honeymoon with another woman. One that he says he didn't enjoy his time in Italy with."

"He said, 'My bad'?" Dalton followed her into the bookstore. Glory and Natasha were sitting on the couch in the front of the store, with Watson on Natasha's lap.

"Now that I think about it, he didn't even imply that it *was* his bad." She grabbed Watson's leash and his tote from underneath the counter. "Natasha, Mom's buying dinner. Grab Junior and figure out where we're eating. I'll run Watson home and drop off this bag."

"I'll walk you home." Dalton took Watson's tote, as well. "I'll carry these. Unless you want me to walk Watson."

"I can carry my bags," Meg insisted, but then she relented. She didn't have the energy. Not after seeing Romain. The night had been perfect before he showed up. Well, except for the one rude reporter. She looked at Natasha. "Text me where you and Junior decide to eat. I'm up for anything."

"You might get your wish. It's Friday, and we don't have reservations." Natasha stood and stretched. "We'll find something, even if it's cold cuts from the local grocery. Thank your mom for the grub."

Out on the street, Meg and Dalton got caught in a wave of pedestrians heading east, toward the ferry. Dalton turned left at the first road that went away from downtown. "I think Natasha will be surprised at what we can find. You have to eat late to avoid the tourists."

"I think she still gets up early with the bakery. She's probably never out late at night," Meg said. The moon was lighting their walk. "I enjoyed working the launch tonight. Lilly has quite the fan base. One woman is going to a second event in Arizona."

Dalton was quiet for a moment.

Meg knew what that meant. "What are you thinking about?"

"L. C. Aster's fan base. I wonder if anyone knew that Meade was stealing from her." He slapped his palm on his forehead. "Now you have me doing it. Looking for reasons that someone would kill the guy. I guess there's a big difference between going to more than one event to show support and killing off someone who was not playing fair with your favorite author."

Meg thought about Dalton's hypothesis as they climbed the stairs to her apartment. It took her a few minutes to get Watson settled. He gave her a sad puppy dog face from the couch. "I won't be gone long."

As Meg and Dalton came down the stairs, Aunt Melody and Uncle Troy pulled up in his truck. She and Dalton walked over to greet them as they climbed out.

"What an event, huh? Nights like this make me wish I was still in the business." Aunt Melody leaned on the truck. "I need to get these heels off and into my slippers. Then I'm having a glass of wine to calm my nerves. Did you meet Sarah? She might be interested in your book idea. Even if it's only to make Lilly happy. It's all about connections."

"I don't know," Meg said as she shrugged. "Right now, it's only an idea of a book."

"You'll probably hit it out of the park." Uncle Troy took Aunt Melody's arm and pulled her to a standing position. "We're going in. Are you guys grabbing dinner?"

"Yeah. Mom's feeding us for the help." Meg loved the way her aunt and uncle fit together as a couple. "I didn't think you were going to the signing."

He shrugged. "I had to go to pick up the princess, anyway, so I thought I might as well see what the fuss was about."

Aunt Melody rolled her eyes. "Whatever. Anyway, have fun tonight. You guys worked hard."

"Avoid any press, okay? Some of the more determined ones might be hanging out at the bars tonight, looking for a local to tell stories." Uncle Troy met Dalton's eyes and nodded.

When Dalton returned the nod, Meg groaned. Why was everyone treating her like a teenager?

As they walked back into town, Meg asked, "So was that 'Have her home by midnight' or 'Make sure you walk her home'?"

Dalton started. "Was what?"

"The look and nod you and Uncle Troy shared at the end of our conversation." Meg punched him lightly in the arm. "Don't act like it didn't happen."

"I interpreted your uncle's stare to be both things. Although I think he doesn't much care to establish a curfew, as long as you're home safe." He rubbed his arm where she'd punched him. "He cares about you."

"He doesn't ask who's walking Junior home." Meg made a point.

"True that. But Junior lives off the island, not above Troy's garage. Besides, your family is beginning to wonder if Junior will find someone dumb enough to want to marry him. Do you know what kind of hours he's working with your dad? If he doesn't find someone at work, he's not going to meet anyone until he's retired."

"She doesn't have to be dumb, only willing to put up with his oddities. He's working so much so he can buy a house and retire early. Then he's going to open his own business. He's not sure what he wants to do." Junior had talked a lot to Meg when she'd been planning the wedding. She'd met up with Dad, and Junior would come along for the meal. Then Dad would leave, and the two of them would talk about their future. It was the most she'd ever talked to her brother, at least as an adult. "Maybe you could set him up with someone?"

"I'm not playing matchmaker for your brother." Dalton reached for his phone, which was ringing. "Speak of the devil. Hi, Junior."

He listened and then nodded. When he hung up, he turned at the next road. "We're heading out to the bay and Marina Taco Tavern."

Meg would have danced with joy at the choice, but she was too tired. "I love that place. Margarita, here I come. Do you think they'd mind if I found a hot tub and had them deliver the drinks there?"

"It would be an interesting end to the night," Dalton said.

Meg turned to look up at his face. He was grinning. "Get your mind out of the gutter. My shoulders are killing me."

"Hard work has that effect on people."

At the restaurant, Meg waited for the orders to be taken and the margaritas to be delivered before she turned to Natasha. "So tell me what happened between you and Meade?"

Natasha leaned her head back and groaned. "What have you already heard?"

"I've heard that you owed him money and he took advantage of that by asking for favors." Meg licked some of the salt off the rim of her glass before taking a drink. Salty, sweet, and frozen. It was the best. "Like driving him to Lilly's the night he died."

"Okay, so you know everything." Natasha glared at Dalton, assuming he was Meg's source of gossip. "I told him that night that I had the money to pay him back and he would get it on Monday. And this was the last favor I'd ever have to do for him."

"Did you wait for him at the house?"

Natasha shook her head. "He was mad that I was going to pay him back. He loved people owing him. It was like he owned them. Anyway, after I told him he'd have his money on Monday, he got out and slammed the door. Then he went in through the back gate at Summer Break."

"That gate's locked," Meg responded. Where had Meade gotten the code?

CHAPTER 14

Sometimes the answer is in plain sight. Cameras are everywhere.

Meg had taken Watson out one last time when she'd got home, then she'd crashed. The next morning she wasn't expected at the bookstore until later, and her assignment for Lilly wasn't due until Tuesday. She slept in. She even turned off the alarm.

A pounding woke her and Watson up. Barking furiously, Watson jumped off the bed. Meg grabbed her phone to check the time. Seven. In the morning. On a Saturday. It had to be her mother. She needed to move farther away. First Romain, now Mom. "Shut up, Watson."

Watson looked at her with sad puppy dog eyes. He was trying to save her life. So he ignored her direction and ran to the door to continue his barking. Meg wrapped a robe around her jammies and went to open the door.

"I take it you forgot we were going this morning?" Dalton stood there in shorts and a tank. He held a large cup from A Taste of Magic. "I've got cookies in the truck to take with us. Along with some water and sodas in a cooler."

"Where are we going again?" Meg didn't bother to try to explain. She had forgotten. So much for planning a fake murder this morning before she went to work. She opened the door wider and took the coffee. "I'm due at the bookstore at three."

"Which is why we're going early." Dalton looked down at Watson. "I take it he needs to be walked."

"Please. I'll get ready. What's the temp?" She eyed his shorts as she sipped her coffee. Dalton wore shorts a lot. She couldn't always just match what he was wearing.

"Beautiful, but take a jacket. I know you can get chilled, especially on the water." He put Watson's leash on the dog's collar. "We'll be back in a few minutes. Go get ready. I want to be out on the water by eight."

"I don't remember agreeing to this," she called after him as he started down the stairs.

After pulling her hair back into a ponytail, she brushed her teeth. She leaned closer to the mirror. Her green eyes didn't look as tired as she felt. Which was a good thing. At least she was alive and acting like it. Not sitting around, stewing over Romain. Of course, it was hard to miss the man, since he'd been on the island to see her twice since he'd come home from Italy.

She decided to split the difference and wore capris and slip-on shoes. Then she put on a T-shirt and topped the outfit with a zip-up sweat jacket with the Island Books logo. She and Junior both had a wardrobe filled with branded clothing from the store. Mom gave it out for birthdays, Christmas, and just because. Which worked well now that Meg was working at the shop. Before she felt like a walking billboard for her mom's business.

Meg walked out of the bedroom, dressed, with a bit of coffee still in her cup. She glanced at the coffee maker, but she knew Dalton probably wanted to leave. He was packing Watson's tote bag. "So it's okay if he comes, too?"

"Sure. Emmett has a dog he brings along to lessons. There's

even a life jacket on board for him." He zipped up the bag. "Ready to go? Do you need to go potty?"

"I hope you're asking Watson," Meg responded as she grabbed her wallet. "Should I take a suit?"

"We'll probably be back before it warms up enough that you'd want to swim." He had his coffee cup now, too. "Do you want to refill your coffee? We can make a pot."

She shook her head. "Thanks, but I'm good. Unless you need more?"

"I drank a pot before I left the house this morning. I've been up since five, waiting for you. This is going to be a blast. Emmett's sailboat is sweet. I'd love to have one like her." Dalton followed Meg out of the apartment with Watson on his leash. He waited for her as she locked the door and tucked her keys in Watson's tote bag. As they walked, he filled her in on all the things about Emmett's boat.

When they got to the marina, the parking lot was halfway full. As she climbed out of the truck with Watson, she asked, "Did people stay out last night?"

"No. This is mostly early birds. Kirk lives on his boat now, but don't tell the marina security. He says he's there until he finds a place or Elaina takes him back. Of course, it's been six months, and neither of those things have happened." Dalton looked back at her and smiled, and Meg's heart squeezed. His blond hair sparkled in the light of the sunrise, and his blue eyes were crystal. Luna was right; he was a good catch. So why hadn't he married anyone yet?

"Are you coming?" He cocked his head as she stood on the ramp to the dock, watching him. "You're not chickening out, are you?"

"Admiring the view." She blushed a little.

He turned and watched the sun rise over Seattle. "We're lucky. We live in a place where we get to view this beauty all the time. You have to take the time to enjoy it."

After boarding Emmett's boat and adjusting the doggy life jacket on Watson, they eased out of the marina and into Eagle Harbor as she watched a ferry come in to dock. Watson sat next to her, his body shaking. She reached down and rubbed his back. "It's all right, buddy. Just a new adventure."

After a while, Dalton eased the boat into a cove at the top of the island and dropped the sails so they would move slowly through the water. After taking out a water bottle, he came over and sat next to her, then offered it to her. "What do you think?"

"It's so quiet out here." Meg nodded to Watson, who had decided he was safe in the life jacket and had lain down to nap. "He was a little nervous, but I think the jacket calmed him down."

"He's less anxious than he was when we took him to the first bonfire. Of course, this is a bigger boat." He leaned back against the seat cushion and lifted his face to the sun. "I could spend days out here hanging. It's always changing, always different, yet somehow the same, if that makes sense. I can imagine the local Native American tribe in their homemade canoes out here fishing and enjoying the sound. Of course, it was probably a lot cleaner back then."

Dalton jumped up and grabbed a net from the side of the cockpit. Then he skimmed the top of the water for a plastic bottle that was floating next to the boat. "People throw all kinds of things out into the water, like it's a trash can. Not everything sinks. And some things do affect the local water creatures."

Meg thought about the night at the bonfire. Nate had been throwing his empties out into the waves. "Your bonfire buddies are bad about that."

"A bunch of us take the time to clean up after the rowdies leave or pass out. We don't want to be banned from the beaches." Dalton took the bottle and put it in a trash bag. "We all do our part, right?"

"It's too bad everyone doesn't feel that way." She hadn't liked Nate, and since she worked for Lilly, the feeling was mutual. But she didn't want to think about him today. This was beautiful. She could see houses lining the edges of the island and wondered what Lilly was doing that day. Jolene would be taking Sarah back to the ferry, and Lilly was probably leaving the island, as well, to grab a flight to Los Angeles. She wondered if her uncle worried that she wouldn't come back. That she might try to skip out of the country.

"Penny for your thoughts. Please tell me you're not thinking about him." Dalton was watching her.

"No, I was thinking about Lilly and her book tour. But what was that about with Romain last night? I think he assumed I would be alone in the bookstore. He can't imagine I'd take him back, right? You're a guy. What's going on in his head?"

Dalton shook his head. "I might be a guy, but what Romain did doesn't make sense to me, so I can't be your Romain whisperer." He paused. "Do you miss him?"

Meg thought about her answer before she responded. "No. Which is weird. I was so brokenhearted I destroyed my wedding dress. Now I'm too busy to even take a few minutes for his apology. I guess being here has cleared my mind. I thought he was the one, but maybe I was jumping into something I thought would work out. I had our entire life planned, but now that I look at it, I'm not sure he was the right man for what I want in life. I was fitting myself into his life. Not creating one together."

"I think that's smart." He was watching Watson sleep now.

"I'm sitting here, boring you with my problems. Sorry. This morning's sail was amazing. I've never been on the water this early, unless I was on my way to Seattle for something."

"I always volunteered for the early shifts when I was in the Coast Guard. It's like being at the beginning of the world when you watch the sunrise in the morning." He stared out at the water, then glanced at his watch. "If we're grabbing some food before you head to work, we better be making our way back. This has been fun."

Meg watched Dalton turn the boat to port and hoist the mainsail for their return to Eagle Harbor, then she realized she hadn't offered Watson water since they'd left the house. "Are you thirsty, buddy?"

Watson's reaction when she pulled out his collapsible bowl told the story. After he'd finished, there was water all over the deck. "Hey, do you have a towel? I guess I took Watson's out of the bag sometime yesterday."

"In that compartment near the wheel." Dalton pointed toward the back of the cockpit. "The water will dry."

"We clean up our mess, right?" Meg didn't want Emmett to notice a problem with his wooden deck and think it was Watson's fault.

She went to the compartment and opened it up. As she pulled a hand towel off a shelf, a plastic bag fell out. Looking at it, she realized it was the registration and insurance for the boat. Emmett must keep it there so he'd know where to find it. As she went to put it back, she noticed that in addition to Emmett's name on the registration, there was a second name. Robert Meade III. She heard Dalton behind her.

"Did you find the towels?" he asked.

She turned around and showed him the registration. "Emmett must have known Meade. Did he owe him money?"

Dalton bit his lip before he answered. Clearly, he didn't want to misspeak. "I don't know. I saw Meade at the restaurant, but it's the best place to eat on the island. He would be there. But why would he put his name on the boat?"

"Maybe he wanted to have collateral in case the loan went

bad." Meg took her phone out of her pocket and snapped a picture of the registration.

"What are you doing?" Dalton took the bag and tucked it back into the compartment. "Whatever financial arrangements that Emmett may or may not have had with Robert Meade are none of our business. I don't want him to stop letting me borrow his boat because you started getting nosy."

"But if he was involved with Meade, that's someone else who could potentially be a suspect," Meg said, then realized she wasn't helping her case. "And who could back up Natasha's story about how invasive Meade was with people who owed money to him."

Dalton was thinking about that point, Meg could tell. But he wasn't convinced. After they had docked and were ready to head to the truck, he blocked her from getting off the boat. "Just don't send that photo to your uncle until I talk to Emmett. I don't want him to be surprised when your uncle stops by to grill him."

"Okay, I can do that. But if Uncle Troy charges Natasha, all bets are off. She couldn't kill anyone." Meg met his gaze, and the two of them stood in silence for a few minutes.

Finally, Dalton blinked and stepped back, letting her off the boat. He took Watson's leash. "Sometimes you are a lot of trouble."

Meg didn't look at him. She'd heard the complaint before. "I know. But I mean well."

She wasn't sure he agreed with her.

Glory was working the store when Meg arrived for her shift. "Hey, where's Mom?"

"Your mother took the day off. She said last night wore her out." Glory grabbed her tote. "And now that you're here, I'm off to Seattle for an art installation. I've been looking forward to this all week. Thank goodness you're here to work the night shift. I'm glad your boyfriend found you last night. It was so crowded I told him he might be out of luck."

Boyfriend? Had Glory missed all the drama about her and Romain? Or did she think they had got back together? "Romain's not my boyfriend," Meg said as Glory passed her on the way to the door.

"Good, because he was a bit of a tool." Glory opened the door and grinned. "Have a great night. It should be quiet since we had such a crowd last night."

As she got everything ready, following her mom's evening shift instructions, Watson settled into his bed, and soon Meg could hear him snoring. Being out on the water must have worn him out. She glanced at her phone. Dalton hadn't texted since dropping her off at the apartment after a quiet lunch. She knew he was wrestling with two arguments. One, he trusted Emmett, and Emmett trusted him. Two, he believed in doing the right thing, and if Emmett knew something that might help clear Natasha, he would want to help his friend.

Meg had the picture. Natasha hadn't been arrested, that Meg knew of, so she'd leave it alone.

Natasha showed up with sandwiches at seven. "Sorry. I got delayed at the bakery. We had a line until six, and then I had to pick up the food. Dalton called and said he was busy tonight. What did you two do this morning that wore him out? He's never turned down free food before."

"We went out on his friend's boat. Do you know Emmett Harding, the chef?" Meg moved her water over to the couch. As Glory had predicted, the evening shift had been quiet, so she'd worked on finishing the mailings that would get sent off on Monday.

"I know of him. I didn't realize he and Dalton were tight. He's been holding out on me. I've been trying to get a reservation at the Local Crab for weeks. My mom loves the place, and her birthday's coming up." Natasha took out the sandwiches and then pushed Watson's nose away from the wrapped food. "Go lay down, buddy. I know your mom has already fed you."

Meg laughed as she pointed Watson toward his bed. "Why should that matter? Watson thinks anytime anyone eats, he should, too. His vet is giving me grief about his weight."

She pushed away the questions she had about Emmett Harding. Right now, she was going to have a nice dinner with her friend.

After they ate, Natasha gathered the bags and then took the garbage out to the dumpster. When she came back in, she leaned on the counter. "So are you going to tell me what happened between you and Romain last night? Is that why Dalton's not here tonight?"

"What? No. I told Romain I couldn't talk. I was busy. Which he should have been able to see. But it's Romain. Anyway, he said he'd call me. I'll think about answering." Meg wiped down the coffee table. "And Dalton's not being here has nothing to do with me."

"If you say so."

Meg glanced around the empty bookstore. The ferry had left; she'd heard the horn blast from the open window. "Natasha, did Uncle Troy say anything about how Meade died? You don't think he's looking at you as a suspect, do you?"

Natasha sank onto the couch and put her head in her hands. Her hair flowed around her shoulders, almost touching the coffee table. Finally, she flipped her head up and stared at Meg. "He didn't say anything. But I'm afraid he's going to. What am I going to do? Robert was in my car. We kind of fought. I mean, he was angry when he got out of the car. If someone had seen that, it could have looked like we were arguing about something. I swear, I dropped him off, and then I took my car home and parked it. Then I changed and went downstairs to the bakery and worked. I made three batches of cupcakes for the next morning before I wore myself out." She closed her eyes.

Meg thought about what she had said. "Maybe there's a way to prove that."

Natasha opened her eyes and sat straighter. "What are you thinking?"

"If they have cameras at the ferry dock, maybe they have them on Winslow Way, too." Meg pulled out her notebook and started writing down everything she thought she needed to talk about with her uncle tomorrow morning. And, she thought, this would make an excellent chapter for the guidebook.

Chapter 15

You might catch more flies with honey, but who wants flies?

The next morning Uncle Troy had left for work by the time Meg got up. Her mom texted her, asking if she was coming to Sunday school. Mom followed up that text with a single word. **Please.**

Meg got dressed, and before she left, she took Watson out. "I won't be long, and we'll go over to Aunt Melody's for lunch, so you can play in the backyard."

Watson didn't look amused. Her dog was used to her being around. She'd gotten him right after the start-up went belly up. Then she'd moved in with Romain, so he'd always had someone around. Between disappointing her mom and disappointing Watson, she'd err on the side of keeping her mother and current employer happy. Besides, she had health insurance because she worked for the bookstore. Those kinds of things are important for a functional adult.

Today she wore one of her sundresses instead of pants. She told herself it was because of the heat rather than the look her mom had given her outfit last week. Meg wondered if she'd ever stop wanting to please her. Her dad? He'd broken that bond by moving out and remarrying. Meg knew that relationships were kept alive by the actions of two people, but he'd taken the steps that had forever broken the marriage.

Like what Romain had done to her. Just before they were supposed to say, "I do."

Overthink much? She was doomed to be single.

After taking Watson back to the apartment, Meg set out on foot for the church. The first to arrive, she waved as her mom pulled her sedan into the parking lot.

And got the look.

Okay, so a sundress wasn't good enough, either. Mom was going to have to deal with Meg's current wardrobe. Meg hugged her after she got out of the car. "Thanks for the reminder text this morning."

"I should have suggested a different dress." Mom rubbed the spaghetti straps of Meg's dress between her fingers. "This looks a little skimpy for church."

Then when Meg didn't answer, Mom pulled a sweater out of the car and put it into Meg's hands. "Here. Wear this. If I know Tina, she has the air turned up to Arctic blast level. You'll be freezing minutes after you step inside."

Meg wanted to believe that the sweater was to keep her warm, but it was Mom offering it. She decided to avoid the fight and put it on. The smell of Chanel No. 5 surrounded her. "Thanks. So where is Sunday school class?"

"Your class is in room three. I'm in the kitchen." Mom locked the car and hurried to the church door. "Come on. I'll show you."

"I thought we were going to the same class," Meg called after her as she tried to keep up.

As Mom opened the door, she turned and pushed a strand of hair out of Meg's face. "Don't be silly. You're in the single young adults class. I've heard there are some nice young men in there that, if you're convinced Romain is out of the picture, you should consider."

"Matchmaking on a Sunday morning? Isn't that un-Christian-like?" Meg grumbled as she followed her mother into the church.

Turning faster than Meg thought possible, her mom leaned in and whispered, "Having a life partner isn't an evil thing. I don't know why you're so against either letting Romain apologize or finding someone new for your life."

"I guess I'm still traumatized from your divorce from Dad," Meg snapped back. She regretted the words as soon as she saw them hit her mom.

"Felicia, I'm so glad to see you and your lovely daughter today." Pastor Sage walked up, and Mom's face went from murderous to angelic in two-point-three seconds. "Meg, I take it you're here for the young singles group. We're meeting in room three today. We have a special speaker on the joy of being single in a couple-based world. Next Saturday we're taking a trip to Seattle, to Pike Place Market, for lunch and shopping. You should come with us."

"I'm sorry. I work on Saturdays." Meg smiled as she started walking with the pastor to the hallway where she'd find room three. "I'm looking forward to the speaker. I need some suggestions on things to do besides work."

Meg turned back and saw her mother watching her walk away. The conversation wasn't over, that was certain, but at least she had a reprieve until after service, and maybe until after dinner at Aunt Melody's. If Meg was lucky, she could run to work and delay the conversation even longer.

One way or another, her mom was going to explain the divorce to her, again. She didn't care, except when her mom insisted that Meg needed a man in her life. A relationship. Time to settle down and make babies. Meg didn't even have a real job yet. Having a family would need to wait. At least until she found the right man. And this time, she wasn't going to settle for someone who only looked good on paper.

She settled into a metal folding chair and smiled as Pastor Sage introduced her to the ten people already seated in the classroom. All women. Young single men didn't seem to know about this group, no matter what her mom had heard. Dalton was working the early shift. A lot of the men at the bonfire were probably still in bed from last night's barhopping. Not that she was interested in finding a soulmate from that group.

As the speaker was introduced, she thought about who her perfect man would be. What he'd be interested in. What he'd like to do. And, most of all, how he'd treat her.

When she was done, she realized the man her list described looked a lot like Dalton.

As they walked out of the room to go to the chapel for services, a woman stopped her. "Hi. I'm Irene. I saw you at the bonfire with Dalton the other night. Isn't it crazy that someone killed Robert Meade? I hated the guy, but, wow, he's dead."

"I'm Meg." She blinked as she took in the question that the small blonde had thrown at her. She'd noticed her in class since she was the only one who had been taking notes during the speaker's presentation. "Are you a local? I don't think I recognize you from school."

"My folks moved here when I was a senior. I hated it, so I begged to be kept at a boarding school in New Hampshire. I went to college at Bryn Mawr and then came home for the summer. I've been working in Seattle since, but housing prices are crazy expensive in the city, so I'm living back home again." She glanced over to where a couple of class members were standing and talking to Pastor Sage. "Do you want to get coffee sometime? I work at home on Mondays."

"That sounds great." Meg needed to open up her friend group. And it would keep her mom from saying she wasn't open to new experiences. And maybe Irene had information about Robert Meade. Okay, so that sounded wrong. Maybe Irene could help her get a different perspective on life on the island as a young adult. "What about tomorrow at ten at A Taste of Magic?"

"I'll see you there." Irene waved at her mother. "Sorry. She must want to talk about something. Probably about my breaking curfew last night. You'd think I was sixteen rather than twenty-five."

As Irene left, Meg made her way into the chapel. Her mom was already sitting in their pew, her Bible open. Meg sat next to her and leaned close. "I'm sorry I pulled the divorce card. I'm fine right now, but I'm not looking to jump into something else. I'll know when I meet Mr. Right."

"Your aunt Melody tells me the same thing. To leave you be. I know how long it took her to find Troy. I don't want you to be lonely." Mom squeezed my hand. "Do you want to grab lunch after this? I'll buy."

"We're not going to Aunt Melody's?" So much for her plan to talk to Uncle Troy.

"She and Troy are attending a show in Seattle. She insists he takes at least one afternoon off during these investigations for them," Mom said as she closed her Bible. "How did you like your class? Oh, it looks like Pastor Sage is starting."

The announcement of the opening hymn kept Meg from explaining that the class would be better described as for single young females. But she'd leave that alone. If her mom thought she was surrounding herself with eligible bachelors, that wasn't her fault.

At least she was getting lunch out of the deal.

Glory reported that she'd been busy that morning with walk-ins from the ferries, but during Meg's shift, Sunday at the bookstore was dead. She had done all the busy work, even neatly stacking all the mailings in boxes to make it easier to transport them to the post office tomorrow. She texted to see if

Mom wanted her to stop by the bookstore and take them to the post office Monday morning, but she must have been napping, as she didn't answer. Meg would call her tomorrow if she didn't hear back.

It was almost five, and Meg had nothing to do. She pulled out the folder with her assignment from her backpack and, using her laptop, made plans on how to kill the imaginary George, who she'd found out was cheating before their wedding.

The writing went fast, even with her needing to check the internet for times, places, and effects of different poisons. By the time Dalton and Natasha showed up with Chinese food, she had the assignment done and printed out. She'd paper-clipped it to the assignment page and saved the file to her laptop. Leaving Natasha to watch the bookstore, she hurried out to walk Watson for a few minutes.

"I'll walk with you," Dalton said as he took Watson's leash.

They didn't talk for a bit, not until they got off the crowded street and started up the hill toward the residential section of town. She glanced at him. "You know I can walk the dog by myself."

He laughed as he looked at her. "I like walking Watson. It indulges all my 'I want a dog' feelings without having to get a dog of my own."

"That weirdly makes sense," she admitted. As long as it wasn't a couple thing.

"You've been strange since Romain showed up Friday night. Are you regretting leaving him?" They turned left so they could walk in a loop and end up back at the bookstore.

"One, I didn't leave him. He dumped me. And two, if I've been odd, it's because I can't figure out if someone I know killed Meade." She rubbed her neck, feeling the tension. "I was going to talk to Uncle Troy today, but he's on a date in Seattle. Maybe that's a good sign that it was an accident. Natasha dropped Meade off at Summer Break, and he slipped on the dock and hit his head on a rock in the water."

"Sounds like a great theory, except, according to the coroner's report, he was forcibly held under until he drowned. And the blow to the head was from a pipelike object. So no accidental drowning." He looked over at Meg, who had stopped walking. "What? The coroner left his briefcase on the ferry when he came back from teaching a class in Seattle. I had to dig to find out who it belonged to so lost and found could contact him. According to them, he's always leaving something on the ferry. Kind of a forgetful professor type."

"Darn, I was hoping this would all go away." Meg turned the corner and headed back downhill. "Uncle Troy needs to clear both Lilly and Natasha."

"The sooner the better." He glanced in the direction of the bookstore. "I heard people talking about Natasha's bakery as the killer's place on the ferry. Rumors are flying about our girl."

"How did they even figure out that she was interviewed by the police?" Meg didn't like where this was heading. Either she would lose her job and Lilly Aster would go to jail or she'd lose her best friend.

"One of the local reporters saw your uncle pick her up at the bookstore the other night. They've been trying to verify her status ever since, but neither she nor your uncle has answered their calls." He lowered his voice as a couple walked by them. "Vi Chin cornered Natasha at the launch party before your uncle kicked the press out, and I think she badgered her into admitting that she was questioned."

"So they published it."

He shook his head. "There wasn't enough for that, but Chin has a social media account, and she posted that she was on the heels of a juicy story and showed a picture of Natasha's bakery.

Everyone put two and two together in the comments. She had a crowd at the bakery snapping pictures, and when she locked up and came out to meet me, they started throwing out questions. It was ugly."

"Does she want to talk about it? Make some plans on how to deal with it?" Meg started walking faster to get back.

Dalton grabbed her arm to slow her down. "That's why I came with you on the walk. Natasha doesn't want to talk about it at all. She wants to have a nice evening with her friends. She asked me to tell you what was going on. And ask that tonight not be an investigation powwow. All she wants to do is have fun with us."

Meg hoped she could keep her mouth shut for Natasha's sake.

Monday morning, Meg was sitting at her kitchen table, watching the main house. When she saw Uncle Troy come out, she hurried down the stairs. She met him at his truck.

"Good morning. Can I ask you something?"

"You just did," he teased as he put his stuff in the cab. "What's going on? Is the plumbing acting up? You'll have to talk to your aunt about that. She handles the rentals."

"Rentals?" They had more than one? Meg shook her head. She was getting off track. "No, I mean, everything in the apartment is fine. Thanks. I wanted to know if you've cleared Natasha yet. And if you have, could you put out an announcement?"

"We don't announce people who aren't charged with a murder," he said. Then he turned and stared at me. "Why do you think your friend is even cleared? Maybe she killed Robert Meade."

"She didn't. And she told you what happened. She dropped him off at the back gate to Summer Break. Then she went back to the bakery." Meg put her hands on her hips. She didn't want her uncle to see that she was shaking. "Can't you examine footage from the camera on the back gate to see if he went onto the property alone?"

He took off his baseball cap with a Bainbridge Island logo on the front. "The camera to the back gate broke a month before the murder, and the repair guy is supposed to fix it this week. If he shows up. Jolene says she's been trying to get him out here for a couple of weeks."

"I can't believe you think Natasha might have killed him." Meg's voice was almost a whisper. She teased, "Have you even met Natasha?"

"Of course I know that sweet girl is unlikely to have done the murder. However, I don't have proof. Meade had his hand on her throat, financially, that is. His lawyer has verified the loan." He moved to get into the truck.

"Did you check the street cameras? They should show a dry Natasha driving her car away at the same time that the gate was accessed. And parking her car at the bakery." Meg pointed out the best-case scenario.

"Why would being dry help Natasha's cause?"

Meg closed her eyes. She'd said one thing too many. She shouldn't know about the medical examiner's report. "Because Meade was held underwater until he drowned. Natasha would have been wet and besides, she doesn't have that kind of strength."

"Tell me you didn't break into the morgue." He leaned against the truck, waiting to hear the whole story before arresting her for interfering with an open investigation.

"I didn't break into the morgue. I haven't even been to Port Orchard since I moved back." Meg held up her hand, three fingers extended, as if giving the Boy Scout salute. "But that's a way to clear Natasha, right? Checking the street cams?"

He didn't respond for a while. Finally, he nodded. "I'm going to check the street cameras. One, because it's a good idea. And two, I hate even thinking anything bad about that girl. But I need a favor from you. You need to stay out of this investigation. It's not safe. Robert Meade wasn't a good man. He had a lot of enemies, which is one of the reasons I haven't figured out who killed him. I might as well throw a dart at a board filled with suspects." He looked her in the eye. "Promise me?"

Meg nodded, hoping that Uncle Troy wouldn't see that she had both hands behind her back and her fingers crossed.

CHAPTER 16

Know your victim, find your killer.

Meg called her mom after she'd finished breakfast. "Hey, I'm meeting Irene from Sunday school for coffee this morning. Do you want me to come by and get the mailings to take to the post office?"

"I already dropped off a load before I opened this morning, but if you want to take the rest this afternoon, that would be lovely. I have something tonight."

"A nap? I called you yesterday, and you were napping."

"I was not." Mom paused but didn't explain what she'd been doing. "Anyway, I need to go. Someone came in."

"Then why didn't I hear the doorbell go off?" Meg asked, but her mom had already hung up. She must be mad that Meg had caught her napping.

Setting down her phone, she looked at this week's plan. Work was back down to normal hours. She'd already finished the assignment for Lilly, but she was still in Los Angeles for the book events. Maybe she'd head over to the campus this week and see if there was someone with whom she could talk about a late financial assistance form. She might have to wait until next fall to enroll, but that didn't mean she couldn't take a night class or two during the next year and get back into the swing of college. She had only two years left to finish. Unless she picked a major with a lot of specific classes. She needed to talk to someone. She blocked off time on Tuesday to drive over to campus. She'd take Watson with her and drive to Summer Break for the assignment exchange first. Then it wouldn't matter when she got back.

And if they got touchy about Watson being in the administration building, she'd take him back to the car or make an appointment for the next week. At least she'd have the course catalog as well as the summer and fall schedule.

With that planned, she realized she needed to leave now if she going to be on time to meet Irene. She packed a bowl, water, and treats in her backpack, then clipped a leash on Watson.

Irene was already seated when Meg arrived at the bakery. She waved, then went up to the counter and ordered coffee and water for Watson. "I have his bowl," she told Natasha. "I need some tap water."

"Are you meeting with her?" Natasha inclined her head toward Irene.

Meg heard a twinge of concern in her friend's voice. "I met her at church yesterday, and we agreed to meet for coffee. Why?"

"No reason," Natasha lied and gave Meg her fake smile. "Just be careful."

"You'll tell me later, right?" Meg said, lowering her voice. Maybe Irene did know more about Meade's death than she'd thought.

Natasha nodded. "It might be old news by then, but you should probably know."

Just like the Bainbridge Island gossip train, Natasha's clues were late and did not provide what Meg needed. She took her coffee and Watson's water and went over to learn more about Irene.

"Thanks for meeting me," Irene said as she glanced over to

where Natasha was helping the next customer. "Making friends here on the island is hard."

"I've lived here all my life, except for my time in Seattle, so sometimes I forget. It was a little cliquey in high school." Meg took out Watson's bowl as she was talking and poured the water into it. He dove in as soon as she set it down.

"See! I told my mom it would be. I think she was upset at the expense of boarding school." Irene picked up her phone and started texting. "Hold on. I want to tell her what you said before I forget."

Meg sipped her coffee as she waited. As soon as Irene put her phone down, she asked about Meade. "So how did you know Robert Meade?"

"He was involved in my job." Irene stared at her phone, and when she got an answer from her mother, her eyes lit up. "Mom says she's sorry about trying to make me part of the community. That sounds a little snarky, doesn't it?"

"So what do you do?" Meg tried to change the subject from Irene's ongoing fight with her mother as Meg shrugged off her jacket.

"I'm in marketing. I work for the cruise lines that call the port home base." Irene smiled. "It's not high-end, but I get two free cruises a year. More and nicer depending on my production." She dug in her tote and handed Meg a flyer. "Do you cruise? You totally should. It's like an all-inclusive resort, but you get to see several ports. Meade told me he was going to buy one, but I called the office, and he never signed up for one. But he told me he did. What a liar. I'm glad he's dead. So do you want to hear about a cruise?"

"Um, no. Sorry." Meg tried to give back the flyer. "Not in my budget right now."

"Oh, I'm sure we could find a plan that's right for you. Besides, it's an investment." Irene went on to explain how her company offered the time-shares of cruises. "One monthly payment and your travel plans are all complete."

As Meg listened to Irene's sales pitch, she saw Natasha giggling behind the counter. This explained her warning. Irene was using Meg's attempt at friendship to sell something. Meg felt trapped. Finally, she finished her coffee and stood. "Sorry to take off on you, but I'm expected at the bookstore. I'm fighting for every dollar these days, so I can't blow off work. Thanks for meeting me for coffee. It was nice getting to know you."

She grabbed Watson's bowl, which thankfully was empty, and left the coffee shop with Watson in the lead. He must have felt her unease while she was chatting with Irene. As she pushed open the door, she heard Irene call out, "You forgot the pamphlet."

Meg started power walking to the bookstore, dodging tourists. Since it was early on a Monday, the sidewalks weren't packed. She hoped she got away before Irene caught up with her.

A hand grabbed her arm, and she turned to find Natasha by her side. "You knew."

"I tried to warn you, but it's hard to say stuff about a customer when they are sitting right there." Natasha fell into step with her. "Don't worry. She's not chasing you, but I bet you'll get a text with a link. And several follow-up calls. Make sure you check caller ID for the next six months. She's persistent."

"And she wonders why she doesn't have friends. She uses them as marketing targets. She hated Meade. He told her he was buying a cruise, then didn't do it." Meg finally slowed down after looking behind her one more time. "Aren't you needed at the bakery?"

"I'm on the way to the station. Your uncle asked me to come down and talk to him again. Irene's a mess. Everyone tells her what she wants to hear so she'll leave them alone. Robert

Meade wasn't the only one. I'm worried that your uncle thinks I killed Robert. I didn't like the way the guy did business, and I was tired of being his driver when he didn't bring his car to the island, but I wouldn't kill anyone." Natasha glanced up the street; the turn to the police station was coming up.

Meg wondered if Uncle Troy had checked the street cams, like she'd suggested. "Maybe this is just to clear you from the suspect pool."

"From your lips to your uncle's ears." They both came to a stop in front of the bookstore door. Natasha hugged her. "Anyway, I'll text you when I'm back at the bakery. If you don't hear from me, come break me out of jail with Dalton, and we'll all go on the lam."

"You're a nut." Meg watched Natasha stroll down the street. She could see that she was nervous, but to anyone else, she probably looked like a young woman heading to her next appointment. Meg knew her friend couldn't have done something like killing Robert. Now she needed to find who had done it, so everyone else knew that Natasha was innocent.

Inside the bookstore, her mom was watching her stand in the doorway. "What's wrong?" she called.

Meg shook her head, leading Watson to the counter. "Nothing's wrong. Why?"

"Irene's mom called and said you ran out of the bakery like your hair was on fire. Irene was concerned." Her mom leaned closer. "Did she ask you questions about the wedding?"

"What? No. Why would you ask that?" Meg took off Watson's leash, and he ran to his bed. "She was in sales mode, and I don't have the money to buy a cruise time-share."

"Oh, I thought you two might develop a friendship." Her mom turned back to her laptop.

Meg snorted. "Yeah, that was the plan. But I guess she's more interested in commerce."

"Don't give up on developing friends here. There are a lot of young people your age. That's one reason I want you to attend Sunday school. To meet people." She peered at her laptop. "I need to keep a pair of cheaters here at the store. I keep putting them on top of my head and taking them home."

"Do you need help with something?" Meg asked, looking over her mother's shoulder. She was looking at an online credit card statement. "Mom? The balance is crazy high. Is that the store card?"

"I told you we needed the Aster launch. Once the accounts settle, we'll be back in the green for a while." Her mom closed out the account. "I hate accounting and projecting. I'm always wrong. Thank goodness I bought the building when your dad and I were still married. He thought it was a phase, but now I couldn't afford rent on this street if I didn't own the building outright."

"Maybe we could sit down and do a projection for the next year. I took finance classes at school. I'm going back this fall, hopefully." Meg glanced at the clock. "If I'm going to get the packages to the post office before Hank goes on lunch break, I better get going. Okay to leave Watson here with you?"

"Not a problem." Her mom reached down and stroked the dog's head. "And, Meg?"

Meg paused before going to the back of the store and met her mom's gaze.

"I'd like you to help me with the business side, too. I used to have your dad to talk out the finance stuff, and now it's all on me. I can do it, but sometimes it's nice to have another opinion." She handed Meg the store credit card. "There's more than enough room for the postage on this."

Meg took the card and tucked it in her jeans. Then she packed up the boxes of mailings she'd organized yesterday. Her mom had made a dent first thing this morning, but she'd need at least two trips with the canvas-sided wagon. Hopefully, no one would get in line after her.

When she returned to the store after the final trip, she took Watson out for a short walk. Her mom had ordered lunch for them. They sat on the couch, with Watson sitting at the edge of the table, watching them unwrap the hoagie-style sandwiches.

Mom sipped her soda and focused on Meg. "What's on the schedule for the rest of the day?"

"Not much," Meg admitted. She was waiting to get Natasha's report on her meeting with Uncle Troy and to hear from Dalton about his chat with Emmett about his involvement with Meade. But her mom didn't need to hear about that part of her life. "I've finished returning all the wedding gifts, so I don't have anything left on my failed marriage to-do list. Well, except for getting the engagement ring into a safety-deposit box. I probably should do that later today."

"I thought you left that at the Seattle apartment?" her mom asked. She hadn't agreed with Meg leaving the ring. She'd thought she should keep it. It was a gift. "Or is that what Romain was here for on Friday? To give it back? It's more of a classy move than I would have expected from the man."

Meg smiled. Her mom had finally realized that she and Romain were over. "He brought it over early last week and left it at the apartment with the rest of our travel money fund. I guess he felt guilty that I'd left it there."

"Well, he should feel guilty. Taking that other woman to Italy and all but leaving you at the altar." Mom sniffed. "It took a bit for me to accept how it all turned out, but your aunt Melody said she'd never liked him. Not one bit."

"You always have the 'hope springs eternal' mindset," Meg told her mom. And given the blush on her mother's face, Meg wondered how well the bookstore was doing. She'd make sure they did a full review and projection sometime next week. She didn't want her mom to lose the bookstore. Then where would Meg work?

She hurried home with Watson, then left him at the apartment while she biked down to the bank with the ring and her documents. She'd looked up what she needed for a safety-deposit box after Romain had dropped off the ring. It wasn't that she didn't trust her neighbors, but they'd had the ring appraised during the purchase, and she knew it was valued in the low five figures. She wouldn't get all that on the secondary market, but she'd get enough. Now she needed to figure out what she wanted to spend the money on. A down payment for a house? Probably, but she needed to finish her degree and start a career before she did anything like that. For now, the ring could sit in a box.

When she got the paperwork all set up, she was escorted into the vault and the bank clerk opened her new box. She took the ring, a pearl necklace, and a few documents out of her purse. Her passport, Social Security card, and original birth certificate all went into the box. Then she placed her grandmother's pearls in and finally reached for the ring box. She opened it and stared at the diamond as it sparkled in the bright light of the vault. It was what she'd wanted. Marquise cut. Platinum band. Simple yet stunning.

It was too bad the ring didn't match the relationship. She closed the box and put it with the other items. Somehow, having a real safety-deposit box made her feel like an adult. More than having an apartment of her own or paying the bills ever had.

This said she was successful enough to have things that needed protecting.

As she walked out of the vault, she saw Emmett Harding sitting at a desk with someone from the bank. Since he wore a suit, she wondered if the man was a loan officer. Was Emmett dealing with the loan from Meade? Or with Meade's estate now?

As Meg stood staring at Emmett, the bank clerk, who had

followed her out of the vault, came to a stop next to her. "Anything else we can help you with?"

Meg realized she was standing there, watching the activity at the front of the bank. No, she didn't look suspicious at all. She smiled and shook her head. "I was thinking about the safety-deposit box. Now, the payment and renewal will come out of my checking account, right?"

The woman, who had explained the process to Meg not more than ten minutes ago, smiled, but her expression looked pained. "Exactly. It's all on those papers I gave you. If you want to come over to my desk, I can walk you through it again."

Meg shook her head. "I'm good. But thank you."

With one last glance at Emmett, Meg walked out of the bank. Before she got on her bike and headed home, she pulled up the pictures on her phone. She scrolled through them, looking for the one of the registration of Emmett's boat.

It wasn't there. Dalton had deleted it from her phone.

The question was why.

She texted him to see if he was working or had time to talk. No response. Finally, she climbed on her bike and headed home.

She wasn't sure why, but right now, she had the same feelings as when Romain had called her from the airport as he was leaving with Rachel. Had Dalton betrayed her, too?

Meg pedaled harder as her mood grew fouler. She hadn't heard back from Natasha. Dalton was ignoring her text. And her mom might be in trouble at the bookstore. Monday was turning into a horrible day. Not to mention the time-share meeting with Irene.

Maybe she should hang out at the apartment tonight and watch movies with Watson.

Instead, when she got home, she turned on the renovation channel for Watson, then pulled up her laptop to her "Sleuthing Guide for Amateurs" document. She'd started an outline, but she decided if she started writing the text for the book, she might see what she was missing in Meade's murder case.

She started the first chapter by talking about her love for Nancy Drew books. The why behind her love for sleuthing. She wrote about the investigations she, Natasha, Dalton, and, for a while, Junior had carried out in middle and high school. She pushed away her negative thoughts about her brother and her friends as she wrote. Then she talked about her life. How she was a start-and-stop kind of person and had tried a lot of new things that hadn't worked out. And how, in her mind, that made her the perfect person to be an amateur sleuth. At least until she could convince someone to pay her for the work.

Then she started writing about the death of Robert Meade III. Her first section was just the facts. Where he was killed. How. And she even included Natasha's involvement, her driving him to Lilly Aster's place. Eventually, she'd change all the names.

Watson nudged Meg with his nose, and when she glanced up at the clock, it was almost six. She grabbed his leash and took him outside. She hadn't brought her phone down with her, so she had no idea if Natasha had texted her. Her uncle's truck was in the drive, but the house was dark, and her aunt's car was gone. They must have gone out for dinner.

She made her way back up to the apartment and started turning on the lights. She locked the door, and Watson, once off his leash, went to drink again from the water dish. It was a never-ending cycle for him. She checked her phone. No missed calls or texts. She texted Natasha, **Everything okay?**

She watched as three dots appeared on her phone's screen, letting her know that Natasha was crafting a response. **Sorry. The bakery was slammed today. I'm fine. Talk later?**

Meg texted back an okay, then set the phone down. "Your aunt Natasha never wants to chat about bad things. We'll give her some space, then make sure she comes to the bookstore on Thursday."

Watson wiped his wet mouth on the rug, then jumped on the couch to continue binge-watching HGTV.

Meg looked in the fridge for something to make for dinner. She decided on shrimp pasta with the vegetables that her aunt had added to Meg's shopping list. Cooking was one of her little pleasures. Although she cooked only for herself on most nights, even when she had lived with Romain, tonight she felt the loss of being part of a couple more than usual.

Chapter 17

Nancy Drew made this job look easy.

Meg had gone to bed stuffed with yummy pasta and hopeful for the new day. When she woke up to the rain, she was glad she'd already planned on driving to Summer Break that day. But did she want to take Watson and possibly have a soaked dog to bring home? Watson loved car rides, so she decided to take him along. Besides, he hated being alone in the apartment. Since they would both probably get wet, she had better bring along two towels. She checked her phone for messages and found nothing.

Meg gathered the stuff she'd need for the day and put it into her tote. After she sat down to drink some coffee and wait for it to not be too early to pop into Lilly's, she went over what she'd written yesterday. It was good. At least she thought so but maybe it could be better. She wondered if the college had a class on writing nonfiction. Maybe that would help.

As she was writing last night, she'd seen the holes in her project. She needed to gather more information, especially about Robert Meade III. *Know your victim, find your killer.* It was a sleuthing guidebook tip. One of fifty she'd developed to help manage writing the book. She didn't know enough about the agent or his life.

That was apparent by the surprise of Natasha's loan. And if he had loaned money to Natasha and Emmett, who else had he loaned money to during the lockdown?

There were probably a lot of businesses that had faced closing without any tourist income, like her mom's bookstore.

She made a note on her calendar to schedule time with her mom to look at the books. Mom had invited her into the business planning. To do that, she needed to know what was currently happening. Having her mom trust her to review the store's financials would help Meg give her advice on future planning and projecting. Something she'd done for the startup. Had the CEO been honest with her about his actual income, she might have been able to keep the nascent business afloat. Instead, he'd lied and taken a large piece of the business pie to keep his home life solvent. Water under the bridge, but she wanted to help her mom.

By the time she'd made plans with Mom to meet Wednesday morning, dodged three calls from Irene about a sale that would end soon, and made a list of people to talk to about Robert Meade, it was time to go drop off her assignment with Lilly Aster. Maybe she'd bring up the subject of Meade, too.

She pulled into the driveway of Summer Break and, leaving Watson in the car, ran through the rain to the door with her folder in hand. She needed to buy a new raincoat. She'd donated her old one in a fit of madness, thinking she'd buy a new one after they got home from Italy. Or maybe in Italy. Now she needed one.

She rang the bell, thankful for the stone arch that kept her and the entryway out of the rain.

Jolene opened the door and waved her in. "I hope you didn't bike here today."

"Nope, I brought the car. I'm heading north after I leave here to get some information about going back to college." Meg paused, realizing Jolene's eyes were glazing over. "Sorry. I've had a lot of coffee this morning. Here's the assignment."

Jolene glanced at the time on the back, then looked at the printed pages. "This looks good. Lilly has your next assignment. She's on the phone with Sarah, but she said to send you in when you arrived. More coffee?"

"No, I'm good." Meg thought it was a good sign that Jolene was now calling her boss Lilly and not Ms. Aster when she was talking to Meg. She nodded toward the office. "Just go in?"

"Yep, she's expecting you." Jolene dropped her voice. "I think she wants to use you to get off the call. Sarah's trying to talk her into extending her book tour by a week. Lilly's not buying it."

Meg headed to the end of the foyer and stopped at the doors that went into Lilly's office. She knocked lightly at the half-open door, and Lilly waved her inside as Sarah's voice came over the speakerphone.

"You can't keep giving your most profitable event to that tiny store on the island. They don't even have the staff to support it. The guy who helped me get water at the event works on the ferry." Sarah was complaining about Island Books.

Lilly rolled her eyes and grinned at Meg. "I hear what you're saying, but I'm committed to Felicia and her bookstore. Small businesses like hers make our lives better. And she hand sells my books. Not like that store you sent me to in LA. The owner wasn't even at my event."

"Carolyn was at a party for a celebrity author who released that week." Sarah sounded aghast that Lilly would even question her loyalty.

"She could have put in an appearance. I had a release that week, too," Lilly reminded her agent. "Anyway, I've got to go. Felicia's daughter is here to help me with some research. Say hi to Sarah, Meg."

"Hi, Sarah. It was nice to see you at the launch," Meg called out. Lilly held up her thumb, letting her know that she appreciated the support.

"Oh, hi, Meg." Sarah paused, and Meg wondered if she was

trying to remember what exactly she'd said about the bookstore. "Lilly, I guess I'll see you in New York on Thursday, then?"

"With bells on," Lilly said, then disconnected the call. "I'm sorry about that, Meg. Sometimes Sarah thinks bigger is better."

"My mom appreciates you doing your launches at her store." Meg's stomach hurt a little as she thought of what might happen if Sarah got her way.

"I'll never change that arrangement. As long as my books are selling and your mom still wants to host the launch, that is." She waved Meg over to the desk. "I've been thinking a lot about your next assignment."

Meg felt her excitement growing. She was going to be doing work on the manuscript Lilly was writing. Maybe as a first reader. "I'm looking forward to whatever you need me to do."

"Great, because it's something I've been needing to do, but I've put it off." She handed Meg a new folder. "I need a list of all the mystery bookstores in the US. I'd love a few in London or Canada, too, but first, we need to cover the States. Please make it an Excel document. You know how to work in Excel, right? Anyway, I need the name, website, phone, address, any sister stores, owner, and author contact information. If you aren't sure it's focused on mystery, put that in the notes. I'd rather have too many than not enough."

"Oh, a bookstore spreadsheet. Are you sure there isn't one out there?" Meg briefly felt the disappointment, then thought about two more weeks, at least, of income being tucked into her account.

"You would think so, but I haven't found one. And check out the book tour listings of at least ten other authors in my genre. That might stir up a new one or two for us to contact for the new release. Robert always pushed me to a few larger venues. Sarah says she doesn't help set up tours—except, it seems, with her friends' stores. I got a new publicist, again, at the publisher. She doesn't know anyone. You'd think I could have someone stable, but no." Lilly pulled out a folder with bookmarks and flyers tucked inside. "These are what I've gathered over the years, but some of the stores aren't even in business anymore."

"Okay, so this will be a moving target." Meg thought of ways she could find the information.

"If you haven't subscribed to the free edition of *Publishers Weekly*, I'd suggest you do that. It will help. I'll try to let you know what I see, as well. I tend to see it and then forget to send the information to anyone. This will be hugely helpful for planning the next tour." Lilly's phone rang. "And speaking of, Sarah is calling again, probably to complain about the stores Robert set up for the New York trip. Like I can do anything about it now."

Lilly waved at Meg as she picked up the phone. "Sarah, what's happening now? You know I'm trying to write before I leave tonight."

Meg knew she'd been dismissed. As she left, the view out the glass sliders caught her attention. From this room, Lilly could see her entire beach, including the boardwalk from the house to the dock and toward the gate. If she'd been here the day Robert was killed, she could have seen him and maybe the attack.

She turned back to ask a burning question, but Lilly was flipping through her planner. "I know I have the owner's name somewhere."

Meg didn't want to interrupt again. Especially not to ask if her employer had seen her former agent drown near her dock. It probably wasn't a work-appropriate subject.

Before she left Summer Break, she gave Watson some water and walked him around the driveway and the house. The rain had stopped, and she could see the sun trying to break through the clouds. Maybe she wouldn't be driving in the rain the entire day.

Summer Break, a three-story mini-mansion, had cedar shake

siding, giving it a coastal feel. The front was completely fenced off, with a gate to the left, which might lead to a trail down to the beach. But from the front, you couldn't tell that the house was even close to the waterfront. Trees surrounded the driveway area and blocked neighbors' views of the property, except in the back.

Meg guessed the houses on either side of Summer Break had windows with views of the Seattle skyline, like those in Lilly's office—views that encompassed Lilly's dock. If someone had killed Meade on the dock, like Uncle Troy believed, maybe someone in one of the two houses on either side had witnessed it. If they didn't, their architects should be fired.

Back in the car, she texted her uncle and asked if the neighborhood had been canvassed, especially those two houses after Meade's body was discovered. She was surprised to see dots immediately show up on her phone's screen, indicating he was typing a response. It was short.

Where are you?

Just leaving Summer Break after meeting with Lilly about my next assignment. I'll be heading to the college next. I have Watson with me. Why?

He didn't answer her question. And his answer was as curt and sparse as his question.

Stay out of my investigation.

Not her monkey, not her circus. She got it. But until Natasha was off the possible suspect list, Uncle Troy was going to keep hearing from her. Even if he didn't respond, she knew he'd at least follow up on her suggestions. Checking out the scene for possible witnesses was another rule of "The Sleuthing Guide for Amateurs." She'd added it last night to the tips list.

She needed to find a way to investigate without Uncle Troy finding out. Stay out of the professionals' way. Or else.

She should write that rule down, as well.

* * *

Meg got lucky. Not only did she get all the paperwork she needed to reenroll, but also her former adviser was having office hours and didn't mind Watson being part of the discussion. Or at least in his office.

"I'm so glad you're coming back. I wasn't happy when you decided to leave school for the start-up. I hear that didn't go well." Professor Valmer had a way of getting right to the point of the conversation.

"No, it didn't." Meg didn't want to go into all the whys and the wherefores. It was water under the bridge. "You can't step into the same river twice."

Professor Valmer blinked and nodded. "Well put. So what are you thinking of majoring in this time? History, English, business, and computer science I think were your top four during your last two years."

"I'm thinking business and English. I'm working part-time for my mom's bookstore and for the author L. C. Aster. I'm working on a nonfiction book, but I'm not sure I'm doing it right," Meg replied.

Professor Valmer laughed as he pulled up her transcript. "Oh, my dear, no one is ever sure they're writing what they should be or the right way. It's called impostor syndrome."

She waited as he looked at the classes she'd completed. Then he printed out her transcript.

"From this, I believe you could still complete an English major with a business minor in no time at all. You've been very eclectic in your course choices. Almost like you planned this all along. I don't think we can get you squared away full-time for the fall semester, but you could take a few classes and come in during the spring semester. Check out the summer schedule and see if there's anything that meets a requirement or sparks your fancy. I'm excited to have you back." He found the page in the degree requirements for a BA in English and then put a paper clip on the business minor requirements. "It might take a bit longer than two years, but I'm sure you'll finish this time. If you keep your eye on the ball. And next year you might qualify for some scholarships."

Meg tucked the college entrance information books back into her tote and stood. "Thank you for fitting me in, Professor."

The older man with salt-and-pepper hair stood to walk her the few feet out of his office. He wore jeans with a tweed jacket over an old rock band T-shirt. Meg had heard that they kept the air down to seventy degrees so the professors could wear suits, which caused the students who showed up in shorts and tanks to freeze during classes. Maybe it was to keep them awake. "I meant it when I said it's nice to have you back. You were one of my favorites."

As she left the building, Meg took a deep breath of the cool air. The rain had stopped, and the campus looked like a sparkling jewel. The grass and shrubs gleamed, their wet leaves picking up the sunlight.

Being on campus always felt like existing in another world. A world where you could try out new things, figure out what you wanted to do with the rest of your life, and read all the books that helped you transition into the journey of adulthood.

Now Meg wanted to earn her degree and to finally have a career that she could count on. Maybe she should have picked a business major with an English minor. But she wasn't sure she could pass the math classes. She'd been the failure-to-thrive child way too long for even her comfort level.

Meg Gates, private investigator. Or maybe she needed a different title. She didn't want people to think she was the one to contact to find out if their husband was cheating. She wanted big cases. And if she solved Meade's murder for her first case, that might even happen.

She and Watson headed home, but not before stopping at the Hungry Onion. It was an old fifties hamburger joint that still had you park your car and wait for your waitress to come to you. The place was a college hangout. It hadn't been remodeled or changed in years, but the food was amazing. Especially the vanilla milkshakes.

As she waited for her cheeseburger and onion rings, her phone buzzed with a text.

Want to hit the bonfire tonight?

She checked the sender line. Dalton. He was talking to her again. But he hadn't responded to the text in which she'd asked him about the picture of Emmett's boat registration. He was good at ignoring things.

Fine. Two could play that game. She was about to respond when her food came. She sipped her milkshake as she looked at the text. Finally, she texted back.

Where should we meet?

I'll pick you up at six for dinner. Bring the mutt.

She looked over at Watson, who was staring at her uneaten onion rings. "Dalton called you a mutt. You should bite him tonight."

Watson looked up at her with full-blown desire in his gaze. He wanted to bite her cheeseburger instead.

She ripped off a bit of the bun that didn't have any sauce on it and gave it to him. "That's about all you can eat from this order. Sorry."

As they prepared to go home, Meg didn't think Watson believed she was sorry. Especially when she got out and threw away the sack with her leftovers. Back in the car, he barked twice at her to show his dismay before lying down in the seat, his back toward her.

Yep, she was getting the silent treatment. She turned up the old rock station that her dad had hooked her on years ago. Dad had wanted to be the next indie rock star. A member of the Seattle grunge royalty. Instead, he'd gotten married and had two kids. Then a successful accounting career and, finally, owning his own business.

And even now, on most weekends you'd find him not on a golf course but in his garage, playing guitar and writing songs.

Meg didn't want that to be her life. She wanted to live her dreams. And if she failed again? At least it would be fast and painless. Not like the failed marriage that had tried to domesticate her father from rocker to family man.

Chapter 18

A good investigator sees the details that others blow off.

The evening was already chilly, so Meg packed a pair of jeans and a hoodie in Watson's backpack. She'd have to find a clump of trees to change from the capris into jeans, or she'd put the oversized hoodie on first while switching into warmer clothes. Of course, she'd probably have to roll up her jeans in order to wade out to the boat. Just the price you paid to play on the water.

Dalton grabbed the backpack as soon as he came to get them. With Watson in tow, they made their way down the stairs and into the truck.

"So how was your day? Did you get a new assignment from Ms. Aster?" Dalton asked as he drove away.

She talked about the new assignment and her trip to the campus to get set up for classes.

"I didn't realize you were thinking about going back." Dalton glanced over at her from the driver's seat. "That must be exciting."

"I have to say I'm looking forward to it." She grinned as they parked in the town lot. "Remind me that I said this in about a year, when I'm tired of doing homework around my two jobs."

"You'll do fine. I think sometimes it takes people time to figure out what they want to do." He parked the truck, pausing the conversation as she got out of the truck and lifted Watson out. "You do know what you want to do, right?"

"Kind of. It's a work in progress," Meg admitted. She waited for him to remote-lock the truck. "Should I have grabbed Watson's backpack?"

"No, we'll come back. I've got us a table out on the Whale Fin patio tonight." He pointed to the restaurant, which was down the street. "A guy from work said he saw a group of gray whales coming this way. I was hoping we could see them from the restaurant or at the bonfire."

"So we're not going to drink and get rowdy with your friends?" Meg followed him down the sidewalk to the restaurant.

"I have acquaintances at the bonfire, not friends." Dalton held the patio gate open for her. "Is that why you said yes? To drink with the rowdies?"

"No, I said yes because I like your company. And it's a good way to figure out who is who on the island. At least in our age group. The age-appropriate class at church turned out to be a female-bonding hour. Which I didn't mind. Mom thought there would be eligible bachelors for me to meet. Instead, I got hit with a cruise time-share presentation."

Dalton chuckled as he followed the hostess to their table. "Irene found a new prospect. She must be over the moon. Did she pull out her laptop for the full half-hour slideshow?"

"So everyone knows to stay away from Irene? It would have been nice to have had some warning. All Natasha did was laugh." Meg sat down, and Watson went under the table to sleep until the food arrived.

"I didn't realize you were looking for a new boyfriend at church." He opened his menu and studied it.

"I didn't say I was looking for a new boyfriend." Meg rolled her eyes. "Mom is the one who was playing the matchmaker card. And don't tell her that the young adult group is filled with women. Otherwise, she'll find something else for me, and Junior will be taking her to church going forward."

As they ate, Dalton watched the sound for any sign of the whales. The silence between them should have been comfortable, but Meg kept wondering about the picture of Emmett's boat registration and why Dalton had removed it from her phone.

Frustrated, she set her fork down. "Look, I know you don't want to talk about it, but why did you delete that picture from my phone?"

He turned his gaze back from the sound to her. "I'm sorry about that."

"That's it? You're sorry? That's not an explanation. How can I trust you if you go behind my back and do things like this? You know I'm already dealing with trust issues." Meg felt her anger building and pressed her lips together. Yelling at Dalton wasn't going to change what had happened. And they were in a public place.

"I'm not Romain," he reminded her. "But I do owe you an explanation. Emmett is a friend, but he's also a client. And he trusts me with his boat. I can't be taking pictures and turning him in to the police because he had some sort of business deal with a guy who wound up dead. I have a responsibility to look the other way unless it's an actual crime."

"How do we know he didn't kill Meade?" Meg pointed out.

"I get that, but, Meg, we don't know he did. And the evidence is less solid than what your uncle has on Natasha. And we both feel like he should be able to see through that." Dalton took a deep breath before he continued. "I told you I'd talk to him about calling your uncle and telling him about the loan. And he did. He went to the bank last week to get a loan to pay off Meade's estate. So he'll be done with him."

"I figured that." Meg picked up her fork and continued eating.

Dalton stared at her. "What do you mean?"

"I saw him at the bank when I set up a safety-deposit box for the engagement ring. Well, the ring and my important papers, which don't even begin to fill up my box. So if you want to put your passport and other stuff in my box, there's room." She broke off a bit of bread and held it under the table for Watson.

"You're asking my papers to move in with your papers? Magpie, I didn't realize we were at that stage yet." Dalton pretended to think. "Okay, I accept, but they get to be in a separate envelope, so your papers can't be all touchy-feely."

Meg snorted, and the heaviness in the air between them broke. "Fine. I see your point about your professional relationship with Emmett. And if you don't need space in my safety-deposit box, I'll ask Natasha if she needs some. Although our girl is much more adult than either of us. She probably already has one."

"I think she does. She had me drop her off at the bank to put something inside her box a few months ago. But she's never offered to share with me." He finished his meal and leaned back. "You're fast becoming the number one friend on the ranking list."

"Whatever," she responded, giving Watson the last of her roll.

He took her hand and squeezed it. "And as a reward for that kindness, look out to your left. The whales are here."

They sat there for quite a while watching as the whales played in the water. Then they swam away from the spot where Meg could see them. She smiled over at Dalton. "I've missed home. I've missed these moments. In Seattle it was all about the rush. Here I have time to think and watch."

"We've missed you, too." He looked over at the waitress,

who then came by with the check. "We better get out to the bonfire, or we'll miss Nate falling over drunk and almost nose-diving into the fire. It's one of his best tricks."

"Besides yelling about *those people* who are ruining his life," Meg added.

Dalton pretended to hit his forehead with the palm of his hand. "How could I forget that?"

Nate and Violet were at the bonfire, but the couple was surprisingly quiet. The group was smaller tonight, and the talk centered around the murder and who would commit such a violent act. Everyone seemed to know already how exactly Meade had died. No one knew who had killed him.

Finally, one guy stood and held his arms wide. "No more sad talk. We're young and alive. Turn up the music."

Dalton leaned over. "That's Blake Adams. He works over at the marina."

"He has good taste in music," Meg responded as she leaned into the chair that Dalton had brought her. Luna was over on the other side of the fire, sitting with a guy but staring at Dalton. "So you aren't dating anyone?"

Dalton smiled and shook his head. "Nope. I'm spending time with my friend right now. Why? Are you trying to get rid of me?"

"More like trying to figure you out," Meg admitted. She rubbed her fingers on Watson's back.

"Good luck with that." He opened a bottle of water and took a drink. "Is Natasha coming?"

"I don't know." Meg glanced around at the people at the bonfire. Natasha had already been here when Meg arrived the last time, but tonight she was nowhere to be found. "I think she's worried about Robert's murder. I know she didn't kill him, and I'm sure Uncle Troy will clear her soon. But that has to be stressful."

As they spoke, Natasha walked onto the beach from the small parking lot on the north side. She had a cooler in her hand as well as a towel wrapped around her waist.

Meg waved. "Speak of the devil."

"I'm going to tell her you called her that." Dalton stood and walked over to Natasha. He took her cooler from her hand.

The man was a gentleman. To her, to Natasha. To everyone. To prove her point, he offered Natasha his chair, which she turned down, spreading the towel next to Meg's chair instead.

"I brought a cake and wine coolers. We're celebrating."

"You had me at cake," Meg joked. "What are we celebrating?"

"Your uncle called me a few minutes before I closed the bakery. My timeline matches up with the street cameras. And my apartment lights go on right after that. So it's unlikely I killed Robert Meade. Or at least I'm no longer the most likely suspect. Your uncle doesn't like being crystal clear on these things. Anyway, I'm taking the call as I'm off his list. And he said I was too short to be a viable suspect, anyway. I guess the neighbor's cameras caught someone fighting with Meade the night he was killed, but the camera view was almost out of frame."

"So they don't know who killed him, but you don't match the killer's body type." Meg hugged her. "That's the best thing that's happened today."

"Besides the whales?" Dalton looked hurt.

"And the cake, especially if it's chocolate," Meg added.

"Of course it's chocolate." Natasha looked between Meg and Dalton. "Wait, you saw whales? Here in the sound? When?"

By the time they called it a night, Meg was feeling more than a little tired. Maybe it was the wine coolers or the second slice of cake, on top of an amazing dinner. She was waiting for Watson to do his business so they could get on the boat when she heard voices.

"I know something's wrong," a woman said to Meg's left. "Why won't you talk to me?"

They were walking toward the parking lot to which Dalton had walked Natasha with her now-empty cooler a few minutes ago. Dalton was waiting for them on the boat.

"Just leave it alone. I can't talk about it," a male voice answered. "I might be heading to Portland for a few weeks. I've got a job lined up, so don't freak out if I disappear."

"Sure. Why would I worry about you?" the woman said as they came around the path and saw Meg and Watson.

"Oh, hi, Meg. Heading home?" Violet asked.

"Yeah, tomorrow's a long day at the bookstore, so I'm getting back." She glanced down at Watson, who stood next to her. "I like to walk him before he gets on Dalton's boat and has bad ideas."

"He's so cute. I bet he never has bad ideas." Violet reached down and rubbed Watson's head.

"Sure. The dog's perfect," Nate muttered as he kept walking.

Violet rolled her eyes. "I better go. The king is in a bad mood tonight."

"It was nice to see you," Meg called after her. Then she turned and headed back to the beach and Dalton.

When they headed back to the marina, she told Dalton about Nate's news.

Dalton glanced toward the shore as she told him. "I heard he got fired from Island Diner last week for not showing up. I guess he's gone through all the employers on the island. Violet needs to dump that loser."

Meg wondered if Nate's situation was more pressing. The guy hated anyone who seemed to have money or was, in his eyes, not a local. Had he fought with Robert Meade and now felt compelled to leave town? It was a possibility. Of course, anyone who was on the island the day Meade was killed could also fall into that logic.

She rubbed the sleep out of her eyes. She was chasing zebras. She'd written the rule for her book last week. *Hoof sounds are more likely a sign of horses than zebras.* Her uncle probably had another suspect besides Lilly Aster now, especially since he'd all but told Natasha that he knew she didn't kill the guy.

When she got home, the lights were off at the main house. Not the time to go banging on the door to ask who was next on Uncle Troy's list of suspects. Or even to tell him that she had a "feeling" that Nate was a killer. Besides, did she even know Nate's last name? Nate, the guy who hung out at the bonfires and dated Violet. She didn't think that kind of evidence would clear Lilly Aster.

She took Watson for one more short walk around the property after Dalton dropped them off. As she waited for him to finish, she saw a light turn on in the main house. Then it went off.

Probably Uncle Troy or Aunt Melody in the kitchen to grab a drink. They wouldn't be watching for her to come home, would they?

Meg and Watson climbed the stairs to the apartment and then headed to bed. Tomorrow was almost here, and she had a job she liked to go to.

As she lay in bed, she thought about her night. Dalton and the whales. Then seeing Natasha at the bonfire, eating the to-die-for cake, and knowing her friend was happy. Maybe coming home hadn't been such a bad idea.

The ringing phone woke her the next morning at eight. Sunlight streamed into the bedroom, and Watson was curled up next to her. He growled lightly when she turned to grab her phone. "Hello?"

"Oh, I didn't wake you, did I? I wanted to let you know that your mom is coming over to have breakfast with me, and I didn't want her to find you in bed. Especially since you had a late night." Aunt Melody was too bright and chipper for this time of the morning.

Meg slid her legs off the bed. "I was getting up."

"Perfect. Then come over and eat with us. I'm making omelets. I got some mushrooms at the farmers market on Saturday that I need to use up. I always buy too much produce there."

After hanging up with her aunt, she checked on Watson, who looked perfectly comfortable, clearly conveying that he wished to sleep for a while longer while Meg showered. It was a good thing they didn't go to the bonfires every week.

She clicked on Watson's leash and headed down to the backyard as soon as she heard her mom's car pull up. Thank goodness for her aunt's warning shot. She was a grown woman, but still, she didn't want her mom griping about her sleeping habits, especially since she'd been out late with Dalton. Bainbridge was a small town.

Inside the gate, Meg let Watson off the lead, and he went to his favorite couch on the porch. She lightly knocked on the patio door and heard Aunt Melody call out for her to come in. When she entered the kitchen, the orange juice and coffee had already been poured.

"This looks amazing."

"I figured you'd like a home-cooked meal. You've been eating out a lot." Aunt Melody winked at her. "How was dinner with Dalton yesterday?"

"We saw whales from the patio." Meg slipped into her chair and sipped her coffee. She needed to change the subject.

Mom stared at her from her spot at the table. "Have you taken the time to talk to Romain since he's been back? I think you should—"

"Felicia, let the girl be. What you want for Meg is for her to be happy. Romain messed up that version of life. Now she has to find a new path." Aunt Melody sat down and put a napkin on her lap. "Now, let's share food and gossip. What have you heard about who killed Robert Meade? Troy has been unusually tight-lipped about this investigation. I'm worried that he truly thinks Lilly might be involved."

Meg listened as her aunt and mom talked about the current investigation and what people around town were saying. Meg had to agree with her aunt. From what she knew, Lilly Aster was the most likely suspect, even if she and Aunt Melody knew that the woman wouldn't have done this. Now that she had Natasha mostly cleared of any wrongdoing, it was time to make sure Lilly was off Uncle Troy's suspect list. And someone else was on it.

Chapter 19

Changing your plan midstream isn't failing. It just feels like it is.

Meg glanced around the empty bookstore Wednesday night and pulled out her laptop. At breakfast her mom had asked her to work another shift. The good news was she didn't have anything else to do. So she'd said yes.

She'd finished all the tasks on her mom's list for the day. She'd even made a sign for a counter display announcing L. C. Aster's newest signed book. Her mother needed to add more Pacific Northwest authors to her signed collection. Maybe Meg should focus on writing a proposal that included a list of possible in-person signing events. Her mom was paying her to be here. She might as well find a way to bring in more customers. And a writing group. And maybe a book club? The island had enough full-time residents to fill a weekly event night. Maybe that would give the area's singles, like Luna and, yes, Irene, a place to meet up that wasn't church or the bonfire. Heaven, hell, or a book club—all meet cute starts for couples in romance novels.

Instead, she decided to work on Lilly's next assignment. A list of mystery bookstores in the United States. She decided to make the country an autofill cell that she could change if she found new bookstores. That way, Lilly—or more likely Jolene, or whoever she hired to set up the book launch events—could sort by location.

For a second, she realized that person might be her. Meg liked the idea of working full-time for Lilly. If she could figure out the benefits part. Maybe Lilly paid for health insurance for her employees. She needed to stop putting up walls to block her dreams. She could deal with the specifics if the dream came true.

She continued configuring the Excel sheet to fit the needs of a writer or assistant. Thank goodness for the classes in computer programs she'd taken at the start-up. She didn't know how to code, but at least she knew how the different office programs worked.

Setting a system up took longer than she'd expected, and suddenly, her stomach was growling. She hadn't had a customer in over three hours, but she had a workable spreadsheet into which she could start inputting data.

First, she needed food. Neither Natasha nor Dalton had shown up with dinner, so she called in a delivery order for Chinese food. Then she fed Watson and, after locking the front door, took him for a short walk. They made it back before the food arrived, and when it did, she sat on the couch and ate.

While she ate, she scanned through her email. She had something from the college admission office saying her application had been received and was being processed, but she was welcome to take part-time classes this summer, before the process was complete. She hadn't even opened the class schedule.

She had four emails from Romain. All with the subject line We need to talk.

She ignored them. She thought about deleting them, but she'd read them later. He had been nice enough to return the ring. She could read a few emails, especially if he was begging for her to come back. It wouldn't happen, but it would make her feel a bit better that he knew he'd messed up. She checked her online calendar. She wasn't scheduled to see Lilly next week, but Lilly had asked her to email Jolene her hours for the week. And her bookstore hours were back to normal. Well, except for tomorrow morning.

She needed something else to keep her busy. Dalton, Natasha, Aunt Melody, and even her mom had filled her hours the first few weeks after she moved home. Now it was time for her to act like she lived here and wasn't visiting and expecting people to entertain her. She had the guidebook to write, but she could work on it for only a couple of hours a day before her brain started to fry. Besides, she needed to do something that didn't feel like work.

In Seattle, on nights when Romain worked late, she'd gone to shows, grabbed coffee, or gone shopping with friends. Friends that now hadn't even called in weeks. Did they think that being cheated on was catching? Or, more likely, had their friendship been one of convenience versus true connection?

As she finished her fried rice, she pulled out the summer catalog that was in her tote and looked at the available classes. Before, with her dad's urging, she'd been focused on getting a degree in business. Now she wasn't sure that was in the cards for her. Instead, she found a class called The History of Mystery. Bonus, she needed the English elective. It was being held for six weeks, on Monday and Wednesday mornings. She wouldn't have to change her work hours at all. Of course, at the bookstore, changing her hours would mean the store would be closed on nights she couldn't work. Not a great way to pay back her mom for giving her a job. She was getting ready to close the shop when Dalton's text arrived.

Cissy's working the Seattle ticket booth tonight if you still want to talk to her about Robert Meade. She hasn't talked to your uncle yet. Hurry and get down here. The ferry's just coming into the dock.

Meg quickly typed an acknowledgment telling him she was on her way, and got her bag and Watson out the door. She locked up and hurried down to the ferry. As they walked, Watson kept looking back, as if asking why they weren't on the road home. After the third time, she laughed and rubbed his head. "We're taking a boat ride tonight. We'll be home soon, in time for your favorite remodel show."

The walk-on line for the ferry was short. Tourists were already back in Seattle, and residents were ready to call it a night. Unless they worked a night shift. The woman in front of her turned, and she realized it was Violet. "Hey, are you heading in to work or play?"

Violet frowned, then recognized Watson and, finally, Meg. "Sorry. It's always weird to see someone out of context. You're Dalton's new girl, Meg, right?"

"Dalton and I are friends. I grew up on the island and moved back." She pulled on Watson's leash, and he sat, waiting to board. Meg tried her question again. "Do you work in Seattle?"

"Yeah, I took on an evening shift to try to save money for my own place. I'm moving back in with my parents again. Nate and I broke up." She glanced out toward the island. "I'm a little shell-shocked. I thought we were on the path to something permanent. Then he tells me he's been seeing someone on the side and I need to move out."

Meg felt for Violet. Of course, she'd had the same experience—well, almost—a month before. "I'm so sorry. I know how you feel. My fiancé basically left me at the altar. Now he's hanging around, trying to talk and, I guess, make up. I'm not buying it, though. I'm better off without him."

Violet blinked several times, staring at Meg. "Oh, I didn't know. Luna said you and Dalton were dating, and I figured you must have met in Seattle. Especially after Nate said you were working for L. C. Aster."

"My aunt knows her and got me the job when I decided to move home. I'm also working for my mom at the bookstore. I'm living in an apartment over my aunt's garage. So yeah, it's kind of a setback. But I'm glad I found out now and not after we had a kid or a house." Meg saw Dalton walking toward them. "Maybe it's a restart, not a setback. You should come by the bookstore some night when you're not working. I bet we have a lot in common."

Violet glanced behind her at Dalton walking up to them. She turned back and smiled. "I'll do that. Just be straight with him if you're not interested. He's a super nice guy."

When Dalton reached them, he smiled at Violet. "Long time, no see. Are you heading into Seattle for some fun?"

"No, work, I'm afraid." She nodded at Meg, taking out her phone. "I'll see you soon."

"Sounds good." Meg turned to Dalton. "You didn't have to come get us. I know how to get on the ferry."

"Yeah, but I have permission to take you up to the captain's deck. I think you'll love the view." He took her arm and turned back to Violet. "I'm sorry. I didn't realize you'd be here, and I only got permission for Meg."

Violet looked up from her phone. "You're a good man, Dalton. Go get ahead of the crowd."

As they walked down the enclosed dock toward the ferry, Dalton glanced behind them once. "I'm missing something."

Meg told him about Nate breaking up with Violet. "She was blindsided."

"Honestly, I am, too. I didn't think Nate had it in him to cheat on Violet. She's too good for him." Dalton opened a door once they were on the ferry, and they climbed the stairs. "I'm beginning to think my sex are all idiots."

"Except you," Meg teased.

He met her gaze, then dropped it. "Yes, except me."

The ride to Seattle was fun. Meg learned a lot from the crew as they maneuvered toward the Seattle skyline. As they got closer, Meg watched the captain and Dalton lock gazes, and then she was hustled downstairs to the main deck.

"Sorry. Jim was breaking all kinds of rules letting you up there, so we needed to get you down before anyone found out. I was in the Coast Guard with him. He's a stand-up guy." Dalton walked her to a side chair where she could still see the lights of Seattle. "We can sit here until we dock. Then I'll take you to meet Cissy. I'll have to leave you there, so don't miss the ferry back."

"Watson would kill me. He already thinks it's past his bedtime." Meg reached down and rubbed his head. "Thanks for doing this."

"The Nancy Drew crew sticks together. Just don't call me Ned." He sat next to her, and they watched the city lights grow closer and closer.

After disembarking, he took her out through a guarded gate and directly to the ticket building. When they stepped inside, two women stood at the windows, but neither one was helping customers. He walked her over to the blond woman on the right. "Meg, this is Cissy. I told her what you wanted to know."

Cissy stood and shook Meg's hand as Dalton left the room. "It's nice to meet you. I'm not sure what Dalton thinks I can tell you. We see a lot of people come through here."

"Well, I'm wondering if you've seen this man." Meg had taken a snip of a picture of Robert Meade on the internet. She held out her cell phone to show Cissy the snip.

"Of course. That's the guy who was killed on L. C. Aster's dock. He was a nasty man. He was always complaining that people were touching his BMW. I guess I shouldn't talk ill of the dead." Cissy rolled her eyes. "He was so easy to hate. He threw his card at me one day to get his ticket. I dropped it, and he griped that I was taking too long."

"He did the same thing to me," the other woman added.

"We get a few regulars to Bainbridge, and most of them are lovely. Like the ex-husband of the writer? He and his new girl are both nice. She even comes over to the island by herself. She loves it there."

"Tabitha and Josh?" When Meg had talked to Tabitha, she'd made it seem like Josh dragged her there so he could talk to his ex-wife. "When was the last time you saw her by herself?"

"Last night. She came on about this time, and I saw her leave after the last ferry docked. I walked over to the same parking garage. She was talking on the phone to someone." The woman blushed. "I thought she was talking to me, but she had in those earphones you can't see. I almost answered her before I realized she wasn't questioning me about my roommate."

Meg tried to steer the conversation back to Robert, but other than both women agreeing he was horrible, she didn't get much.

Cissy checked her watch. "You better get going before you miss the ferry."

"Oh, wait. I remembered something. The last day... I guess it must have been the day he died." The other woman met Meg's gaze. "He was actually in a good mood. He was talking on the phone when he came to get a ticket. He waited for the change, then smiled. And then he said something weird."

"What?" Meg and Watson paused at the door, eager to get back to the ferry.

"He said with this information, she'd have to stay with him. The golden goose didn't need to be slaughtered, only penned up." She waved her out. "You better run."

Her pathway took her along a row of windows through which she could see the Seattle-bound passengers leaving the ferry. As she watched, Romain hurried through the people, looking at his watch. What had he been doing on Bainbridge Island? Had he been looking for her? Again? Maybe she needed to read his emails.

After she boarded the ferry, she settled onto a bench, with Watson lying on the floor. Meg thought about Meade's words. He'd had his hands in a lot of pockets. Could he have been talking about Natasha and his loan? Or Lilly and her books? The one person he hadn't been talking about was Emmett Harding. He'd said *she'd* have to stay with him. If Meg bet on anything, it would be that Meade had been talking about Lilly. Especially since she'd fired him earlier that week.

It was more evidence that she could give to her uncle. If it all didn't point to the two people she didn't want on his suspect list.

This sleuthing thing was harder than it looked on television.

Watson woke Meg the next morning by barking. Someone was at the door. She pulled on her robe and opened the door to find Uncle Troy standing there, a sheet of paper in his hand.

"Do you want to tell me what this is all about?" He shook the paper at her.

Meg turned and went to start coffee. She couldn't have this conversation without it. "I talked to Cissy last night about Robert Meade. I would have brought the information to you sooner, but I wasn't sure what it meant. Sometimes I need a few hours or even days to find out if it even applies. Do you want coffee, too?"

He frowned and shut the door behind him. "Don't tell me you're investigating Robert Meade's murder. I thought I told you to stay out of it."

Meg pulled two cups out of the cabinet and then sat down at the kitchen table. "I'm confused. If you didn't know I was investigating, you probably didn't know about me talking to Cissy. So why are you here again? Is Aunt Melody out of coffee?"

"No, your aunt isn't out of coffee. She gave this to me after feeding me a full breakfast, including omelets and juice. I should have known to be suspicious when she made monkey bread this morning." He rubbed his face. He took a seat at the table, then he pushed the white paper toward her. "Your mother found this in the trash at the bookstore. Please tell me you were venting and Romain isn't in danger."

"Why would Romain—" Meg started, then looked down at the page. It was a copy of her assignment for Lilly Aster. She pushed it back to her uncle and stood to pour the coffee. "That was a writing assignment from Lilly Aster. She wanted to see how my mind worked when I was asked to plan the perfect murder. I realized after I'd printed this copy that I hadn't changed Romain's name. I didn't want anyone to get the wrong idea. This is fiction. Not a murder plot."

Uncle Troy waited for her to bring over the pot and fill both cups. As he waited, he scanned the document again. "It's a good plan for a murder."

"Thanks, I think. Anyway, it was an assignment. What's Mom doing going through the trash, anyway?" She resumed her seat at the table.

"According to your aunt, the paper fell out of the trash can and was under the counter. Your mother found it when she was sweeping. Then she got worried." He sipped his coffee. "So how is your job with Ms. Aster? Are you learning a lot?"

"A lot about mystery and murder, yes. And a little about the book business. She's on a whole higher level than any author I've met before. Yet she's so down to earth. She wants to write a good story." Meg sipped her coffee. Watson was sleeping on his kitchen bed. She'd have to take him out soon. He was a good dog, but even well-trained dogs had their limits.

"You don't think she killed Robert Meade." The question didn't sound like a question, at least not to Meg.

She met her uncle's gaze and shook her head. "I don't believe that is possible in this world or in a fictional one. She's too nice. I'm willing to bet on it."

"You kind of are since you go over there once a week." He leaned back in his chair. "I suppose you need the job to afford to pay rent, right?"

Meg nodded. "But it's not only that. I'm learning. I'm engaged. I'm loving work for the first time in a long time. I can be creative and yet useful."

"I'm happy for you. I don't know who else to chat with to get your favorite author off my suspect list. She said she was writing and didn't even look up at that amazing view all day."

Meg thought about her promise to Dalton. Maybe she could steer her uncle toward another suspect without mentioning Emmett Harding. Besides, Dalton had said Emmett had already talked to Uncle Troy.

"Have you looked at Meade's financials? If he loaned money to Natasha, maybe he made loans to other people. Ones who didn't want to or couldn't repay him."

CHAPTER 20

People may not like you or your questions during an investigation. Including your friends.

Dalton brought pizza over to the bookstore after Natasha arrived. He sat the pizza down on the table, and when Meg went to open the box, he slammed it shut again. "Tell me you didn't tell your uncle about Emmett."

"I didn't tell him about Emmett. I did point out that if Robert Meade had loaned money to Natasha, maybe he had loaned money elsewhere."

"Which is the same thing," Dalton said, but he moved his hand away from the box and they all took a slice of the thick-crust kitchen sink pizza inside. "Okay, I'll agree with your technicality. Besides, Emmett told me he'd already talked to Troy and he has an alibi. He was cooking with his crew the afternoon Meade was killed. There was no way he left the kitchen. They have proof. He was making a training video for new employees on the current menu items."

"Congratulations. Your friend isn't a killer. I didn't say he was one, but if Meade made two loans, he might have made more. And maybe to someone who didn't or couldn't pay it back." Meg took a bite of her pizza slice, taking off the olives.

Natasha looked at Meg and Dalton. "Who's going to say they're sorry first? You know I can't stand the tension."

Dalton caved. "You were right to tell your uncle. And thank you for leaving Emmett's name out of it."

"You're welcome." Meg reached for another slice, but this time, Natasha held the box closed.

"And . . ." She stared at Meg.

"And I'm sorry I broke your confidence without telling you about it." She stared Natasha down. "Can I eat now?"

"If you mean it, yes." She moved her hand away from the box. "I'm glad we settled that. I didn't kill Meade, and Emmett didn't kill Meade, so who did?"

"I've been thinking about that. All roads seem to lead to Lilly Aster," Dalton said and held his hand up when Meg started to deny the idea. "So why does someone want us to think it's Lilly?"

"And who? Who would benefit if she went to prison?" Meg saw where Dalton was heading with the idea.

Natasha grabbed a pen and started writing on the pizza box. "Well, there's her new agent, Sarah, but she only makes money if Lilly's free and writing. And her assistant, Jolene, would lose her job. As would you."

"So we have a list of three people who wouldn't want Lilly to go away. I can see Sarah killing to be Lilly's new agent. I wonder if Uncle Troy talked to her?" Meg got up and grabbed a notebook for Natasha. "Here. Use something that won't smell like pepperoni tomorrow."

Natasha grinned and took the notebook. "Thanks. Sarah wouldn't be framing Lilly, but she can't be counted out on the 'killing Robert' list."

"Maybe Jolene's the same way," Meg said thoughtfully. "She's protective of Lilly. She didn't even call her by her first name when she was speaking to me until she accepted me into the group."

"We need to talk to your boss and see if she has an alibi. If we can take that possibility off the table, then the other blocks might fall into place." Dalton served the last three slices of pizza, putting one on each person's plate, then stood up to take the box to the trash.

"It's kind of like the game Clue. We need to show each other our cards so we can figure out who didn't kill Meade, which will tell us who did." Natasha's eyes were wide as she realized she hadn't practiced what she preached. "I was holding back my cards from you guys. I'm so sorry."

"You were worried about what people might think if you told us that you drove Robert Meade to Summer Break. Now that you've told us what was going on, Uncle Troy can check out who else Meade loaned money to and maybe find the killer." Meg didn't want her friend to feel bad about her omission. "Besides, what goes on in your business isn't our business."

"Unless it makes me look like a murderer," Natasha corrected. "I'm so glad you're back, Meg, and we can get together like this."

"Hey, I stopped by the bakery at least weekly to see you. I can't help it if you didn't tell me what was going on." Dalton came in from the back, with Watson in tow. "I took the mutt out with me."

"It's not the same if all three of us aren't together," Natasha told him. "It feels like that summer before Meg and I went to high school. We were thick as thieves then."

"Not to break up the lovefest, but it's time to close up the bookstore. We need a plan for where to go next." Meg finished her last bite of pizza as she stood to throw away her paper plate.

"When does your boss get back in town?" Dalton grabbed the trash bag and cleaned off the rest of their mess.

"She should be back tomorrow, but then she leaves on Saturday for a couple of days." Meg tried to remember the schedule that Lilly had sent her of the book tour stops and her travel plans.

"Can you see if we can talk to her tomorrow morning? I've got the day off." Dalton glanced around the store. "Is this the last of the trash?"

"Check the break room, but I think so. I'll text her tomorrow morning to see if she can see us. I hope I still have a job when we're done talking." Meg locked the register and put the keys in her tote.

"Okay. Then turn off the lights, and I'll lock up the back as soon as I dump this trash. I'm walking both of you home. First stop, A Taste of Magic bakery and apartment." Dalton disappeared into the back.

"He's been working at the ferry too long." Natasha laughed as she handed Meg the notebook. "I added Josh and Tabitha to that list of people who might be better off with Lilly gone. I don't think Tabitha likes how close Josh is to his ex-wife."

Meg tucked it into her tote and grabbed Watson's leash. "I think you're right about Tabitha. When I talked to her, she made Lilly sound weak, like she couldn't get by without Josh's counsel. I don't see her that way at all."

"Maybe there's more to that story," Natasha said as Dalton came in from the back room.

"What story?" he asked as he took the leash from Meg and clicked it on Watson.

As they left, Natasha filled him in on what they were talking about.

"I don't know. It seems like a far-fetched way to get rid of an ex-wife. Why not kill her?" He paused when they reached the bakery. "We'll wait for you to get inside."

"Okay, Dad," Natasha teased as she hugged Meg and then Dalton. She gave Watson a pat on the head. "I was serious about how much I love having the gang back together. Bonus, now we also have Watson to keep us company. I've missed this."

They watched as she went up the side stairs and then unlocked her door and turned lights on as she moved through the apartment. After they started walking, Dalton paused and looked at Meg. "She's right. I missed this."

"You left the group once you and Junior hit high school. You two guys were too busy hanging out, playing football, and dating the cheerleaders, as I recall," Meg reminded him.

He smiled at her and pulled her jacket closed. "I was an idiot."

As they walked to Aunt Melody's garage, they talked about the houses they passed and the plantings in the front gardens. Meg's mind, though, was on what he'd said. Had they been dating while Meg thought they were hanging out? Or was this his slow-burn move into a romance when she was ready? Whatever was going on, she agreed with Natasha and Dalton. This was nice.

She'd been thinking about her Seattle friends, and now she realized she'd never had friends as steadfast as these two. People she could tell anything to without judgment. Sure, she'd get a lot of teasing, but they didn't judge her. And they'd come with her family to move her home. Her life might not be the one she'd planned—or, more accurately, like any of the lives she'd planned—but it was good. And right now, that was enough.

She suddenly realized they'd stopped walking. Dalton was watching her. "I'd ask what you were thinking about, but I'm not sure I want to know."

Meg smiled and took Watson's leash from his hands. "I was thinking how nice it is to be home."

Dalton was back at her door at eight thirty the next morning. Meg met him with a cup of coffee in a travel mug.

"Sorry to get you up so early on your day off, but Lilly said she could talk at nine for a few minutes, and then she has to get ready for a day of publicity interviews. Which works since I need to open the bookstore at one thirty."

Meg grabbed her tote and her cup. Leaning in, she called to Watson, "Be good. I'll be back soon, and you can come to work with me."

She locked the door, and they headed downstairs.

"We could bring him if you want." Dalton looked back at the door.

Meg shook her head. "I think I'm wearing him out. In Seattle we stayed at the house most of the time. He had three short walks a day. Romain didn't like me to walk too far out of our neighborhood. He didn't think it was safe."

"Your ex seems to have had a lot of rules." Dalton held her car door open.

Meg snorted. "You have no idea."

"So you aren't going back?" Dalton asked as he climbed into the driver's seat and started the engine. "Your mom thinks . . ."

"My mom wants me to be happy. She thought I had that with Romain, because I never told her half the things that went on. I thought that was what couples did, adjust to each other's oddities. But as I found out, I was the only one adjusting." Meg stared out the window as they drove through the neighborhoods to reach Summer Break. "Have you thought about how we're going to ask Lilly about killing Meade?"

He shook his head. "I guess rip the Band-Aid off and hope she doesn't kick us out?"

"I think I have a better idea. Let's bring up the loan and the power that Meade was holding over our friend Natasha. Which lets her know we're not looking for dirt." Meg bit her bottom lip as she thought about the conversation she was about to have. "Hopefully, my work has been good enough that she doesn't fire me on the spot."

"She'd be a fool if she did." Dalton reached over and squeezed her hand. Then he held it for a second too long.

She took a breath and glanced down at his hand as he released hers.

"We're here. Here goes nothing." He pulled into the driveway.

Lilly Aster stood on the steps, watching them. She waved them over, then looked back at the truck. "You didn't bring Watson?"

"No. He's been going a lot. I thought he could use a break," Meg explained as they followed Lilly around the house to a pathway that led to the back. "Where are we going?"

"I wanted to get outside since it wasn't raining. I'll be locked in my office for hours today once the release interviews start. The good news is the book's doing well. The bad news is the book's doing well, so Sarah has all these requests for interviews. The life of an author, right?"

As they cleared the house, the trees opened up, and Meg gasped. It was the same view that she'd seen from the office windows, but somehow, being outside in the middle of it made it that much more beautiful.

"You have a lovely spot here," Dalton said.

Lilly nodded and motioned to the table with chairs that sat near the Olympic-sized pool with a built-in hot tub. "Let's sit here. I had Andrea set up coffee and baked goods. I had a feeling that this wasn't about work."

After they all took a seat at the table, Meg met Dalton's gaze, and he nodded. He was letting her take the lead in the discussion. "It's not about work. I love my job. I want you to know that first and foremost. And I don't want anything I say to jeopardize it."

"Meg, I'm not a wilting flower, even if people tend to treat me like one. You want information. About Robert Meade's death." Lilly poured them all coffee. "It's a dark roast with a little bit of chocolate flavoring. I don't know how they do it, but I haven't used cream or sugar in years since I found this. It's here, though, if you want."

Meg lifted her coffee cup and took a sip. Lilly was right. The coffee blend was amazing. "Well, we do live in the land of coffee, right?"

Lilly laughed and broke open a muffin, then buttered it as it gave off steam in the cool air. "So true. I enjoy having you around, Meg."

"Thanks. I hope that doesn't change."

Lilly took a bite of the muffin and moved the basket toward Dalton. "Eat. I take it you're Meg's emotional support guy in this meeting."

His eyes widened at her quick understanding of the situation as he took a muffin. "I am. Thank you."

"Go ahead, Ask what you came to ask."

Meg swallowed. Nancy Drew would have been much cooler in this situation. "Where were you when Robert Meade was killed? It looks like you're the one with the most to gain from his death."

Lilly finished another bite of muffin. "Does it look that way? I'd fired the man. Yes, I'd found he'd been stealing from me for years, but I'd already talked to my attorney, and we were making arrangements to sue. We'd put liens on his cash accounts, which was probably why he came over that day to talk to me. He never found me. I was at a rental I have on the other side of the island."

Meg frowned. "You use a rental? Rather than working in your office? I don't understand. It's beautiful, and you have so much room here."

Lilly glanced over at Dalton, then reached over and patted Meg's hand. "I love how naïve you are. It's not a bad trait. It's quite beautiful."

"I don't understand," Meg stammered. She was missing something. Something that, judging from the blush on his face, Dalton had already figured out.

"I have a rental that I use when my ex-husband comes to visit. It sounds strange to say it aloud, but I'm having an affair with him. He comes once or twice a week, and we go to the rental." She glanced over at the dock where Meade was killed. "I was there all day, and when I came back, Jolene had found Robert in the water. Josh and I were together all day. He's already talked to your uncle."

Meg sipped her coffee. That was the one thing she hadn't expected.

"Your aunt told me that you and your friends were mystery sleuths when you were young. I suppose now you're looking into Robert's death?" Lilly finished her muffin and glanced over at the basket. Then she shook her head and turned back to Meg, sipping her coffee instead.

"We are, but we're not getting very far. Every time we turn around, we find one more person that wanted him dead." Meg smiled at her boss. "I'm glad you're no longer on the list."

Lilly's watch alarm beeped. "So am I. But now I'm afraid I need to get inside. My stylist and hairdresser will be here soon, and I need to jump into the shower. Please be careful looking into Robert's death. The man had some unsavory friends. A fact I've also shared with your uncle."

Meg started to stand, but Lilly waved her down. "Stay and finish your coffee. This view is too beautiful not to enjoy. I have so few visitors to share it with. Once this book is launched, you and your friend should come back for dinner one night. I'd love to hear about how your investigation is going. Good luck."

With that, Lilly rose from her seat and headed back down the pathway to the house.

After she was out of earshot, Meg turned to Dalton. "I didn't expect that."

"Me neither. She's charming. I can see why you enjoy working for her." Dalton leaned back and studied the view. "And she's right about the view from this spot. It's amazing."

Chapter 21

Sometimes going back to the beginning helps you see what you're missing.

Dalton came upstairs with her when they arrived back at the apartment. They hadn't talked about Lilly's news since she'd left them on the patio. He took Watson outside as Meg made a new pot of coffee. Aunt Melody had let herself in, left a box of cookies on the counter, and put several things in Meg's fridge. Including a small ready-to-bake lasagna and several plastic containers of pre-cut vegetables.

Meg pulled out her notebook that Natasha had made notes in last night, sat down at the table, and wrote down Lilly's alibi. Which also took Josh off the list of suspects, since they were together. When Dalton came back inside with Watson in tow, she was still staring at the list of names. "I feel like we're missing something. That we know the answer, but we haven't put the dots together to see the animal shape."

"I loved those puzzles in elementary school. I always tried to guess what it was without the lines," he said as he poured them coffee. "Oh, and the next time you have a salary discussion, make sure she throws in a few bags of that coffee with every paycheck. It was terrific."

"I know." She pushed the notebook aside and took the cup

he offered her. "Thanks for going with me today. I'm not sure I would have had the guts to question her if you hadn't been there."

"I have no doubt you would have. Besides, she knew why we were there. Your aunt has been touting your mystery-solving prowess to your boss." Dalton spotted the cookies. "Are those for something special?"

"Go ahead. Aunt Melody came in and dropped them off, filled my fridge, and probably changed the sheets on my bed, along with sweeping and dusting and starting my laundry. I need to remind her that I'm an adult. And I will in three or four months." Meg smiled as Watson jumped on the couch. She'd left the television on, and it was still playing the remodel shows he liked.

"You're lucky to have people who love you," Dalton said as he took a seat at the table, his coffee and a cookie in hand. Then he changed the subject. "So now that Lilly's off the suspect list, who's next?"

"That's the question, isn't it? Josh was up there, but she alibied him, too." Meg flipped through the opened notebook and scanned the page with the notes from talking to Cissy at the ferry terminal. She tapped the page with her pen. "I forgot to ask Cissy the last time she saw Josh on the ferry, but now that's a moot point."

"For Josh, but what about his girlfriend? Tabitha? It would be a long stretch to kill someone, thinking Josh and Lilly wouldn't alibi out. It's not the smartest move. I would have killed the cheater and tried to frame Lilly for it."

"Good to know. The woman who works with Cissy mentioned that she'd seen Tabitha by herself. I'd assumed it was her coming over late to meet up with Josh. Now, after Lilly's confession, I'm not sure." Meg glanced at her watch. "Do you want to have lunch with me? I'd love to put that lasagna in the oven and eat it before I go to the bookstore. Unless you have plans."

"I'm working the later shift today, so that would work out great for me. I can walk you to the bookstore on my way to work." He glanced down at his clothes. "I'll have to run and change at home, though, after that."

"If you have time, that would be fun. I hate to make it and only eat one piece. Although, I might need my strength, since it sounds like I'm going to have to find my way home all by myself tonight." She put the back of her hand on her forehead. "Oh, my, how will I survive?"

"Brat, I was going to ask if you wanted to ride over on the ferry after you close and chat with Cissy again to see if she remembers anything more about Tabitha." He rolled his shoulders. "Magpie, I'm not convinced that it's a strong motive, but if you're getting your strong Nancy vibes about her, I could be wrong."

"I love hearing you say you might be wrong." She stood, opened the fridge, and pulled out the pan of lasagna. Aunt Melody had put a note on the top. *Bake for an hour at 350°F.* Meg checked the clock. "We should be done eating long before we need to leave for work."

Dalton grabbed a pen and looked around. "Do you have an extra notebook? Let's go through this step by step from the day Robert Meade was killed."

"I'm putting that in the book—something about going back to the beginning when you get stuck." Meg went to her desk and pulled out another spiral notebook. She loved them. Every fall she went to the back-to-school sales and bought supplies. She even had colored pencils and crayons. "You know what I need? A whiteboard, where we can post all the facts and see what jumps out at us. I think in notebooks, clues can get lost in the wave of words."

"I don't think your aunt would like us pinning things up on

her walls." Dalton looked around at what was available. He pointed to a corner of the living room. "What's in that box?"

"Winter clothes. I need to get a plastic tub and go through what I have. Why?" Meg watched as Dalton stood up, crossed the living room, and took the box into her bedroom. When he came back, he was opening up the cardboard box to make a board. "Your bed was made, so I dumped it all there."

"I tell you, Aunt Melody makes it feel like I'm staying at a five-star hotel with room service." Meg waved him over to the table, and for the next thirty minutes, they scoured the notes, putting clues and even the names of alibied-out suspects, like Natasha, on the board.

Meg stared at it as they put the last name on the board. "I hate seeing her name there."

"I know. I do, too. But maybe she knows someone else who Meade had loaned money to. Have you asked her? Or asked your uncle again about Meade's financials?" Dalton grabbed the small piece of cardboard that they'd cut off because it kept falling over, and drew a line down the middle.

"What's that? And no, I haven't asked my uncle to divulge to me confidential information from an ongoing case. Do you want me to be kicked out of my digs?" She stood and watched him add points along the line.

"It's a timeline. Here's where Meade was murdered. You saw him twice before that, on the ferry on moving day and at Lilly's house. What date was that?" He made a note of the ferry sighting, leaving room for more events to be added before that date.

For the next fifteen minutes, they added events to the timeline. Events like Natasha driving Meade to Summer Break. He also put in the year Natasha took the loan from Meade. He made a note in his notebook. "I need to ask Emmett when he took out the loan. That's going to be uncomfortable."

"Just tell him we're working on a project to find Meade's killer before the police do. Everyone wants to be part of a secret investigation." The oven timer went off. She stood and took the pan out of the oven. "We need to let the lasagna set for a few minutes, so we have time to finish this."

Dalton glanced at his notes and then back at the timeline and the murder boards. "I think we have everything. Since your aunt likes to make herself at home, do you want me to keep this at my place?"

Meg shook her head. "She won't rat me out. Besides, she wants Uncle Troy to find someone besides Lilly to have on his suspect list. I'll put this behind the boxes I haven't unpacked and tell her to leave them be since I need to sort out things to donate and throw away."

"Or put a sign on the boxes so she sees you have a plan." He went over and glanced at her weekly schedule on the desk. "You like things in order."

"It helps me keep track of things." Meg snapped a picture of both boards and sent it to both Dalton's and Natasha's phones. "I don't have a regular job, where I go in the same time every day or even do the same thing. I have the book project, which right now, only you and Natasha know about. I don't want Lilly to think I'm using her."

"Got it. Except how much work have you done on this book?" Dalton asked as he cleaned off the table so they could eat.

"Hey, being creative takes time. I'm thinking about the book a lot." She didn't want to admit that all she had so far was a partial first chapter and a list of tips and tricks. "I know it's a long shot to get published, but if I don't even write the book, it definitely won't happen. I'm going to add in what we did as an exercise."

"I'm not dogging you. I'm saying I didn't see any time set aside for writing on your schedule. You need to set aside time to work on that, too." He opened several cabinets and finally took plates out of the last one. "I know you can do it. You need to try."

Meg stood there, staring at him.

"What? Did I say something wrong?" He paused as he opened the last drawer to find the silverware.

She shook her head and wiped away the tears before they fell. Romain would have laughed at her before dismissing the dream. Not help her plan time to pursue it. "No, you said all the right things. Thank you."

He grabbed forks and set them on the table. "Well, if you're done with your existential crisis, can we eat now?"

Meg went over and blocked off an hour the next morning on her paper schedule. She set down the pen. "Now we can eat."

While she was at the bookstore, she thought about the case. Was the perpetrator simply a jealous girlfriend? Dalton was right. It was a stretch, but the only other possibility besides Lilly or Jolene was someone Meade had lent money to. Emmett had an alibi, and Meg hoped that Natasha was totally off her uncle's suspect list.

A text popped up soon after she'd arrived. It was from Dalton.

Emmett says he took out the loan four years ago. And that he thought Robert Meade had another loan besides Natasha's. He said Meade bragged that he had saved Emmett from buying the bakery so that he could open the Local Crab. And that he'd made a mistake with the third loan. All he had was interest in an old truck and a bunch of old carpenter tools.

Meg texted back. **So he loaned money to an islander who ran a construction company?**

That's what Emmett thought. He apologized for not knowing more. He asked when the two of us were coming back to the Local Crab. I guess he doesn't hate me.

Meg thanked him for asking Emmett. She knew it had been hard for Dalton. He liked being on the outside, especially when it came to questioning friends. Then she texted her uncle and asked if he'd found information about a third loan from Meade to an islander.

This time she didn't get a text back. She got a phone call. "Don't be mad," she said when she answered her uncle's call.

"I asked you to stay out of it." He didn't sound happy at all.

"I'm not digging into things that might get me into any trouble. Unless Meade was connected with the mob or something. Does Seattle even have a mob?" She smiled and waved when a customer came in to browse. She used her hand to cover the phone and called out, "Let me know if I can help you find your perfect book."

"You're at the bookstore? Not wandering around Bainbridge, breaking into homes and checking car plates?" Her uncle sounded a little less angry. "And no, there's no organized crime syndicate in Seattle that I know of. But not everyone follows the laws, especially when you get around the drug culture."

"I'm trying to stay out of harm's way, but I knew about Natasha's loan, and I was wondering if there was a third." She was trying to keep Emmett out of the discussion.

"You say third, which means you also know about the loan to Chef Harding." He rolled his eyes but continued on with the discussion. "There was a third loan, but Meade's accountant said that the guy never made payments, so he had Meade write it off last year for his taxes. He had told the accountant that the guy didn't have a pot to . . . Well, he didn't have any money or property."

"Do you know who the loan was made to?" Meg waited as she heard papers shuffling on the end of the line. Uncle Troy must still be at work.

"A local. Hold on. I have the report here. My detective went through this information. And it was . . ." He whistled. "Of course it was."

"You found the name?"

"Nate Baldwin. Violet's boyfriend. The mayor is not going to be happy." Uncle Troy groaned. "Small towns, big egos."

"Nate and Violet broke up. She's upset about it." Meg thought about what Violet had told her when she'd seen her in the line for the ferry. Where would Nate have run into Robert Meade? "He worked at the Local Crab. That must be where he met Meade."

"Probably, but Meade did him a favor and wrote off the loan. Why would he kill him?" Uncle Troy paused, and Meg heard a phone ringing in the background. "Your aunt's calling. I need to take this. Meg, thank you for the information, but I've got this investigation handled. I'll find the killer. I promise."

He hung up before she could say anything else. Uncle Troy wasn't happy with her, but she had more things to add to the timeline. And more questions. If Nate was a possible murder suspect due to the loan, what would be his motive for committing murder? Unless he didn't know that Meade had written off the loan.

As Alice would say, things were getting curiouser and curiouser. She went over to see if she could help the new customer find the perfect book. At least her mind would be taken off finding a killer.

At ten she closed up shop, and she and Watson walked to the ferry to ride over to chat with Cissy. This time, Dalton didn't come to find her until they were almost at the Seattle terminal. "I can walk you to the ticket office, and then I have to get back to work. Just come back the same way. If you get confused, have Cissy walk you past the guard at the front entrance."

"I have been here before," she teased and then updated him quickly on what her uncle had said.

"Nate did come into some money a few years ago. He said a relative had passed. I'd heard him talk about starting a construction company, but he never implemented it. By the time he got everything in place, the lockdown happened, and no one wanted a handyman in their house." Dalton walked with her to the place where they would disembark. "Nate always had bad timing."

Cissy met them at the walkway and instead of going into the ticket booth, she took Meg a different way to the break room. "I need coffee to stay awake for the rest of my shift. Do you want some?"

"That would be great, but I have Watson with me." Meg glanced down at the dog, who was excited to be somewhere new.

"No problem. They like pets here. During lockdown, most of the ticketing staff brought their dogs in. We had a lot of time to walk them. It was pretty slow." She opened the door to a brightly lit break room and nodded to a table by the window where you could see the sound and the Ferris wheel.

When Cissy brought back coffee, she also had a bowl of water on the tray for Watson. "I didn't know if you wanted sugar or cream, but I can go back."

Meg took the water and put it on the floor, then took a seat. "I hope he can hold it for the way back."

"We have a pet area next door. They set it up nicely for employees. I think they felt bad calling us into work as essential workers. So they increased our perks." She put the cups on the table. Before she sat down, she asked again, "Cream and sugar?"

"No, I'm good. As long as it's good coffee. And it smells like it is." Meg took a sip. "Mmm."

"I tell you, we get perks. And our benefit package isn't bad, either. Dalton's is better since he actually works on the ferry. I think they're worried about the boat sinking or being bombed, so they pay better for those positions." Cissy moved the tray to another table. "But you came to ask me more questions."

Meg pulled out her phone and found the picture of Tabitha that she'd taken the day she'd talked to her at A Taste of Magic. "Your coworker mentioned seeing Tabitha, but have you seen her much? I wanted to make sure we were talking about the same person. I can show you a picture of her boyfriend, too."

"Lilly Archer's ex-husband. Yes. I know Tabitha. She's always coming with him, and she's very clingy. If she could wrap herself around him like a snake, she would. She's always giving me an evil eye when I sell him the tickets. Like I could make him fall in love with me with a glance or a touch of my hand. Like that old movie about the woman who saves the life of the guy she's in love with, but he doesn't know she exists."

"*While You Were Sleeping*. Yeah, I know that one." Meg smiled at the comparison. She hadn't seen Tabitha with Josh, but she could imagine her acting jealous. Probably having a hunch about the affair, but not knowing about it. Sometimes people get a feeling. Meg hadn't with Romain, but she'd heard from more than one person that they had sensed something was wrong before they had proof. "So she came with Josh, Lilly Archer's ex-husband."

"Yes and no. Sometimes late at night, I'd see her getting a ticket alone. She always wore her hair in a ponytail and dressed in a hoodie and jeans to disguise herself, but it was her. I could tell by her eyes. She has mean eyes." Cissy frowned as she remembered something. "You know, now that I think about it, Josh, the ex, used to come without her, too. He didn't dress any differently, but he wouldn't meet my eyes unless he was with her. I hadn't realized that until now."

Meg sipped her coffee. Why would Tabitha come over to the island at night? Alone? That didn't make sense. Now that she knew about Lilly and Josh, his solo ferry rides made sense.

Cissy stood. "Is that it? I need to get you to the pet area and walk you back to the ferry. Then, with this magic elixir, I'm going to try to stay awake until we close the booth. They frown on us sleeping at the window."

"Sorry. Of course." Meg followed her to a nice patch of grass in a gated area where you could let your pet play. It even had a divider for big and little dogs. Watson watered a bush, then came back to her, ready to head home.

Cissy walked them to the ferry. "Stop by anytime. Maybe we can double-date sometime. My boyfriend works on the ferry, too, so we'd have to coordinate schedules, but it would be fun."

She walked away before Meg realized what she'd said and could correct the misperception that she and Dalton were dating. A misperception everyone seemed to be having.

She texted the information about Tabitha to Dalton and Natasha, adding a question to both reports. *Who was she meeting with on the island at night?*

Dalton was the only one to reply before she got off the ferry.

What do we know about Jolene?

Chapter 22

Even when you think you're right, you may be wrong.

Jolene. Meg hadn't even considered her a suspect. She'd found the body. If she'd killed Robert Meade III, wouldn't she have built an alibi and let someone else find the body? And how had Dalton pulled her name out of thin air after hearing that Tabitha had been meeting with someone on the island without Josh?

She texted him a few times after she got home, with no reply. Natasha said that tomorrow she'd bring dinner to the bookstore after she closed her bakery so they could talk.

Dalton showed up at her door at seven on Saturday morning. "I've got the day shift today, and the ferry is going to be crazy with the farmers market and a show at the art museum, so I don't have much time. But I wanted to let you know what I'm thinking and ask you not to go over to Summer Break today to talk with Jolene."

She held open the door and waved him inside. "Coffee's ready, and Aunt Melody dropped off blueberry scones as soon as she saw me take Watson out at six. She's anxious about the case, and when she's anxious, she bakes. I'll take the leftovers she gives me. So how did you get to Jolene?"

"I started wondering who would know about Meade's misdeeds. And maybe about Lilly's. If Meade had tried to leverage knowing about the affair to keep his job, Jolene might have protected her employer. You told me that she worships Lilly Aster." He poured coffee into a travel mug and grabbed a scone before sitting at the table. He wore his blue ferry uniform, and his hair was still wet from the shower. Even this way, he was pretty cute.

Meg shook her head and stopped thinking about Dalton. Everyone was getting in her head. Especially Crissy and the double date comment. Maybe she'd ask Dalton and he'd tell her that they weren't dating. They were friends. Meg sat down at the table, with the murder board propped up on a chair so she and Dalton could see it from the table. She'd printed out the picture of Tabitha and put it on the board. She'd even printed a picture of Jolene. The other pictures, besides the one of Nate, all had yellow sticky notes with an *A* written on them. They all had alibis. She hadn't been able to sleep last night after the coffee on the ferry, so she'd added to the board. Meg had put a pink sticky note with an even bigger *A* on Natasha's picture.

"I didn't say she worshipped Lilly. She is dedicated, though." Jolene's picture was on the board as the person who'd found Robert Meade. Should she be added to the list of suspects? "There is no evidence pointing to her except the fact she might have a motive to try to protect Lilly. Knowing about the affair would explain why Meade thought Lilly would forgive his actions and take him back as a client."

"Just don't go talk to Jolene today. I'm not working tomorrow morning. I've got the late shift again. I'll go with you to talk to her in the morning."

Meg stood up and pulled out her weekly schedule. "I'm going to church with Mom in the morning. Come over at noon and we'll go then, unless Aunt Melody pulls us into brunch.

Then we'll go afterward. And maybe Uncle Troy will let slip what he's thinking."

He finished his scone and stood. He met her gaze and asked, "So we have a plan?"

She nodded. "We do. Have another scone for the road. Maybe two."

"They're amazing. I'm not sure why you're giving them away." He took two, and Meg handed him a ziplock bag to put them in. "I'll see you tonight at the bookstore, and we can plan our questions."

"Sounds perfect." Meg refilled his travel mug, then watched as he headed down the stairs for work. Then she grabbed Watson and went down to talk to her aunt. Her uncle had left around six thirty, after Aunt Melody had dropped off the basket of scones. Maybe Aunt Melody knew more than she was saying. Lilly had to have told her about the affair. Meg would lay money on that.

When she knocked on the kitchen door, Aunt Melody was already standing on the other side. "Oh, I was coming out to sit and drink one more cup of coffee. I've got an online book discussion at ten, and I don't want to be jumpy. Can I get you a cup?"

"I'll get it. The scones were amazing, by the way. Dalton says thanks. He ate three."

Meg went into the kitchen and found a cup. After she filled it, she noticed her uncle's notebook on the table. She opened it and read the notes he'd written from some sort of meeting. There was a list of suspects. But instead of scratching off suspects and their alibis, he had put a big *A* after their names. Natasha's name was there, but so was the *A*. She marveled at how similar her sleuthing process and her uncle's official process were, at least on paper.

He had a badge and a reason to ask questions. As she ran down the list, she saw that Jolene's name was there, with no *A*.

So her uncle considered her a suspect. She wondered what evidence he had against her.

She pulled out her phone and took a picture of this page in his notebook. Then she closed the notebook and went back out to talk to her aunt.

Gossiping went better with coffee.

Aunt Melody was as concerned as Meg was about Lilly Aster. As she talked, she rubbed Watson's head. Meg assumed with Watson here, her aunt's need for a dog of her own might ease, but maybe not. Maybe they'd wind up with two dogs, one for her and one for Uncle Troy.

"I'm probably breaking a confidence, but I need someone to talk to. And I can't talk to Lilly. She's too worried that what she says will get back to Troy. I wouldn't do that, but here I am, talking to you. Maybe her fears are warranted." She took a sip of her coffee. "Anyway, the day I talked to Lilly about Robert Meade threatening your mom and her bookstore with pulling the launch event, she told me she was firing him. They'd already found the fraud he'd committed, and she was going to fire him before she signed a contract for the next book. He'd been coming over on the ferry for days, trying to get her to sign the adjusted contract, but she'd kept putting him off. She'd decided to hire security for the next day, and she fired him on the porch, with the guard watching. She told him she knew he'd been stealing from her."

"That must have been awful." Meg remembered how threatening he'd been the day she showed up for her first assignment.

"It was, but it was long overdue. Lilly called me afterward and told me what a relief it was that it was done. But then he called the next day and told her he'd be over for her to sign the contract the next day. Or else he'd tell everyone about Josh." Aunt Melody leaned back. "Of course, the first thing Lilly did was call Josh. He came over, and they went to their rental for the night. She told him about Robert's threat, and he told her he didn't care. He was going to break up with Tabitha, anyway. He loved Lilly. He's been going with her on book tour this time. I have to say, she's happy about it."

"So what happened with Robert?" Meg felt like she was missing something.

"He never showed up until Jolene found him in the water by the dock." Aunt Melody leaned closer. "Troy says you've been investigating this. Have you figured out who killed that awful man yet? Troy knows about the affair, and their alibi holds up. Street cams show them driving to the house and not leaving until after Jolene called them. And they have food delivery people who verified they were there around the time of death. Thank goodness for Island Diner and Josh's love for breakfast."

Meg thought about the loose ends that her aunt had tied up. Lilly and Josh, she'd known about, but Uncle Troy had verified their alibi. They hadn't killed Meade. Tabitha didn't have a reason to, unless she could pin his death on Lilly. That left Jolene and Nate, along with any other suspects her uncle had.

Meg leaned forward with her elbows on her knees and asked the question she didn't want to ask. The one Dalton had asked her. "What do you know about Jolene?"

Meg had promised Dalton that she wouldn't talk to Jolene without him. But after hearing her aunt's story, she wondered if Jolene had been protecting her boss. Would she be in all that much danger if she went to talk to her? Lilly hadn't done the deed, so there was nothing to protect. Unless Jolene had killed Robert Meade with her bare hands.

As Meg thought that idea through, she decided not to take a trip to Summer Break before going to work at the bookstore. There was no reason to go up to a potential killer and poke the bear. Besides, if Jolene hadn't killed Meade, accusing her of murder might affect their working relationship.

Solving crimes surrounded by friends and family was hard, especially when some of them were perfect suspects. She was going to have to write this sentence in bold when she added it to the guidebook.

As she was finishing up the chore list at the bookstore, the bell over the door jingled and Jolene came inside. She looked around, found Meg, and made a beeline toward her. She had a folder in her hand.

"Meg, I'm so glad I found you. Lilly told me that she told you and your friend about Josh. You need to keep that to yourself. It's covered under your NDA. I need to talk to your friend, too. We'll pay him to sign the NDA."

"Jolene, neither Dalton nor I am going to spread the news that Lilly's seeing her ex." She nodded to the couch. "I need to talk to you, though. Do you want some water or coffee?"

Jolene laughed as she sat down. "I'm trying to cut down on the caffeine. My therapist says I'll be less anxious if I slow down. And now I've told you I'm in therapy. I don't understand why you're so easy to talk to. Are you a witch or something?"

Meg sat next to her. "Far from it. My only superpower is to choose the one path that won't continue. I fail at everything I do. Of course, I hope that doesn't happen while working for Lilly. I love doing the assignments. I can't believe how many mystery-focused bookstores there are."

Jolene pulled out her phone and made a note on it. "I've got a folder on my computer I'll send you. It's all the bookstores that Lilly has visited since I started working for her, dates of visits, names of owners or contacts, and contact information. It might help."

"Thanks. It sounds like you were on top of it." Meg wondered why Lilly had asked her to do the spreadsheet.

This time the laugh sounded harsh. "Hardly. I'm good at looking like I'm in control, but I'm overwhelmed. It's one of the things I'm working on in therapy. I was the one who talked

Lilly into hiring Jessica, the girl before you, and then she was a mess. I was skeptical about hiring you. But you've been great. I hope I haven't been too hard on you. I can be friendly."

Meg took a deep breath. Jolene was opening up with her, and now Meg was going to slam that door shut. "I wonder if you can tell me about finding Meade. Had you talked to him that day?"

"On the phone. He called on his way to the island, and I told him Lilly wouldn't see him. She was done. I gave him her lawyer's number. We were building a case to sue him." She leaned against the couch. "I didn't tell him that. But he insisted that he could make this all go away. All he needed was five minutes with Lilly."

"Did he tell you what he was going to say?" Meg figured he was going to blackmail her, but having Jolene say it would be better.

Jolene closed her eyes as she began to talk. "He knew about Josh. He'd gotten a call from someone with a tip. I think it was Josh's girlfriend. I talked to Josh about breaking up with Tabitha, but he said it was the perfect cover. Besides, they helped each other with their careers. He said it wasn't serious and he'd stopped sleeping with her so she would get the hint." She opened her eyes and looked at Meg. "I know you haven't met him, but he's Lilly's kryptonite. He's also an idiot. Truly. Of all the men she could have fallen for, she finds him."

"You love who you love, I guess." Meg wanted to steer the conversation back to Meade. "So Meade came to the house?"

Jolene shook her head. "He came but I didn't let him in. I called Lilly and told her that he was coming to the island, and she said to ignore him. If he showed up, not to even answer the door. I went to my room and worked on a knitting project, another one of my therapist's ideas, and screened the calls. He called twice. His first message was that he was at the ferry terminal and needed a ride. Then he called and said he was at the back door, but no one was answering. I watched him on the security feed, but soon he gave up, flipped off the camera, and left."

"Did you give that tape to Uncle Troy, I mean, Chief Miller?"

"We turned over everything, and I told him what I told you. After Meade left, I got in my car and went down to Marina Taco Tavern and ate lunch. I drove back to Summer Break around three. I went down to the beach to walk and clear my head. That's when I found the body. I called the police. The neighbor, Alice Clark, was walking the other way, and she stayed with me until your uncle got there. I know what you're asking, but I didn't kill Robert Meade. Even though I wanted to, several times."

After Meg gave Dalton's phone number to her so she could talk to him about signing an NDA, Jolene stood from the couch, signaling she was ready to leave the bookstore. She gave Meg a quick hug. "Thanks for listening. You're almost as good as talking to my shrink."

After Hurricane Jolene had left the store, Meg wandered around the shelves, looking for a new book to read. The bell rang again. Meg hadn't had this many customers since the week after Lilly's new release event. "I'll be right there. Feel free to look around."

This time, Natasha called out. "I brought dinner. Where are you?"

"Set it up on the coffee table. I'll be right there." Meg grabbed a recent true crime book from the shelf and took it back to the counter. She'd scan it to see if it could help her write the sleuthing guidebook. Maybe she needed to study more than the active investigation to get a better understanding of how to solve the crime. Especially since she was down to one suspect, who seemed to be in the wind. Then she went to the couch, where Natasha was setting out fish and chips for them.

"I need to start chipping in for these meals," Meg said as she sat down on the couch.

Natasha finished setting things on the table and folded the bag that the food had come in. "It works out. You paid the night after the book-signing event."

"No, Mom did. Technically. I still need to get reimbursed for that . . . as soon as I find the receipt. It was fun having the four of us out together. I don't think we've done that since you and I graduated and the boys took us to dinner in Seattle." Meg smiled at the memory. "Junior was our official college guidebook. He told us everything we needed to know that first year and what frats to avoid."

"Junior is always trying to help." Natasha nodded, focusing on her fries. "Anyway, I was craving Proper Fish, so I got you one, too. Dalton texted that he is working late. I think we'll see him in a few, but he said he ate on the ferry."

They ate in silence, enjoying the food, and then Natasha picked up her phone. "That murder board is sick. You're good at this. Maybe you should get a degree in criminal justice and go into law enforcement?"

"I don't know. Maybe. I'm not good with authority. You know that." She dipped the fish into the sauce. "And there's a fitness component, which would mean I couldn't eat like this three times a week. I need to join a gym or something if I'm going to continue to eat my way through the island."

"You're grieving a loss. You're supposed to be eating. If you were depressed, you wouldn't eat anything." She nodded to the phone. "So Jolene or Nate? That's the answer?"

"Jolene came in today and alibied herself. She was eating at Marina Taco Tavern at the time of the murder. I'm sure Uncle Troy has already verified that. So now it's Nate, but according to Violet, he's left town."

"That's not true. I saw him today." Natasha pointed a fry at her for emphasis. "He's still here. I heard Violet had to move back in with her folks until she saves up enough for her own place. I think she's leaving Bainbridge, though. She says the guys here, except Dalton, are lame."

"Everyone thinks Dalton is amazing. Why isn't he married or in a relationship?" Meg finished off the fish and looked at the pile of fries.

"I think you know the answer," Natasha said as she pulled out her notebook. "So Nate's on the list because he hates newcomers?"

"Seems a little thin, right?" Meg brightened. "He also had a loan from Meade, but that got written off, so yeah, still a little thin."

"Well, let's dig a little deeper and see what we can find out to prove he didn't kill Meade. If we get him off the list, we'll need more suspects, but so will your uncle. There are a few reasons someone would kill someone else. One, they're crazy. Two, love."

"Three, hate," Meg added.

Natasha nodded, touching the third finger on her outstretched hand. "And four, money."

"Is that it?" Meg tried to think of more reasons. "I guess survival is another one, but that's an extreme, Donner Party situation."

"So five. And we can take off survival, unless it was to save a secret. But that has to have another component. Like money or love, right?"

"Keeping a secret? I'd put that under survival. Especially if the secret would blow your normal life up." Meg stood and grabbed a notebook from the counter. She wrote down all the reasons to commit murder that they had come up with. "These will make a great chapter for my book."

"That's amazing, and I'm glad to help, but let's get back to Nate. He was cheating on Violet, but he's already let that cat out of the bag. I'm surprised there hasn't been more than one person. Nate's never been good at monogamy."

Meg snorted. "That's probably because Violet's dad is the mayor. He doesn't want to be arrested."

"Okay, so it wasn't a secret from Violet, but maybe the other person didn't want the secret being let out." Natasha tapped her finger on the table. The fries had gone cold, and she tucked them back in the bag. Then she held her hand over Meg's. "Are you done? Watson's drooling over there, and I think he's going to pounce."

"Food's a strong motivator for anyone," Dalton observed as he walked into the bookstore. "What did I miss?"

Chapter 23

Sometimes the Fates put you on the exact path where you need to be.

"You missed dinner, for one." Meg pointed to the now empty bag. "And a visit from Jolene."

Dalton groaned as he sat down. "I know. She called me. Three times before I was able to take a break and call her back. She's bringing over an NDA tomorrow to my house, so I won't tell anyone what Lilly said about Josh."

"Do I know what Lilly said about Josh? If not, you need to tell me now, before you sign. Are they paying you money?" Natasha leaned forward, interested in the gossip.

"She told me she has to pay me to make the NDA valid, so I told her I'd take the money. She's giving me five thousand. Don't judge. It's going into my home-repair fund. I might be able to refinish the living room this year. If the furnace doesn't go out before I spend the money."

Meg whistled. "I should have told her the info wasn't covered under my NDA, but they're paying me well, anyway. I shouldn't be greedy."

"You still didn't tell me what Lilly said," Natasha prodded. "Hurry, before Jolene rushes in here and forces the money on you."

Dalton grinned. "You already know. Lilly has an alibi. She's having an affair with Josh, and she was with him at the time of the murder."

"Maybe I shouldn't have put that on the murder board." Meg pressed her lips together. "I need to read that NDA I signed."

"Okay, so Josh wasn't in love with Tabitha. And she was coming over here at weird times without him. And Nate was sleeping with someone besides Violet." Natasha stared at the three names she'd written down on the notebook in front of her. "Is anyone else seeing lines of attachments?"

"Just because Nate was sleeping with someone besides Violet, that doesn't mean it's Tabitha. I mean, seriously, how would he even meet her?" Meg shook her head. "I bet it was one of the bonfire girls."

"You make them sound like a club." Dalton held up a hand. "Besides, I can answer that. I saw Nate hitting on a blonde with a Southern accent a few months ago at Island Diner. Junior and I were having dinner. I walked through the bar on the way to the head. Nate hangs out there when he's not working, which is a lot of the time. You said Tabitha looks like a Miss Georgia?"

"Yeah. Hold up. I have a picture." Meg flipped through her photos and then handed Dalton the phone. "That's her."

He stared at the picture. "I felt bad for Violet. This woman's a knockout, and it shows even with her dressed in jeans and a T-shirt. Violet's pretty but not beautiful. This was the woman. Nate must have thought he won the lottery. She's way out of his league."

"I bet he'd do almost anything for her," Meg said as the three of them exchanged glances.

"Love. Our motive is love?" Natasha finally asked, breaking the silence. "You are putting these motive ideas in your book, right? It makes everything clearer when you look at it through that filter."

"I think on both ends. Tabitha was mad at Josh for using her as a cover for the affair. And Nate was so in lust with Tabitha that he'd do anything for her. The only question is, why kill Robert Meade rather than Josh or Lilly?" Meg rubbed her face. "I'm tired, and my head is pounding."

"And it's ten. Let's clean up and get out of here. Natasha, don't leave. We'll drop you off on the way to Meg's apartment. I'll grab the trash." He grabbed the bag from Proper Fish and stuffed napkins into it before heading out to throw it away.

Natasha caught Meg's gaze as they cleared cups off the table. "Does that answer your earlier question?"

"Stop it." Meg lowered her voice. "Let's focus on who killed Robert Meade, so Uncle Troy doesn't throw you in jail to get the case off his open list."

"He wouldn't do that." Natasha followed her into the break room, where they put the cups in the dishwasher and Meg started it. "Right? Tell me you're joking. Your uncle isn't going to charge me with killing Robert, is he?"

Dalton came in from the back and locked the door behind him. "She's joking. If he was going to charge you, he would have held you in jail for seventy-two hours, while he made his case against you and got the DA to sign off."

Natasha looked stricken at the idea of spending time in a jail cell.

Dalton pulled her into a hug as he laughed. "Come on. Let's go home. We'll all meet at the bakery tomorrow at nine to figure out how to prove this long shot. At least enough for Meg's uncle to take over. Right now, I think he'd laugh us out of his office."

"Sometimes you have a mean streak, Dalton Hamilton. And don't think I don't see it." Natasha followed him out into the shop while Meg turned off the lights.

* * *

The next morning, the knock came right at eight thirty. Meg was used to Dalton being early, so last night she'd set her alarm for seven, which had given her time to be dressed and ready before he surprised her. She filled his cup with coffee and then went to answer the door.

Romain Evans stood there. He wore his typical weekend casual outfit. Dockers, a polo, and a light blazer on top. He wore old brown wingtip shoes. Dalton was right. Romain dressed like an old man. "Good morning, Meg. May I come in?"

"No, you can't. I don't invite evil into my house. It's kind of a new rule. Why are you here, Romain? I think we've said everything we need to say." She set the cup on the table next to the door and leaned on the doorway, blocking the entrance.

He stepped back, surprised. He'd moved toward the threshold, thinking he was coming inside, but now he looked unsure. For the first time in the years that she'd known him, he appeared utterly flummoxed.

It made Meg happy that she'd stunned him. When he didn't speak, she asked again. "Why are you here?"

"I was wondering if you'd sold the ring yet. I wanted to ask for it back." The words fell out of Romain's mouth quickly.

Meg stared at him. "I don't understand."

"Rachel, she loves the ring. I'm going to ask her to marry me, so I wanted to know if I could have it back. I'll give you money for it. Not what we paid for it, of course, but I need the ring back. Rachel doesn't know I returned it to you."

"I'm confused." Meg reached over to her desk, where his note still sat. She lifted it and held it out for him to see. "This says you felt bad for what you did, so you gave me a hundred dollars from our travel cash and the ring to try to make up for it. Now you're telling me you want my ring so you can use it to marry the woman you already took on my honeymoon? Am I understanding the sequence of events?"

He blinked. Obviously, he hadn't expected any response besides Meg giving him the ring back.

Meg's gaze traveled past Romain, and she saw Dalton standing at the corner of the garage. He was leaning on Romain's Tesla and grinning at the exchange. She shook her head.

"No, you cannot have my ring, even if you want to pay me twice what we paid for it. That is *my* ring. The one with which you pledged your undying love for me. Besides, if you wanted to give it to Rachel, why did you bring it to me? I'd left it for you. In your tuxedo. The one I helped you pick out for our wedding." Now Meg was curious. She didn't feel mad so much as tired of the games. "I did the right thing once. Then you did. I think we're done."

"Rachel and I got in a huge fight in Italy. I guess I kept complimenting you on the hotel and the plans you made for us. She thought it was rubbing our relationship in her face. So she left a day early and flew back. I thought it was over. When I came back and found you'd left, I wanted to talk you into coming home. Giving you the ring felt right."

Meg rolled her eyes. "Let me guess. Then you made up with Rachel."

"And she doesn't know I tried to get back with you. If she did, she'd flip out again." He shook his head. "She's very intimidated by you."

"As she should be," Dalton commented from the bottom of the stairs. He was still leaning on Romain's new car. "Meg's an amazing woman. Too good for the likes of you."

Romain whipped his head around to glare at Dalton. "Stay out of this."

"I'm just watching the show," Dalton replied, holding up his hands. "Nice car."

"Stop leaning on it," Romain grumbled.

Meg moved to close the door. "Goodbye, Romain. Have a

great life with Rachel, until she finds someone better. Which shouldn't be long."

Romain leaned forward. "Meg, come on. Be reasonable. Sell me the ring."

"I'd love to, but I threw it in the sound the day you gave it to me," Meg lied.

"You what?" Romain swallowed hard.

"I got on the ferry and dropped it in the water midway to Seattle. That way I'd never be tempted to go back to you." She smiled and closed the door in his terror-stricken face. *Explain that to Rachel!*

Dalton came in about five minutes later. He nodded at the full cup of coffee now sitting on the table. "Is that for me?"

"Of course. Is Romain gone?" Meg glanced out the side window that looked over the parking lot.

Dalton laughed. "He left. I think he was frustrated that he couldn't race the engine and burn rubber in his electric car as he left. I'll give him props that he at least tried. Did you really toss the ring?"

"Of course not. That thing is a down payment on a house. Or it can at least fill up my emergency fund. He gave it to me twice. I wasn't going to give it back for Rachel's sake. She got him. I got the ring. I got the better deal." Meg handed him one of the cookies that Aunt Melody had dropped off sometime last night, when she was at the bookstore, along with milk and more sparkling water. She loved her aunt. "At least I know why he kept sniffing around here. I can't believe he thought I would hand over the ring. Again. I'm so not the girl who left Seattle anymore." As she spoke, they both took a seat at the kitchen table.

"That girl would have given him the ring?" Dalton broke the cookie in half.

Meg thought about past Meg. "I hate to say it, but I think

she would have. He controlled our lives. He made himself bigger while he made me feel smaller. I would have thought he was right and I owed him the ring. But now he tells me that Rachel wants it and that this should be enough for me to give it back. I'm sorry. I can't see myself doing that anymore. Rachel can design her own ring."

"I'm proud of you for standing up to him. I worried about you when we moved you home, but when I saw what you did to the dress, I knew you'd be fine. The old Magpie was still in there, waiting to be let out." He reached out and squeezed her hand. Then dropped it.

"I'm glad you were amused. My mom is still trying to find a seamstress who will agree to try to piece the dress together again. The problem is they're all telling her it's not worth the money she'd have to fork out to get it done. I'm done with that dress. If I ever get married, I'm getting a new dress. And a new ring." She finished her cookie, then dusted off and showed her empty hands to Watson, who was watching her eat. "Sorry, boy. It's all gone. So how do we prove or disprove that Nate killed Robert Meade?"

Happy with the subject change, Dalton pulled out his notebook. "I've got some ideas. We need to see where Tabitha was on the day of the murder. Or maybe that whole week. And maybe Meade was in the wrong place. Did Nate ever meet Josh? Maybe Tabitha sent him to kill Josh. Or he thought killing Josh would get him the girl."

"You've done a lot of thinking on this since last night," Meg responded as she glanced at the clock. "We're supposed to be at the bakery at nine. If we're walking, we need to leave soon."

"Let's walk. You need to calm down a little after your exciting morning." Dalton tucked the notebook back into his pocket.

"Don't tell me what I need. I've had enough of that lately." Meg paused when she saw Dalton grinning at her. "You're a jerk. You're trying to get me riled up. Should we take the murder board and timeline?"

He shook his head. "Probably not. I don't think other customers would love seeing the visuals."

Meg giggled. "I hadn't thought about that. Besides, what would we do if Tabitha came in and saw her picture on the board as a suspect?"

"That would be awkward." He grabbed Watson's lead. "Get what you need and let's get going. You have to work tonight."

"Don't remind me." Meg grabbed all she needed for the day, including Watson's treats. She'd already stocked his dog food for his night meal at the bookstore. They were making a new routine and a new life—time to get rid of the old.

As they walked to the bookstore, she thought about the Nate and Josh theory. "So you've seen the two of them together at least once, Tabitha and Nate, I mean?"

"Yeah, but I don't hang out at the bars much. I never know what shift I'm going to be working, so being at the bar late doesn't work for me. I wonder if Junior has seen them together. We talked about how out of Nate's league Tabitha was the first night I saw them. Let me give your brother a call." He pulled out his phone.

Meg listened in on Dalton's side of the conversation. First, they caught up and made plans for their next meetup. Then Dalton asked about that night. Junior talked for a long time, with Dalton adding an occasional yes or wow. Finally, he grinned at her. "Thanks, dude. You gave me what I needed. I'll call you next week to finalize our plans."

After Dalton hung up, he looked at her. "Not only has your brother seen him with Tabitha several times, but Nate also told him about this hot girl who was going to move him to Hollywood to get him work as a stunt guy. Junior asked about Violet, and Nate blew him off. Said they both needed to get rid of the exes so they could move on with their lives."

"Get rid of the exes? Nate dumped Violet. I wonder if he thought he took care of Josh, too." They arrived at the bakery, and Natasha waved them in. They all gathered around a table in the back. Meg continued her musing with Dalton. "But no, he knew Meade because of the loan."

"I have news. Nate and Tabitha got in a fight in front of Island Diner a few minutes ago. She told him she wasn't interested in seeing him anymore. That he was a loser and to leave her alone." Natasha poured them coffee as she chatted. Then she joined them at the table. "Serena was there getting food before she went home to crash. She bakes for me from midnight to seven. While she was waiting for her food, she watched the whole thing. And then she called me."

"Did they mention Robert Meade?" Meg couldn't believe their luck. Someone had witnessed the couple turn on each other.

"Not by name, but Nate told her he'd taken care of his end of the bargain. Tabitha laughed and told him his plan was stupid and only got him out of debt." Natasha lowered her voice as a customer came in. "Then she said he could deal with this island insanity on his own. That she was done with it all."

Natasha left to help the customer. Dalton whistled. "I knew Nate was an idiot, but do you think he thought killing Meade at Summer Break would cause your uncle to arrest Josh?"

"I think it's time for us to talk to Uncle Troy about our suspicions. He can talk to Nate and see if he can rattle him. The mayor will be thrilled to have Nate out of his daughter's life. Tabitha had to be the mastermind of the plan. Nate wouldn't be able to put this together."

"I wonder if Tabitha knew Robert Meade. Maybe she had an outstanding loan, as well." Dalton opened his phone and scrolled through Tabitha's social media account. "And there it is."

He handed the phone to Meg. It was a picture of Tabitha and Meade at a charity event for Young Seattle Writers. At the table, as well, were Lilly and Josh. "This could be how Meade knew about Lilly and Josh. Jolene said he was trying to blackmail her. And we all know that Meade liked to use the people who owed him money for favors."

"And it could be how Tabitha found Nate. I can't believe she walked into a bar and picked the one man who also owed money to Meade. She could have used him to solve two problems in her life. The loan and her cheating boyfriend." Dalton leaned back. "The dots all fit, but we don't have real evidence."

"I bet my uncle does." Meg smiled as she pulled out her phone and dialed Uncle Troy's number. When he picked up, she said, "Hey, can the Mystery Crew talk to you for a few minutes at A Taste of Magic? We'll buy the coffee."

Chapter 24

When you're done, you find out you have more questions....

It took a few days and a lot of interviews and reviewing local camera feeds as well as those on the ferry, but soon Tabitha and Nate were charged in the death of Robert Meade III. Lilly showed up at the bookstore the next Thursday night with bags filled with a full dinner and dessert from the Local Crab for five. She'd asked Meg to invite Dalton and Natasha, and she brought Josh along with her.

"I wanted to thank you three for helping Troy find Robert's killer. He told me that you put the clues together for him, so all he had to prove was that they were around the island that day. Felicia said we could close the bookstore for the night, so lock the front door and put up the sign and let's eat." Lilly started unloading the bags. "This is my favorite restaurant on the island. I adore Emmett's selections. He's always adding something new."

Dalton met Meg's gaze as she remembered the fight, no, disagreement, they'd had about letting her uncle know of Emmett's connection to Robert Meade. Dalton grabbed a chair from the back so they'd all have a seat, then said, "Well, it didn't hurt that Nate was so mad about her dumping him that he told Chief Miller all about Tabitha's plan and how she'd leaked the information about you two to Meade."

Josh shook his head. "I knew that Tabitha was determined to win, no matter the cost, but I thought that was in career matters. I didn't realize she played hardball in her personal life, too."

Lilly laid her hand on his chest. "You're lucky that she wanted out of Meade's loan program more than she wanted you dead for cheating on her."

Josh's eyes widened. "I didn't think of it that way. I guess I'm going to have to stay with the woman who kills people on paper rather than in real life. You don't have any research on new methods of murder you need to perfect, do you?"

They all found a seat around the table.

Lilly laughed as she dished up some of Emmett's lobster mac and cheese. "Not at this moment. But someone might be more worried about my research assistant and her plans to kill off her philandering fiancé."

"Don't bring that up. Uncle Troy already had a fit when he read the plans I wrote for your assignment. I hadn't changed the names in the version he read." Meg rolled her eyes, thinking about her uncle's visit to her apartment. "I swear, working for you is never boring."

"I'll take the boring parts of the writing job," Lilly said as she passed the mac and cheese. "I like losing myself in my characters' world while I enjoy myself with friends and family in this one. I'm sorry Jolene couldn't make it tonight. She's in Seattle, at a show she's wanted to see forever. That woman works too hard."

Meg watched as the group chatted about the island and work and then got on the subject of books. The scene was straight out of her daydreams, the ones she'd had when Aunt Melody told her she'd gotten her a job with *the* L. C. Aster. They might not be best friends now or ever, but she already had Natasha and Dalton for that. *The Mystery Crew rides again.* The guidebook to being an amateur sleuth might not be as easy to write as she'd assumed, but the process was going to be fun. Because she wasn't alone. She had a community.

Dalton met her gaze from across the table and smiled at her.

And maybe there was room in her heart for more than just friendship. Again.

Murderous Mac and Cheese

When I imagined the death of Robert Meade, I wanted my victim to be sleazy, opportunistic, and plain mean. And Robert turned into all those things. From the moment he showed up on the ferry, I haven't liked him. I hate to say I'm glad he's gone, but the relationship between an author and an agent is sacred. You have to trust that they always have your best interest at heart. I'm not sure Meade even had a heart. And he probably kicked puppies off the page. And if there is organized crime in San Francisco, where Meade had his office, I'm sure he had his fingers in that pie.

So here's a mac and cheese that's good enough to serve with lobster. Or with chunks of cooked lobster gently swirled into the cheesy goo. Enjoy.

Lynn

Prepare 4 cups of dried elbow macaroni according to the package directions. (I put it in boiling salted water and cook for 10 minutes.) You want the mac to be al dente, and not too tender, since it will cook more during the baking process. Drain and set aside.

Preheat the oven to 325°F. Butter a 9" x 13" baking pan and set aside.

In a large, heavy skillet, melt 4 tablespoons butter over medium heat. Add 2 tablespoons all-purpose flour, 1 teaspoon salt, and ¼ teaspoon freshly ground black pepper and stir constantly to make a roux. Let the roux cook for 2 minutes, stirring constantly to make sure it doesn't burn. (This is the same roux that goes into my sausage gravy and milk gravy.)

Next, add 1½ cups milk and ½ cup half-and-half to the roux. (If you don't have half-and-half, use 2 cups whole milk.) Whisk the milk mixture until it thickens enough to coat the back of a spoon. If you want your mac and cheese a little spicy, stir in 1 teaspoon chili powder, or to taste.

Fold 1 cup shredded cheddar cheese into the milk mixture. (I like to mix and match whatever cheese is in my fridge.) Stir constantly until the cheese has melted and the sauce is smooth. Next, fold the reserved macaroni into the cheese sauce.

Spoon half of the macaroni and cheese into the prepared baking pan. Sprinkle with ½ cup Cheddar cheese. Next, spoon the rest of the macaroni and cheese atop the Cheddar, and then top with ½ cup Cheddar cheese.

Bake for 15 to 20 minutes, or until the cheese on top has melted. Enjoy.

Acknowledgments

Sometimes the muse works in mysterious ways. Michaela Hamilton, my editor, and I were working on titles for another book. If I remember correctly, it was one of the Survivors' Book Club recent releases. *Confessions of an Amateur Sleuth* came up as one of the options for the title of that book. The team at Kensington loved the idea. Not for the title of the book I'd turned in, but for a new series, set on Bainbridge Island. We batted around who Meg Gates would be, and to my agent Jill Marsal's surprise, we started contract negotiations.

Life is like that, and you have to be ready to zig or zag at the right moment. Big thanks to Michaela, the Kensington team, including our Cozy Coordinator Queen, Larissa Ackerman. That's not her real title, of course, but she's amazing at herding authors at events and getting our books out to the world.

As always, I need to acknowledge the work of my agent, Jill. Not only on my contracts but also on the many rough drafts she reads, always with a willingness to give her sage advice. She's made me a better writer.

Much love to my husband, who keeps me fed and gives me grief about living life outside the office. And love to the pups, of course.